THE LOOK OF A STORME

The Storme Brothers
Book Three

Sandra Sookoo

ARE YOU SIGNED UP FOR DRAGONBLADE'S BLOG?

You'll get the latest news and information on exclusive giveaways, exclusive excerpts, coming releases, sales, free books, cover reveals and more.

Check out our complete list of authors, too!

No spam, no junk. That's a promise!

Sign Up Here

www.dragonbladepublishing.com

Dearest Reader;

Thank you for your support of a small press. At Dragonblade Publishing, we strive to bring you the highest quality Historical Romance from the some of the best authors in the business. Without your support, there is no 'us', so we sincerely hope you adore these stories and find some new favorite authors along the way.

Happy Reading!

CEO, Dragonblade Publishing

Additional Dragonblade books by Author Sandra Sookoo

The Storme Brother Series
The Soul of a Storme (Book 1)
The Heart of a Storme (Book 2)
The Look of a Storme (Book 3)

CHAPTER ONE

August 15, 1817
Ipswich, England

"Of all things holy on land or sea," Brand breathed with no small amount of exasperation in his voice. When his three best mates glanced at him from around the tavern table as he entered the public dining room, he held up two letters. "My family apparently can't leave me in peace." Granted, this was the first round of missives he'd received since landing in the town following his retirement, but still.

"Tear 'em up then, Captain," his friend George suggested with a shrug. "It's not as if they worried over you while you were fighting."

"True." Word from the Stormes in London had been few and far between while he'd been away fighting against Boney's forces. By necessity, for the post couldn't very well deliver to the middle of various seas and oceans. Not to mention the two years he'd been officially decommissioned from the Navy where he'd sailed through port towns until he found a place that felt like home. Of course, he'd been tight-lipped regarding his whereabouts, but there had been a reason—or four—for that. Francis Hildenbrand Storme—Captain Storme—dropped heavily into the one empty chair around his customary table with his fellows. "Might as well read them before I consign them to the fire."

"Why?" asked his closest friend, John Butler. "It can't be good news. You remember when you last heard from your mother."

"I do." A twinge of pain and loss briefly gripped his heart. The previous time he'd properly heard from his family had been when his mother had notified him of his father's passing over two years before. But he'd been embroiled in his own professional troubles and couldn't attend to familial matters. When he hadn't turned up in London—that they knew of—an angry letter from his oldest brother Andrew had followed with blistering words and accusations, designed to bring about feelings of shame and guilt. It had at that, but Brand had buried them deep inside, for he hadn't the time to give them their due. But then, Drew had always been an arse. "However, I'm curious. I have a feeling I'll regret finally forwarding my direction to Mother." He'd made that decision a couple of months ago. This was the first time he'd received letters from home since the news of his father's passing. Did he even consider London that after all these years? He touched a fingertip to the small compass he wore on a cord about his neck beneath his clothing. Yes, perhaps that was so. London wasn't as welcoming as his current location. Ipswich in Suffolk was pleasant enough that he wouldn't hare off to the capital anytime soon.

If ever again.

Still, they'd written. That had to mean something. Except the words of his fellow humans couldn't be trusted and oftentimes did more harm than good. Absently, he moved his fingers to the black leather strap that kept the eyepatch in place over his left eye—or, rather, the empty socket, sewn up with alacrity by the surgeon on the recuse vessel.

His mind jogged to the end of his naval career. During the horrible time of London hearings and the court martial that had followed the Battle of Grand Port on the Isle de France in the Indian Ocean, he'd met and had fallen hard for a lady—the daughter of an English admiral—only to casually overhear a handful of words at a ball that had shattered his heart and forever solidified his decision to never marry. Especially if a woman couldn't stomach his permanent disfigurement.

His lips tightened into a thin line as familiar bitterness churned in his belly. Yes, there were too many foul memories in London now, but there was the same amount, if not more, rattling around in his brain. Yet they no longer served him and didn't deserve his attention. Ruthlessly, Brand shoved all of that into the back of his mind with everything else he refused to think about or let himself feel. Emotions were dangerous to a man's health and position; it was best to pretend they didn't exist. Wasn't that the ultimate lesson his father had imparted?

"Captain, are you still with us?" George's question yanked Brand from his musings.

"Aye." He focused on the envelopes. "Let's get to it, shall we?"

George, with his coarse voice and his graying-brown, scraggly beard and eyebrows that made him look like a fur-trapper in the wilds of America instead of a seadog, lifted his tankard. "A new round for us all if your mother demands you return to the bosom of the Storme family."

Philip, a reed-thin young man more full of misfortune than grace, nodded. "And roast beef if she wants you to marry!"

As laughter went around the table, Brand nodded. "Aye, you're on." He grinned, for the three of them—him included—would do anything for a dare or challenge. He settled more comfortably into his wooden chair despite the carved spindles that dug into his back. "Let's see." After breaking the seal on the first letter, he took it from the envelope and unfolded it. His mother's flowing and flowery script covered the page. "Definitely from my mother," he grumbled, for it didn't look good for him or his coin. "What now? Some imagined crisis?"

Well, that won't be enough to convince me to come to London. With cold dread tripping down his spine, he began to read.

Dearest Francis…

God, why couldn't his mother ever remember he detested both his names and that she needed to call him Brand?

It is time for you to come home to London. If one listens to on-dits, you are continuing to create scandal in Ipswich, and have been since you arrived. That simply won't do. You need to learn how to be a civilian and an upstanding member of the ton in London—without dragging the family name through the muck. Also, I'd like you to marry and settle down, perhaps start a family, as your brothers have done.

"What?" His exclamation was met with blank stares, for of course his mates hadn't been treated to him reading the letter aloud. Once more, Brand gawked at the sheet of stationery.

Andrew married a lovely woman in Derbyshire a handful of weeks ago. Phineas plans to wed a wonderful lady here in London in mere days. They met at a society function. If you depart from that godforsaken place in which you've taken up residence as soon as you receive this missive, you could arrive in time to witness the event. I'm sure he would love to see you. Of all my boys, you and he used to be so close…

What the devil had occurred in his absence? Never did he think his brothers would marry, especially Finn, not after he'd received wounds during Waterloo that had left him paralyzed. His eyebrows raised. Not even raging curiosity could budge him from his contentment in Ipswich, but a niggle of doubt crept into his being. Had he made an error in judgment staying away so long? Not having answers to the many questions circling through his mind, he returned to the remainder of the letter.

In any event, you three boys need to reconcile your differences now that you're grown and moving forward onto new paths. Our family is desperate for mending. Don't follow in your father's footsteps and let misunderstandings and hurt feelings come between you. Once you're home, we shall do the rounds in society, introduce you to eligible ladies. It's not so crowded in Town just now, which means you'll enjoy it better... and there won't be too many ladies to turn your head so you can fully concentrate on the right one. Andrew will return after Christmas, so you and I can have time to ourselves.

I miss you. Please do the right thing and come home, Francis. You're no longer that reckless young man I said goodbye to when you left for war. I've missed you.

Love,
Mother

"Of all things holy on land and sea," Brand whispered as he lowered the paper to the scarred wooden tabletop.

George grunted and took another swig of his beer. "You said that already when you first arrived."

"Well, it bears repeating." Did he appear as confused as he felt with his insides knotted up as they did whenever he thought about his father or his brothers? "I don't know where to start." Why the devil would he wish to leave Ipswich and the freedom or fun he had therein? He glanced at his best friend John and shrugged. "Mother wishes for me to come to London."

A cheer went around the table and George grinned. "Next round's on you, Captain!"

"Aye, I promised that." He gestured to a buxom barmaid. "Another beer for my mates."

She nodded and her doe brown eyes found his. "Whatever you say, Captain." The invitation in those dark depths was obvious. "I'll give you that and more."

Brand ignored her. He wasn't in the mood for flirtation or finding a shadowy corner to explore beneath her skirts.

Perhaps later, for she *was* a looker and he *had* angled for a moment of her time over the past week. Didn't matter to him what a woman's rank or position in society—or out of it—was. If they were attractive enough and disease and lice free, he'd bed them.

John Butler—a tall, barrel-chested man who'd sailed with Brand for years—leaned back in his chair. His disheveled golden hair winked in the sun. "Is that what you want to do?"

"Hell no. It's jolly fun here." He rolled his eyes. "No responsibilities, no one nagging me about manners or marriage." He paused and grinned. "And it doesn't lack for bed partners."

Jovial laughter went around the table, for it was no secret that doxies, village maids, and the local female gentry alike adored a man of adventure and the seas. All of that came with the added benefit of no outraged fathers claiming ruination of their titled daughters and demanding a quick trip to a parson's mousetrap. The women of Ipswich were discreet enough, but they also knew he wasn't the marrying kind. A bit of slap and tickle was what they—and he—desired. Nothing else was ever discussed or implied. Both parties walked away satisfied… in more ways than one.

That was exactly how Brand liked his dealings with the opposite sex. He wasn't one to find himself tied into domestication or the fetters that marriage brought.

John frowned. "Then write your mother back and decline her offer."

"She hinted that I should settle down and marry."

Another round of huzzahs circled through his group.

Philip pounded the table with a fist. "Roast beef for dinner!"

"Aye, I promised that also." Damn, but his pockets would find a dent before the day was out.

John chuckled. "Bad news, eh? If she only wishes for you to land in a nuptial contract, moving there is not an option. You could visit and should, of course, but you've a life here in Ipswich now."

Not for the first time did Brand wonder about John's upbringing and life before he'd joined the Navy. The man had told him just enough for an introduction, but the rest didn't matter, for they'd become fast friends over the years and neither had brought up their pasts for whatever reason. Their relationship didn't hinge on such things, and Brand wouldn't push if the other man didn't wish to share. Lord knew he had enough things on his own conscience that might throw him in a bad light that he didn't want others to know. He wasn't one for needless words; perhaps they weren't ether.

"True," he finally responded to his friend. Still, the news contained in his mother's letter rankled. "Apparently, my brothers have found love. Drew is married, with Finn entering that state in a matter of days."

He remembered them as rough and tumble boys growing up. They'd had adventures as boys do and had fallen into a fair amount of trouble. In school, as their interests divided, he'd drifted apart from the other two. As adults, and especially once their father had died, he didn't care to spend time with his siblings. Drew was a pompous arse, had been even before he'd assumed the title of earl, and always had their father's attention. Finn had been the sensitive middle one in need of affirmation. Of the two, Brand was closest to Finn, but they each carried their own wounds and demons, which meant an enormous divide; Mother doted on him. Probably still did, but once Father purchased a commission for him, he'd left home in short order.

And I was left behind, forgotten without expectations.

With nothing to do except create—or chase—scandal depending on his whim, Brand had set the London *ton* on its ear with his rakish ways. Had it been a bid for attention? He scoffed. Doubtful, but having all eyes on him and tongues wagging wasn't a bad thing. That penchant for skirt-chasing and dare-entering had eventually embarrassed his father to the point that he'd acted and issued an ultimatum. Gladly Brand had joined the navy and fought against Boney's forces with all the aplomb with which he'd done everything else.

It didn't curb his taste for women or scandal, but at least those things happened far enough away from England's shores that his family wasn't bothered by them. Not to mention he'd been a damned good sailor.

He chuckled with the memories. "I regret nothing," he told his mates, though they'd not been privy to his thoughts. However, now that he understood himself better, he needed a proximity to the sea; it made him happy and calm, ready for sailing at a moment's notice on his sloop he'd named *Charlotte*. As an homage to a particularly gifted lover he'd had years ago. If one named a boat after someone, they'd never be forgotten, or that was what he'd like to think.

He'd seen too much death in his life. No one deserved to be forgotten to the ages.

John frowned. "Pardon my slowness, but did you say Finn is to be married?"

"I did." Brand set his mother's letter aside in favor of taking a swig of his own beer.

"Even though he's confined to a Bath chair without the use of his lower half?" Astonishment threaded through the man's tones.

"Aye."

Philip gawked. He shoved a long hand through his reddish-blond hair. "How's that then? From what you said, his prick doesn't work."

Another round of laughter—ribald this time—filtered through the group. Brand shrugged. "Not sure, but there's a story there, don't you think?" No matter how much curiosity to know how his brother had done it burned in Brand's gut, it wasn't enough to prompt him to return to London. As soon as he set foot there, his mother would attach herself and he'd never find an escape. He held up the second letter. "Might as well see what the man himself has to say." While his three friends looked on with varying degrees of interest, he cracked the seal and removed a slip of paper from its envelope.

Dear Brand,

I'm certain Mother implored you in her letter to come to London, but if Ipswich is making you happy, by all means stay there. For far too long you and I have followed someone else's orders, both while in the service and beneath Father's thumb. Now that the war is over, and Father is gone—God rest his soul—we're done with those chapters in our lives. There is no more need to dance attendance on others' whims.

Brand's eyebrows soared again. Now that was a different tack from his brother. What had occurred to change his thinking?

Life is too precious to cater to everyone else—Mother included—instead of your own wishes and dreams. I almost threw away my chance, nearly lost it to depression and my own stubbornness, and no, I refuse to write about it here. If you want to know, come for a visit.

"I'll be damned," Brand whispered. "Finn's found his independence and a backbone." Curiosity flared again, and he delved back into the letter.

Furthermore, don't overly analyze your disfigurement or your time in service or anything else that has the tendency to lay you low and cause doubts. They will curtail your growth and stunt every good thing that might come your way. We witnessed horrors, this is true, but they don't define us. Neither do our injuries. Nor does our position within the Storme family. Regardless of what Drew says, you and I are not his adoring acolytes. It's my fondest hope you'll come to believe all of this as truth.

Brand frowned. He once more fingered the eyepatch. The women he bedded never seemed to be put off by his hindered eyesight or the patch, but none of those liaisons were deep or permanent. He flirted and charmed his way into their beds. Once the deed was done, he moved on; he didn't know of their lives and they remained ignorant of his. With the exception of the woman who'd stolen—and smashed—his heart. She hadn't been able to move past him having one eye. She wouldn't fathom a life married to a man without a title or a secure livelihood. Yet... a vague ache set up in his chest. There was a loneliness there that went bone deep. Would he ever know a woman for longer than it took to bring her to release a couple of times? More to the point, would he ever meet—and trust—one who'd love him for the man he was?

"Bah!" Where had those thoughts come from? He needed none of that. Annoyed, he returned to the letter.

> *No doubt Mother has informed you of my upcoming marriage. Yes, it's true. I'm set to wed in a few days. I'd love to see you but not at the expense of your wellbeing. I also learned that the hard way. Perhaps we can come together for Christmastide. I've overhead snippets of Drew's plans, which he has neglected to share with Mother for the moment, to spare her emotions. He wishes to repair the Storme family's connections now that he's wed, and his wife is increasing. If this is true, it will be nice to see our cousins again.*

"What the devil does that mean?" Brand could almost see an eyeroll in the letter, for Finn's words were that real while his own mind spun at the implications. He hadn't seen his Storme cousins for more than half his life due to some contretemps between their fathers. No one had ever spoken of what had happened, and eventually, the story was consigned to the past.

> *Regardless, little brother, enjoy your life and keep scandal to a minimum. No need to upset Mother while she's busy trying not to worry about you. If you have the chance for a bit of happiness—the kind that's not found in chasing skirts and servicing your prick—to ease the burdens of the war and its aftereffects, take it. Hold on to it tight, for it's fleeting, but when it's right, it'll knock you on your arse and change your life.*
>
> *Finn*

"That was even more startling than Mother's letter." Carefully, Brand folded the missive and tucked it back into its envelope. He glanced at John. "It was interesting to say the least."

His best friend shrugged. "You know how family is."

"I do." He snorted. "Yours too?"

"Not as disparate as yours, but they mean well. My father is…" The bigger man pressed his lips together. "He's a difficult man. Baron or not, he makes life difficult, but I suppose he can't help it." He stared at Brand over the rim of his tankard, his eyes full of regret and sadness. "He's worried, I suppose. And afraid. Those two things manifest as anger at times. But times weren't all bad. He's a good sort when he's of a mind to remember how things used to be."

One of these days he'd have his best friend's story, but not just now. "Do you return to Surrey then?" He'd had no idea John was loosely connected to the *ton*, but now his refined way of speaking and the elevated cut of his clothing made sense.

"Not soon, but eventually, when I've got the courage and the temperament. Ipswich has been my home for a while now, and I'm not anxious to leave the reprieve here." He shot Brand a wry look. "It seems I'm a coward when not on the sea."

"Aye, aren't we all." It wasn't a question. While in the Navy or even running supplies up the coast in his sloop, there was nothing he couldn't do, but on land? Insecurities abounded. He worked hard to never let them show because in the back of his mind, his damned father's words rang loud.

Englishmen don't show their emotions, Francis. The moment they do, a man becomes vulnerable and weak; he loses face with his peers. Never give away your standing like that.

John nodded. "The only way I'd leave in the current moment is if you plan to continue your naval career and need a crew. I'd give up a visit to Surrey for that." A hopeful light gleamed in his tawny eyes.

"My military days are over. Not by my say, that is." Brand traced the leather eyepatch over his left eye socket. He'd been part of the defeat in Grand Port in August, 1810. God, it seemed both so far away and yet as if it had happened yesterday.

When his ship had been disabled by heavy cannon fire, it had been boarded by the damned French. During the war, the scum had seemingly reached all over the earth. Hand to hand combat ensued, but he'd defended his ship and crew until the very last. Lost his eye from one swipe of a dagger. Nearly lost his life as well but for John Butler's interference and quick thinking. After that, he'd been rescued with his remaining crew. British reinforcements patched up his wounds aboard their ship. A court martial followed once they'd returned to England, where he'd answered for losing his ship to the French.

Eventually, he and the other captains were cleared of any wrongdoing, but the damage to his reputation and career had been done. He was asked to retire; his days in service over. No commendations, no medals, for the King wouldn't soon forget such a resounding defeat, especially in the same year as he'd been defeated by America on the sea. Brand had nothing to show for all he'd done except for the bloody missing eye. At least the bastards in charge of the government had let him keep his rank.

Not wishing to bring such scandal to his family's doorstep, he'd gone to Ipswich, the home of his faithful first mate John. He'd used some of his coin to buy a sloop and then proceeded to enjoy the hell out of his life and keep the memories at bay.

And there he'd remained for three years, content to indulge in scandal, taking odd sailing jobs when he needed coin, doing whatever he pleased, all the while avoiding the life he'd used to have in London.

Damn, but he missed his command and his fellows. "No, my Navy days are done, my friend. I have only boredom and skirt-chasing to fill my days now, but God I miss adventure and daring."

Murmurs of agreement went around the table. The barmaid returned—Molly was her name, he recalled—with four tankards on a round, wooden tray. Each time she placed one on the table, her breasts were on display in the low-cut bodice of her dress.

The men openly ogled her charms. Molly left with a blatant "come hither" stare over her shoulder directed at Brand, which earned him an elbow in the ribs from George.

"She's a brazen baggage I'll wager you can find adventure with," he said with a leer.

Brand rolled his eye. He accepted the cards Philip dealt, for that was how they spent most of their afternoons. "I'm not in the mood."

Philip snorted. "You're always randy. What ails you?"

"I'm of a mind to think over these letters." Word from home had ruined his libido and had swamped him with unwanted ennui. Besides, he wasn't all that certain Molly *was* disease-free. As much as he might lust after her in some moments, he still believed in being careful.

"You know, we could give you a challenge and place a wager on it," George said, his expression nonchalantly sly as he looked over his own hand of cards.

"Oh? What on?" Brand straightened his spine as excitement trickled down. At least it was something.

His friend gestured at the window. A woman trailed after a man clad in a black suit through the street, clearly having been shopping if the number of bags and boxes they each carried was any indication. "The clergyman's sister."

"What of her?" Brand had seen her around the town a few times, but a woman of her views and drab looks didn't interest him. "And isn't he a missionary?"

"Does it matter?" Philip asked.

"No."

George winked. "The objective is to kiss her."

"What? *Her?*" Brand glanced more closely out the window as she passed. Nothing about her tempted him, for even in the summer's heat she wore a brown spencer, and her dress was two sizes too large. To say nothing of the hideous, outdated straw bonnet that hid her face and hair from view. Perhaps it was an effort to hide.

George settled more comfortably into his chair, his cheeks rosy either from his plan or the beer. "You brag about being able to charm any woman into a kiss upon first meeting. Why *not* her?"

"Indeed." Philip nodded with enthusiasm. Even John grinned, for they'd all heard the stories. "Perhaps they'll visit the traveling fair tomorrow. Her brother is always trying to convert their souls."

Both the preacher's presence at the fair and the thought of kissing such a creature as his sister soured Brand's stomach. Surely there was other game to be had in town. Yet, he never could turn down a challenge. "What's the prize? I won't do it if there's no motivation."

This time it was John who spoke. "One hundred pounds. We'll all chip in." When each man nodded, his grin widened. "That's enough motivation, eh, Captain?"

"Not bad." That was a hell of a sum, and the fact the three were willing to split it said volumes to their friendship with him. "It'll join my savings to buy a bigger craft than my sloop." Which would let him go farther out to sea and perhaps away from England permanently. A new life in a new part of the world. Now *that* was a dream. "What sort of kiss?"

His friends exchanged glances. George said, "Full lip contact. Tongue, if needed to make her knees weak. We'll be watching."

"And if I lose?" The task, while not impossible, wasn't exactly easy. A missionary's sister wasn't the same as a buxom and willing barmaid. No doubt she'd be frigid and bristling with maidenly virtue. He'd probably earn a slap for his efforts.

"*You* pay *us* the one hundred pounds." Philip hooted with laughter. "At least our rent will be caught up."

For long moments Brand glanced around the table at his closest friends in the world. They'd formed a surrogate family for him while in the Navy. "What the hell? Challenge accepted." He grinned. "Now, how do I manage it?"

That was the question, but the proposal had beaten back the lurking blue devils.

CHAPTER TWO

August 16, 1817
Ipswich, England

MISS ELIZABETH HAYHURST turned nine and twenty with no fanfare, no celebration, and nothing to mark the day as special. She wasn't surprised, of course, since that was how she'd ushered in every other birthday she'd ever had. It was vanity to think otherwise or to wish to live one moment with all eyes on her. Or, heaven forbid, buy a new gown that wasn't out of style or too big.

But, oh, how she could dream!

Yesterday, she and her brother William had gone shopping for monthly supplies, but never once had he mentioned her birthday. It still grated. A tad out of sorts, she walked behind William—nearly ten years her senior—as they entered the meadow where the traveling fair had set up. Not a half mile in the distance, the sunshine glimmered off the River Orwell. What must it feel like to board a boat and sail to points and ports unknown? How embarrassing it was to have lived in Ipswich for a year and never set foot on the water.

I do know this for certain: I will not leave here without going sailing once.

It was another thing William thought of as a sin—putting

oneself on a boat for the specific purposes of entertainment or leisure. If life were up to her evangelical brother, no one would do anything except read the Bible and minister to people he considered in need of saving from condemnation. He took pleasure in yanking someone's soul from the fiery pits of Hell and turning them into religious accolades for his brand of faith. Elizabeth believed in *some* of his strictures to a point, but the others were too fanatical and invasive for her tastes.

Unfortunately, since their parents had died five years prior in a church fire, and without any other family to speak of, where William went, so did she. The war had taken her only hope of marriage—thanks to her brother, men steered well clear of her—and now her future was rather bleak and murky. She had no choice but to accompany William wherever he decided to minister.

Her brother had been a parson since she was a young girl still in the schoolroom, and now that he'd become a devotee of the evangelical movement, he bounced around all corners of England and had never settled until he'd found his calling as a missionary. Soon he would leave for India, and since she had no other prospects, she would accompany him.

Whether she wished it or not.

Despite all of that, she thanked God every day that her ill-health and her doctor had decided Ipswich was what she needed for a while. The views were beautiful and for the most part, she could ignore William's zeal while walking through the town and around the area to strengthen her lungs.

With a sigh, Elizabeth dabbed at the perspiration on her upper lip with a finger of her glove. The August sun was hot even for late afternoon, but her gown of heavy linen in an old-fashioned floral print did nothing to allow for air circulation. Neither did the equally outdated spencer, but William had insisted she wear it, for modesty's sake, of course. Scandal might break out if a man spied a bit of her bare arm. An unladylike snort escaped her. How modest would it be if she succumbed to the heat and collapsed into a heap? Would he notice or would he continue his mission to convert the faithless and keep them from hell?

Stop that, Elizabeth. Such uncharitable thoughts.

They'd come more frequently of late, for over the course of the year she'd grown increasingly out of sorts with her life, but she made no effort to quell them. For once in her life, she wished she could wear a pretty gown that was currently in fashion with short sleeves and matching frivolous slippers merely to discover what it would feel like. Surely that didn't make her vain; it certainly wouldn't change her existence that much. She'd had a long time to think about such things and determine if they were a sin or not.

William glanced over his shoulder. "Are you feeling quite well, Elizabeth?"

Aside from the need to faint from the heat? "Yes. My lungs don't hurt quite as much as they did before. I credit that with walking every fine day."

"Good to hear. You must do everything you can to heal quickly, for we travel in a month's time."

"I haven't forgotten." For her recovery, William had brought her to Ipswich, though he'd grumbled about it the whole time. She needed to regain her strength after suffering a particularly violent bout of pleurisy last winter. Her doctor had warned that too much excitement or a lack of exercise could see a relapse, and that breathing clean air away from the pollution of London was vital to her recuperation, else they'd need to bleed her with leeches.

Again.

Or worse, keep her in a room away from everyone else until her lungs healed. A shiver racked her body. Never would she allow that. Leeches were bad enough, but isolation? She might as well pray for death. At the moment, she was strong and capable, had been since May, but then boredom had set in. It was time to test the limit of her lungs and perhaps enjoy life before she might travel with William. Though, she suspected the climate and conditions in far-flung India might tax her health more than the journey there, and she'd never verbally said she wished to go with her brother. Not that he'd ever asked her opinion. He never did, for according to him, women's minds weren't capable of difficult decisions. She shoved the thoughts from her mind, for it wasn't good to dwell on uncertainties or bitterness.

"Don't dawdle, Elizabeth," William said. "There is much to do." In his somber black suit and white clergy collar, and with a well-worn Bible clutched in one hand, he was every inch a country vicar. Why he refused to settle down with a wife, or find a living in England, she couldn't fathom.

It would certainly be much easier—and cooler—here than in India. Perhaps he's driven by something I can't understand.

But in some ways, she did, for she had secret dreams and aspirations as well. The fact they went directly against the views of the church sent knots into her belly. Elizabeth hastened her steps and caught him up to walk at his side. "We've been in Ipswich a year. It's pleasant and idyllic with all sorts of people in the town and countryside. Why not find a living nearby? I can just as easily keep your house here." She nodded as if to encourage him. "It's a good sight better than London, and I adore the slight tang of saltiness in the air if the wind is right."

"I don't care for the sea." William kept walking. Of course he wouldn't give her idea a thought. He never did, so why would he start now?

"No?" The urge to needle him grew strong, and not even grace could help throttle it. "I find it invigorating. Something about the sea calls to me. Since we've been here, I've felt its pull." She allowed a small smile. "I'd love to learn how to sail."

He grunted. "You'd do well to stay away from temptation."

Dear heavens. According to her brother, *everything* that wasn't reading the Bible or listening to a sermon was a temptation. "What do you assume the sea will do to ruin me?" Every day during her walk, she watched boats of all shapes and sizes depart the port to sail down the River Orwell and farther into the North Sea. Where did they go? What did those men sea while on their trips?

Oh, to have such freedom!

"Not the sea, sister dear; the men who sail it." William glanced at her with concern in his blue eyes so like her own. "Bounders, all of them. No good can come from knowing a sailor, and Ipswich harbors a few rotten reprobates."

"Surely not all. There are good men everywhere, just as there are bad." She nodded to a few young ladies they passed. The three were garbed in pretty dresses of varying pastels with stylish bonnets that didn't have the excessively large brim that blocked her vision. They giggled and sent curious looks at William, for after everything, he was still a fine-looking man, and eligible. What she wouldn't do to have a couple of friends. It would certainly make life more interesting and would save her from being alone with her thoughts. "It's not good to tar every man with the same brush."

"Honestly, Elizabeth, such talk isn't Christian." Exasperation echoed in his voice. "Especially when there are so many souls to save in this town. I can feel their sins in the very air we breathe."

"Be careful, William. You are not above sin yourself." She frowned. Why couldn't a person have concern for the lost and find joy in their surroundings or fellow inhabitants? "I'm curious about the inhabitants of Ipswich, though. The stories sailors must have to tell! Can you imagine life not connected to land?" What must that feel like? "There is so much world beyond the horizon. I often find myself sad I'll never experience it."

"Allowing your mind to dwell on things outside of the church will lead you down the wrong path."

"Toward what?" If that path held excitement and possible adventure, she most certainly wished to explore it. Anything was better than watching the world go by while she sat embroidering an endless supply of baby gowns for infants she'd never hold in her arms. That was her project currently, for there was no end to babies belonging to the poor in Ipswich, and they all needed clothing. Babies arrived regardless of one's circumstances.

"Ruin and scandal most certainly." William grunted. "You need to find a godly man to keep you busy, so these types of rebellious thoughts won't rot your brain."

Indignation twisted up her spine. "So you won't have the responsibility of me?" When he didn't answer, she continued. "I had a man once, or at least the *promise* of a husband, but the war took him regardless that he was a chaplain."

Jacob had been nice enough and most certainly polite who adored his vocation, but there'd been no excitement between them, no certain feelings that might sweep her away into scandal. Their engagement had been arranged by William. Jacob had never stolen a kiss, let alone wanted to do anything else with her. Only once had they held hands. As suitors went, he was quite dull. Perhaps it had been an unanswered prayer he'd been taken from her, for she couldn't imagine a lifetime with him.

Was it too much to ask that God might send her the man she needed, despite everything? To date, it hadn't happened, and so she continued to embroider baby clothes. Still, her brother's attitude rankled. "Perhaps this time around I'll choose a more daring man." Where had that thought sprung from? "A man who is so different from Jacob the whole of my attention will be on him. Then you won't need to worry about me."

William shook his head. "Marriage is not supposed to be thrilling. It's to glorify God and further the species so that the Word might be spread."

At the last second, Elizabeth tamped the urge to scoff. "Only a nodcock would think that." No, she certainly hadn't gained control of her tongue. Guilt threaded through her insides. If one chose to take William's opinion as fact, that meant there was not time for sailing or fun or laughter or a bit of naughtiness that happened between a man and a woman. Then why would anyone wish for such a union? "There is no reason a woman can't have enjoyment in the wedded state along with someone who shows the proper respect for the Lord. Life is not made up of absolutes. Indeed, that's the glory of it."

At least, that had been her hope. As of yet, she'd not seen evidence of it. Men were either wicked and broken, or dull and essentially married to the church; there was no in between. All the more reason for her to expand her boundaries.

"Good heavens." Her brother came to a stop with a grunt. "Elizabeth." He dropped his free hand on her shoulder. "God doesn't appreciate such cheek in a woman."

"How would you know? To my way of thinking, the Creator is vastly mysterious." It irritated her William was bullheaded and thought himself the authority in religious matters, or even life for that matter.

"I am a man of the cloth." Fervor lit his eyes. "The church should be taken seriously and somberly. The Word isn't something to make jest of."

"I'm not making light of it." Elizabeth resisted the urge to stamp her foot like she had as a young girl when she argued with William. "I'm merely stating that believing in God should bring a sense of peace and happiness. It should light a person from the inside out. Why shouldn't a man, someone sent from Him, make a woman feel that prior to their wedding and even beyond?"

My goodness, but I've grown bold since this morning. Perhaps having yet another birthday had empowered her, for she refused to pass another year without having found a purpose.

A slight curl to William's upper lip warned of his displeasure. "You are naïve if you think so." He shook his head. "Life doesn't work like that, and I don't want you making a spectacle of yourself. You have an image to maintain that reflects upon me." Admonition rang in his tones.

Only part of the statement was truth, and she immediately ducked her head. "I beg your pardon." Was there anything else for her in this life than docilely keeping his house and looking after him until she reached her dotage? Eventually, he would marry and have children. What would become of her then?

Surely that couldn't be all God would give her.

He patted her shoulder. "You are forgiven." As if he were the end-all of such a thing. "When we settle in India, I will pick a husband for you from the Englishmen at the fort nearby or perhaps an East India man. It will be a good enough match."

"Do I not rate more than good enough?" At the last second, Elizabeth stifled a sigh of annoyance. "And it will relieve you of your duty to me."

"I am your only living relative, so that responsibility falls to me. I want you settled."

"But not happy."

"The only true happiness comes from above. You'll never find it in a man."

Frustration swept over in her a wave. "Then why wait until we reach India?" She couldn't help arguing; it was *her* future after all. "Find a match here in Ipswich and leave me be."

"Give you over to a fisherman?" His tone suggested she might be swallowed whole by a whale. "I think not."

"There are more than fishermen here."

"I said no."

"Ah, I see." Elizabeth crossed her arms at chest level and took a step back from her brother, breaking their connection. "*You* still have need of me, for who else would keep your house or clean your clothes or cook your meals for no pay and less thanks?" When she arched an eyebrow, a slight wash of red rose over his collar.

"It's your duty as a woman of the church." He tightened his hold on the Bible, his gloved fingers digging into the cracked leather cover.

The bald fact and his unwavering belief in it brought quick tears stinging her eyes. She blinked them away. "As if I have no value unless I'm subservient to the church or a man's needs," she said quietly. Yes, this was the life she'd been born into and what she'd watched her mother live every day of her life, but that didn't mean Elizabeth had to accept it. There must be more to a woman's existence than that.

Yet, what would she do with herself? What were her own dreams?

She wished for marriage, of course, but not to become a maid-of-all-work for a man or to only bear him children.

What of being cherished and loved for the woman she was instead of what she might give? What of finding companionship and affection and most of all humor? What of finding the freedom to be the woman she could be with a man's support? What of discovering for herself if the act that was whispered to be a fate worse than death or a duty to be performed was exactly that? Surely not, for why would so many couples marry in order to couple, and why would others seek the thrill of the sin of adultery?

Oh, there were so many questions about life to which she didn't have answers but staying stuck where she was wouldn't help with any of them.

"Don't look to people for your reward, Sister. Your treasure does not lie here on Earth." It was the typical noncommittal answer a man of William's type always gave. "Now, I must follow the work mandated to me. The fair is teeming with activity and people just now. Shall we meet back here by teatime?"

With a start Elizabeth glanced about the immediate area. All around them, visitors to the fair laughed and chatted in gay fashion. Delighted screeches from children rang in the air. Savory and sweet scents tickled her nose from food carts. Flashes of brilliant color from the traditional clothing gave life to the meadow grass and the backdrop of the river. Brightly decorated wagons were arranged in a large, wide semi-circle throughout the fairgrounds. Tent-like stalls lay interspersed between them where vendors sold their wares.

"Of course." Could she find a bit of fun before she needed to depart for India? "I wish you good luck in your conversion attempts."

"I don't need luck, sister dear. God is on my side." But he grinned and headed off toward the hub of activity.

She frowned. Didn't God look after the best interests of *all* people, no matter what they had done? In His eyes, weren't folks equally precious regardless of their heritage and beliefs? What gave William the right to think his way was the only true path?

The magnitude of her thoughts stole her breath. If her brother knew, he'd immediately drag her to the church and demand the elders lay hands on her to banish the demons in her head who sought to poison her mind. Thinking differently didn't mean there was something wrong with her or that she was evil.

Something must change!

With a sigh, she walked toward the heart of the fair. What to do first that would banish the ennui that suddenly plagued her? As she moved steadily forward, she passed a group of men who nodded. Their clothing styles varied, and two of them wore jackets that fit their shoulders better than the others. A pair of gray eyes—or rather one eye—met hers from one of the men. The black leather eyepatch he wore on the left side gave him the rakish air of a scoundrel. She quelled the urge to smile as a faint tickling sensation invaded her belly. Such a silly reaction to someone she didn't know. The heat must be playing tricks with her. With quickened steps, she continued toward a wagon on the far side of the fairgrounds. As she drew close, a wooden sign proclaimed, "Fortunes told."

That's exactly what I need, and William should be none the wiser.

In short order, she found the owner of the wagon sitting at a small, round table near the rear of the vehicle. The older woman gestured her over and then pointed to a wooden stool across from her location. "I am Vadoma."

"What a pretty name. I'm Elizabeth."

"Ah. A proper English name. You wish your fortune told, young lady?" The soft, rasping voice held a faint Romani accent that put Elizabeth in mind of far-flung places she'd only dreamed of. An orange scarf covered her graying black hair. Golden spangles on her orange and yellow gown caught the sun, as did several bangle bracelets on her wrists.

"Yes, please." She rooted in her reticule for the required pence and offered it to Vadoma as she sat on the stool. "It's all in fun, right?"

"That depends on what you believe." The coin vanished into a clever pocket sewn into the front of her gown. Full, bell-shaped sleeves allowed for air flow while Elizabeth felt cooked alive in her pelisse and its tight fit. "Take off your glove and give me your hand."

"All right." She did as instructed and then offered her right hand, which Vadoma took between her own.

"You are no stranger to hard work and labor." It wasn't a question. "Yet there is a softness to your soul and a yearning in your heart that others cannot banish."

How could the woman possibly know that? As her heartbeat accelerated, Elizabeth stared in fascination. Vadoma held Elizabeth's hand in one of hers, palm upward. "What are you searching for?" she asked in a whisper as the fortune teller scoured her palm.

"Your truth. The yearning beyond what's proper perhaps, eh?" She winked before returning to her work. For a few long moments, Vadoma studied her palm, occasionally tracing the lines with a forefinger. Then, she nodded as if having gotten confirmation from an unseen voice. "Do not put stock in the opinions of others. Your life is your own."

"What does that mean?" Elizabeth whispered. She raised her to Vadoma's.

A twinkle appeared in the deep brown depths of the woman's gaze. "To seek the life you desire, you must change your path *and* your thinking. Do something you've never done to reap the results you've only dreamed of."

"Why must you talk in riddles?"

"That is all I see." Vadoma dropped Elizabeth's hand. "But I will tell you the change will start at this fair."

"How? Is there magic here?" What would William say to that?

"Magic? No, but there are possibilities, and you have come to a fork in the road." Vadoma waved her fingers. "Go, now, and meet your future."

Speechless with questions dancing through her head, Elizabeth stood. "Thank you." With haste, she donned her glove. What had the woman meant by her words, and had she really seen a vision? Not paying attention to where her steps led, she wandered. What was it she truly desired from life?

Barely had she moved away from Vadoma's wagon when she ran into the hard wall of a man's chest, her bonnet fell from her head and for one instant, the man's arms went around her to steady her balance. "Oomph!" She clutched at his elbow. "I'm terribly sorry." As she looked upward into his face, she sucked in a breath. The same gray eye she'd seen before stared back at her. He was one of the men she'd passed earlier.

"I'm not, for such an accident put a pretty lady into my keeping." The tenor of his voice was pleasing and sent a shiver down her spine. As he grinned, she couldn't help but gaze at the most sensual pair of lips she'd ever seen on a man outside of a statue. "Come with me for a moment."

"Why?" Her head fairly spun from the unexpected contact as well as his heavy-handed use of flattery. No one of her acquaintance, not even Jacob, had done that. Heat blazed in her cheeks, for without the bonnet's brim, the sun was quite warm, but bemusement got the better of her and she kept pace with the man despite the crowds.

Before she could utter a word, he tugged on her hand and pulled her inside a stall that stood empty of goods or a vendor. She was alone with a strange man who smelled like sandalwood, citrus, and leather. "What are you—"

He cut off her question by taking her into his strong, powerful arms and lowering his lips to hers. At the age of nine and twenty, the day of her birthday to boot, Elizabeth Hayhurst was treated to her first kiss, and she didn't quite know what to do with herself.

Oh, my stars! It's both heaven and hell.

CHAPTER THREE

A S KISSES WENT, it wasn't his finest.

Though Brand applied finesse to that one meeting of mouths, the woman stood stiff and still as a board, her arms dangling at her sides, her eyes wide open and staring into his face, shock and confusion warring for dominance in those blue depths.

His friends were watching from across the way. If he didn't apply himself to this kiss and take it deeper, he'd lose the wager. Relaxing his hold on the missionary's sister, he pulled back to better look into her face. A pretty flush stained her ivory cheeks. A few strands of her dark brown hair had escaped from the tight knot at the back of her head to frame her round face. No, she didn't appear undone enough for his liking. "Well, that won't do at all."

The delicate tendons in her neck moved with a hard swallow. "No, I suppose it won't." The words were rather breathless as she stared at him, torn halfway between flight and fainting.

Those melodious tones gave him pause. Beneath the horrid, drab, ill-fitting clothing, and the unremarkable hairstyle, she was a fetching thing. Obviously the first kiss had caught her by surprise. The thing to do was try again, and this time he'd give it some stick. "Shall we have a repeat, then?" When he drew her close to his body a second time, she uttered a soft protest and wriggled out of his hold.

"I rather think not." With shock still firmly in her eyes, the woman fled from the stall. She soon melted into the crowd.

"Damnation." Brand rubbed a hand over his chin. At least she hadn't slapped him. He stepped from the stall, and when his gaze alighted on her abandoned bonnet, he stalked over the ground. Quickly retrieving the headgear, when he straightened, his fellows had joined him. All wore expressions of mirth. "Out with it, then. Tell me I've failed."

George snorted. "Failed, hell. Captain, you barely got started." A snicker followed the statement.

"That's so." Philip nodded. "Never thought I'd see the day when the charming, lauded Captain Storme couldn't kiss his way into a woman's good graces."

John shrugged. "She certainly didn't melt into your arms." He met Brand's gaze. "Isn't that what you always say women do? With just one kiss you have them eating out of the palm of your hand?"

Another round of laughter erupted between his fellows.

"*Et tu, Brute?*" Brand asked of his best friend.

"What can I say? You do tend to brag excessively about your conquests." John looked about their circle. "Since she ran from you as if the hounds of hell were after her, I'd say you lost the wager fair enough."

"He did indeed," George inserted. He thrust out a hand. "Pay up."

"You know I'm good for it." When his mates stared in expectation, Brand sighed. "Fine." He delved his free hand into an interior jacket pocket and withdrew a slim leather pouch. The clink of coins echoed as he tossed it to John. "There's an even hundred pounds there. Divide it up as you see fit, but I demand another chance."

"That's not allowed, Captain." Philip shook his head. "You already lost the wager." He accepted his portion with a grin.

"I'll have that kiss; I know it." What the devil did he want it for now? There was no more wager, no purse of coin to win, so why the deuce did he care? Something he'd glimpsed in the dark depths of her sapphire eyes called to him, something more than the shock and the fear, something he doubted she was even aware of, and, by damn, he wished to see that tiny spark kindled, to discover what it might become.

Though he'd touched her lips for a brief moment, the softness in those two pieces of flesh had set his imagination soaring. He wanted another taste, for no other reason than to find out if there was fire buried within the missionary's innocent sister.

Philip and George exchanged glances brimming with speculation. They gestured John close and then they three held a whispered conversation. Finally, when the knot broke, George counted his share of the wagered coin and then shoved the lot into a pocket.

"We all agree the wager is over and you lost," John began, but the twinkle in his eyes didn't bode well for Brand. "However." He held up a hand when he would have protested. "We propose a new one."

He tightened his fingers on the brim of the monstrously ugly bonnet. The sound of cracking straw reached his ears and he relaxed by increments. "Such as?"

George took up the narrative. "Since we are all aware of your skill with the ladies, we realize kissing is probably beneath you and you might not have had a correct advantage."

"Thank you for that. I'll admit catching a woman by surprise is unorthodox—"

Philip cleared his throat, interrupting. "This new wager hasn't anything to do with kissing."

Despite himself, Brand's interest piqued. "Go on."

"We're offering you five hundred pounds if you can seduce and then bed the woman." The cheeky grin on Philip's face begged to be knocked off, but Brand quelled the urge.

Nothing to do with kissing? Are they mad? Kissing is the first step to seduction. "What's the timeframe?" Not that it mattered. He knew his skill and was quite confident in his ability to charm any woman between the sheets, except... the missionary's sister represented a larger challenge than normal. A few kisses or stolen caresses wouldn't do it.

John shrugged. "For a man of your talents? Let's say a week. From today."

God, sometimes his friends were bastards. Brand narrowed his eyes. "A week to bed a woman who ran away from a kiss." It wasn't a question.

George's deep belly laugh sent a few looks their way from passersby. "Shouldn't take much effort on your part, eh Captain? Or are you fearful that a woman with high morals might prove your Waterloo?"

"Do shut up," he growled. Though her rebuff and subsequent running still stung, Brand slowly nodded. "A week, then." He wasn't accustomed to having his overtures ignored by a female, and the fact she had both intrigued him and annoyed the hell out of him.

Why?

The three conspirators nodded.

"How will you know I haven't lied about giving her a round of slap and tickle?"

"It might be rote to you, but no doubt Miss Hayhurst will look and act differently. "Virgins always do." He winked, and Brand wanted to land the man a facer for no other reason than he could.

Was that true, though? Experienced or not, bold or shy, didn't all women wished to be pursued and wooed? And wasn't it a matter of how a man touched and talked to a woman that prompted her to act a certain way? With a narrowed eye, Brand regarded his friends. "I'm not convinced your statement is sound."

George shrugged. "Fair enough. It's your funeral, for if she confesses to her brother regarding whatever you'll do, he'll come after you with all the wrath of a summer storm."

"Fine." He shoved a hand through his hair. The fact the three would bear witness to his efforts made his skin crawl. The last thing he needed was an audience offering pointers. It would make his quarry that much more skittish. "I'd best start by returning this." When he held up the bonnet, he tamped on a shudder. A week in which to seduce and bed a missionary's sister. Was that even possible? It might take a month merely to persuade another kiss.

"Good luck, Captain." John saluted him. "I have every faith in you."

"I appreciate that." He clapped his best friend on the shoulder. "Else I'll be forced to take on a slew of odd jobs in order to pay you boys for the wager." Five hundred pounds was an exorbitant amount, and even though his older brother Drew was an earl, he refused to borrow coin from him. Especially for something like this. Admitting to the wager in front of his family would prove the height of embarrassment. He touched the brim of his hat. "That being said, I don't intend to lose." It might take extra effort on his part, but he would have her in his bed in less than the specified week.

He eventually tracked the woman to ground by a small corral containing goats, of all things. She stood at the temporary fencing with her arms folded on the top wooden rail, her gaze focused on the cavorting animals within the pen, but he doubted she actually saw their antics. As Brand crept closer to her position, he discerned a thin sheen of perspiration on her upper lip and a trickle of the same at her temple.

Yes, the summer's afternoon was hot, so why the devil was she dressed as if she'd suddenly take a chill?

With nothing for it except beginning a seduction that would lead to bedding her, Brand softly cleared his throat as he came abreast of her so that she was on his right side. At least then he could see her better. "Miss Hayhurst, you dropped this." As she startled and half-turned to glance at him, he held the bonnet out in offering. The faintest hint of apple blossoms reached his nose. It suited her, light and teasing, yet apple trees were strong in storms.

Would she be the same in a fight against him?

"Oh!" Her eyes roved his face briefly before she dropped her gaze to the bonnet he held. "Thank you." With a fair amount of hesitation, she took the hat and then haphazardly fit it onto her head.

More's the pity, that, for it hid her hair as well as shielded her face in profile from him. For the first time in his life, Brand didn't know what to say. He'd never apologized to a woman for stealing a kiss; neither had he been rejected for the same.

She rushed into the yawning gap of silence that had sprung between them. "How did you know my name?" Deftly, she manipulated the drab brown ribbons into a bow beneath her chin.

"Uh…" Finally, Brand shrugged. "Everyone in town knows who you are."

"Why? I've done nothing to call attention to myself." Confusion threaded through her dulcet tones.

That was painfully obvious. If she desired notice, she would have dressed better. "I expect that's directly related to your brother." It was the truth. "He's rather… abrasive in his deliveries of sermons."

Another truth. A month back the missionary had tried—and failed—to convert the fisherman and random sailors like from Brand's set into finding religion and God. None of the men took kindly to the fire and brimstone preaching, nor to the assumption they'd all burn in hell if they weren't saved. Since then, Mr. Hayhurst had become an object of ridicule and someone to be avoided if at all possible. Of course, the feeling must have been mutual, for the clergyman hadn't returned to the wharf or dock areas.

"Oh, I quite agree on that point." When Brand's eyebrows raised in question, she turned toward him and peered up into his face, which gave him full view of hers. "William's tactics are often too forceful and demanding. I've told him before that he needs to find common ground with those he wishes to minister to, but he firmly thinks his ways are best."

How interesting, and how handy to know she wasn't of the same ilk as her brother. "You don't hold his same mandate?"

"While I believe it is beneficial for everyone to have some sort of a relationship with the Creator as well as attend services regularly, I think there are other, more delicate, ways to present the Gospel so the message is broadly received. Good works certainly help." A certain merriment and intelligence twinkled in her lake blue eyes, and it tugged at his notice. "However, no message will be received unless the subject is ready to hear."

Fascinating. Where he assumed she would be as dull as her clothing, her words presented a completely different picture and spoke to an intelligence that transcended church matters. He flashed what he hoped was a winning smile and moved a tad closer to her. "What of you, Miss Hayhurst? Are you one who considers herself married to the church or do you harbor secret dreams that have nothing to do with godly pursuits?"

A pink blush stained her cheeks. She dipped her head, and once more the ugly bonnet hid her face. "I rather think it doesn't matter. My brother is doing his work, and my time is best spent helping in that regard or the other charities I assist in." Her body stiffened, and once more she prepared for flight. "If you'll excuse me?"

"What if I don't?" he asked softly and dared to put a staying hand on her forearm. The muscles tightened beneath his touch.

"I beg your pardon?" Her chin went up and consequently her gaze met his again.

"What if I don't excuse you?" Brand repeated the question but couched it in his most charming tone. "I've found myself rather enchanted by your company at the moment."

Really, seducing a woman didn't require much effort on a man's part. He merely needed to give her all his attention and pay her lavish compliments, tell her what she'd always wished to hear in her heart of hearts. After that, she'd let down her guard and kisses would follow. The jump between that and bedding was negligible. If all went well, perhaps he'd have that five hundred pounds in hand earlier than a week.

"Oh." The blush on her cheeks deepened. "I… I don't know what to say."

All the better to keep her at sixes and sevens because then commonsense wouldn't come into play. Brand once more applied his most winning grin. "Perhaps we should talk somewhere that doesn't host the smell of goat excrement?" When he offered her his crooked arm, her eyes rounded with shock. Was she so untried that she'd never been singled out by a man before? "I promise not to bedevil you in any way," he said, his tone cajoling.

She worried her bottom lip with her teeth, which called his attention to her mouth. The top lip was slightly less full than the lower. What would it look like if she genuinely smiled? "Are you a sailor?"

That was an odd question. "I'm retired from the Navy." He concentrated on her lips. Was she susceptible to corruption, and if she was, could he teach her all the carnal things she could do with those lips?

"My brother doesn't like sailors or men having anything to do with the water or boats."

What the devil was so evil about boats? Curiosity churned in his gut and scattered his inappropriate thoughts. "To each his own, but the last time I checked, I wasn't asking your brother for a stroll. I've asked you."

"Oh!" Tentatively, as if she feared he were a snake ready to strike, Miss Hayhurst reached out her hand and laid her gloved fingers upon his sleeve. "We shouldn't go far. My brother will worry."

That she'd decided to do something for herself? Of course he would. Brand knew the man's type. Though he shrouded himself in matters of the church, he probably treated those in his inner circle with less care than he should. Did she toil for him in the name of godly obedience? Had she been told there was nothing else for her in life? It left a sour taste at the back of his throat.

With care so he wouldn't spook her, Brand drew her away from the goat pen in favor of walking past the large semi-circle of brightly colored wagons.

"I'd like to apologize for kissing you earlier." If he were to properly seduce this skittish woman, he needed to be the type of man she'd no doubt dream of. "I knew it was wrong, but I did it anyway." He glanced at her, but her focus remained straight ahead. "Perhaps I was swept away by your beauty."

An unladylike snort escaped her. "You're having me on." She drew them both to a stop and removed her hand from his arm. When he turned to face her with a frown, she tilted her head up and met his gaze. To give her credit, after the first curious sweep of his eye patch, she never peeked at it again. "Despite my brother's position as well as mine, I am in possession of a mirror. I know exactly what I see each morning, which means you're lying, mister—"

"Captain. I'm Captain Storme." It was important that she knew he wasn't some layabout sailor. "And no, I'm not. You have a certain… look. Slight changes to fashion and grooming would bring out your natural beauty."

God, what gammon! This woman cared nothing for gowns or fripperies or curling rags. She would forever remain a sparrow in the midst of colorful songbirds… and promptly be forgotten.

"A captain. How marvelous!" The unexpected excitement in her reply surprised him, for he'd fully expected her to comment on her appearance. "Have you a ship?"

Obviously, she knew nothing about him. The fact left him slightly annoyed, for everyone in Ipswich had heard of him. He was rather a local hero—scoundrel—of sorts. "Not any longer. But I do own a modest sloop called *Charlotte*."

"Oh, the freedom you must have, to leave the land whenever you please and sail the water until that call fades." Her eyes had darkened slightly to sapphire. "What does it feel like?"

Once more, his eyebrows raised of their own accord. "I beg your pardon. What does *what* feel like?" The abrupt change in subject matter taxed his brain.

"Being upon the sea. Swimming in it, sailing it, having it around you, letting it take control." Her voice had gone a touch breathless as she spoke. That yearning he'd glimpsed in the backs of her eyes earlier had bobbed to the forefront. "I've always suspected it has a mind of its own and can tell when a sailor has an affinity for it."

"Yes, that is quite true." But he didn't wish to discuss the sea or sailing with her. Not right now or so soon in the conversation. Certain pieces of groundwork needed to be laid, which would make the seduction that much easier later. "How long have you been in Ipswich?"

"A year."

"You came from London, I assume?" Her speech patterns were too refined for anywhere else.

"Yes, but in the winter, I suffered from a horrid bout of pleurisy that weakened my lungs to the extent I nearly died." She shrugged. "The doctor told me to come here to take in the sea air, that it might help."

"Has it?" The thought that she wasn't strong in health tightened his chest. She seemed timid but not ailing.

"Very much so. I'm almost at full strength. Which is why I'm anxious to see and do as much as I can in Ipswich before I'll leave with my brother to India."

"You're leaving?" That would squelch all his own plans.

"In a month. Unless…"

"Unless what?" He clenched his jaw. It was maddening to try and talk with her.

Elizabeth met his gaze. "Unless there is a compelling reason I should say. As of yet, I have no path of my own nor a direction, so this is what I must do."

"You are not a slave; do what you wish."

"Perhaps. One of the travelers told me I was at a fork in the road."

What the devil did that mean? Surely she hadn't had her

fortune told. "The same can be said of us all." His mind reeled at the information he'd taken in. If she were truly to leave, he had to work quickly to win the wager. When confusion clouded her eyes, he continued. "However, if we may return to the matter at hand?"

"Which was what? I've quite forgotten in the excitement of discovering your title."

Indeed, and he would use that to advantage soon. "The kiss, and my apology therein."

"It *was* rather shocking."

"But interesting nonetheless?" Perhaps it was vanity on his part, but he hoped she'd like some of it.

"I shouldn't think so."

"Is that Miss Hayhurst the woman talking, or the views of the church and your brother rattling about your head?"

"How dare you!" She retreated a step. "Regardless, decent men don't go about stealing kisses. It's not proper." With a hand, she fanned her face.

"Perhaps not, but if we don't take a chance every now and again, how will we ever change our fate?"

This time, it was *her* eyebrows that shot into her hair line. Speculation filled her eyes. "Change our fate. Have you had your fortune read, then?"

"No, of course not." Conversing with her was rather convoluted. Taking pity on her, Brand delved a hand into his interior jacket pocket and then handed her a pristine, folded handkerchief. "You seem to need this."

"Thank you." She wasted no time in dabbing at her upper lip and forehead. "It's rather warm today."

"Next time you venture out, leave the spencer behind, and wear a dress made of lighter material. You'll faint before too long."

"If it were up to me, I would. However, William says a woman should always deport herself with modesty. That means limbs should remain covered regardless of the weather without the chance of seeing through fabric."

"Oh, botheration." Then it was true. The clergyman sought to impose his will upon his sister. "Seeing a woman's bare arms will not drive men to insanity." Feeling a tad desperate, he turned her about. "Look around. Every female at this fair wears short sleeves and wrist gloves. None of them want to wilt into the meadow grass like you will do soon." He dropped his hand from her person. "Couple that with the ponderous headgear and it's no wonder you're struggling."

"A woman of the church shouldn't mirror herself after the world," Miss Hayhurst said softly. "I'm to set myself apart in order to be a beacon."

Brand clenched his jaw so tightly he feared his teeth might crack. He'd been wrong. Seducing her wouldn't be as easy as he'd thought. At this rate, he couldn't see himself convincing her of anything in a week. "Dressing for the weather doesn't make you a sinner."

"I sometimes wonder…" When she didn't finish the thought, a muscle moved in his cheek.

"In any event, I find myself fascinated by you, Miss Hayhurst." That wasn't a lie. She was a conundrum, a riddle he wished to solve if only to streamline the seduction, and he needed to move this mockery along. "Will you meet me here at the fair tomorrow around this time?"

A gasp escaped her. She looked up into his face. Shock once more lined her expression, coupled with a very faint wash of hope. "You wish to see me again." It wasn't a question.

"Yes, of course. Why shouldn't I?"

"I've been in Ipswich for a year and no man has ever shown an interest."

No doubt largely to her brother's tight control as well as the same methods the church employed on females. To say nothing of her off-putting appearance. "Perhaps it's time to change that."

Confusion clouded her eyes. "I'm not certain I can."

"Do you want to?" When she didn't answer, he shrugged as if

her acquiescence didn't really matter. "Life is full of risks and rewards. You must decide which one you want, and if you have the courage to embrace the future based on that decision."

"Meaning?" She clutched the handkerchief in her hand. The longing in her face was more pronounced as she warred with herself and thoughts that had no doubt been ingrained into her from childhood. In that one instant, he and she were more alike that she knew. Except her prison was of religion's making while his was a trap of the aristocracy.

Both cages, still.

"Come tomorrow afternoon or don't. I intend to find adventure in my day, nonetheless. If you want that as well, all the better." Brand touched a finger to his hat brim. "Enjoy the remainder of your day, Miss Hayhurst."

Oh, yes, she'd been well and truly hooked, but only a woman of fortitude would wish to move forward into scandal. Which one would she choose to be? Despite himself, he was anxious to discover that answer.

CHAPTER FOUR

August 17, 1817

E LIZABETH SMOOTHED HER hands along the front of her navy dress. It was plain and without fripperies, but it was the most cheerful of her gowns and it fit her form to a certain extent. Plus, it featured short sleeves even if they were without nuance. Would the captain think it too drab and dreary?

Put him from your mind, Elizabeth. That kiss was a one-off experience. He's a rake.

Though the reasoning was sound, logical even, she couldn't help but allow her thoughts to dwell on Captain Storme. His name held mystery and the lure of far-flung adventures. Was he as captivating and treacherous as his namesake? And oh, he was so handsome! That midnight black hair of his, shot with gray and given over to a devil-may-care style beneath his top hat. The cut and quality of his clothing signified he was no ordinary fisherman, as did the cultured tones and his way of speaking. Never had she seen such broad shoulders. The remembrance of the banked strength she'd felt while in his arms during the brief kiss or when she'd laid her fingers on his sleeve sent a delicious chill of delight coursing down her spine.

Why had he kissed her? Not for one moment did she believe the gammon he'd fed her about being swept away with her beauty, for she certainly wasn't pretty. Relaxing her eyes, she caught her reflection in the window glass. A soft snort of derision escaped. No, her mousy brown hair in its severe knot wouldn't drive any man to desire.

So *why* had he done it? Especially when there'd been many other women who'd attended the fair yesterday. The not-knowing would soon drive her mad. Drat her innocence and shock, for that one kiss might have been her only chance to experience such a thing.

I should have enjoyed myself or attempted to kiss him back, but I didn't. Fear had caused her feet to run. Even now, guilt from that fleeting kiss buffeted her insides. What would the church elders do if they caught wind of her indiscretion? Would they consider her sullied or soiled, ban her from doing good works in their name?

"What are your plans for the afternoon?"

The sound of William's voice startled Elizabeth out of her thoughts. Unease knotted her stomach muscles as she looked across the small parlor at her brother. She'd been standing at the window, gazing out into the tiny garden where her orderly rows of vegetables were flourishing. He'd spent the last couple of hours answering correspondence as well as writing a sermon he planned to orate if he could gather enough people in the town square.

What plans indeed. She'd told the captain she would meet him. Was that a wise choice for a woman who'd had it drummed into her over the years that ladies should be demure and subservient, who should never utter an opinion of their own, who should follow whatever dictates that the head of her household demanded? "I thought to visit the traveling fair again."

She kept her focus on the garden while questions circled her mind like ponies on a loop. The rented house had been more than cozy, and she'd enjoyed it this past year. Once she and William departed for India, she'd be sad to leave it. What would happen to her vegetables and flowers when she was gone? Would the next set of occupants take care of them like she would have?

She sucked in a tiny breath. Perhaps she didn't wish to go abroad. If she managed to work up the courage to say so, could she stay on in this house? But without coin to manage the rents or any other expenses, how was it possible? *Perhaps I can take a position in town as a governess or teacher or—*

"Whyever for?" The annoyance in William's voice scattered her musings. "We were there yesterday, and from my experience, not many of the sinners found therein were receptive to the message." A bit of a whine had set up in his tone. He truly despised it when he didn't have his way, and ego told him he was one of God's chosen or that he alone was better—more divine—than everyone else.

Whether it was true remained to be seen.

Elizabeth bit the inside of her lip to keep from grinning. Immediately, guilt broke over her, for such thoughts weren't charitable or an example of God's love. Yet William was just so… outrageous at times. "It's not like you to give up so easily, Brother." This, coming hard on the heels of the failed fishermen conversion, must stick in his craw. "Perhaps you should go a second time, but do so in a mindset of friendship." Though, that would put a dent into her own plans. What would he do if he saw her conversing with Captain Storme?

"No." He shook his head. "Not today. I thought to speak with some of the people in the tavern. Harlots and drunks are easier to sway than those who already believe in a religion, but I *won't* give up." The soft clink of china on china spoke to the fact that he finished his tea. "A stronger message is needed, I think, with *those* people."

As if fishermen or the folks who made a living on the sea were as dirty as the muck he accumulated on the soles of his boots. And women who had no other choice but to make a living on their backs were humans beneath the mantle of supposed sin. Had he no compassion? Elizabeth narrowed her eyes while anger needled her chest. "Or perhaps a softer message would help," she added and turned around to face him. "The more you try to ram convictions down anyone's throat, the more they will resist." Truly, her brother's views on Christianity were somewhat cracked. "Being told time and time again they are sinners and destined for hell, that they don't matter, won't help your cause; it will only push them away."

"Fear is a good motivator, Sister. That's what these people need most, and the only way to reap the number of converts needed to curry praise with the movement."

Ah, so that was *his* motivation. Somehow, she didn't believe his earnestness in ministering to the people in India. Everything William did was a ploy to elevate his rank in the church. What else was he after? Not knowing, Elizabeth couldn't quite tamp the urge to roll her eyes. "Perhaps you should try love instead, in addition to understanding. Isn't that what God's Word tells us to do? As well as being a light and an example for others to follow?"

"Bah! The masses don't need coddling and neither do they need kindness. They need to know without a doubt their souls are in trouble." William glanced up from his notes. "You are in a mood today." He narrowed his eyes. "Has something untoward occurred since yesterday to cause you to become outspoken? I must say, it's not becoming."

Who was he to say how she should act, feel, or respond? The heat of anger slapped at her cheeks, but she tried to shove her quick reaction away. It wouldn't do to show herself as anything other than a proper, Christian woman lest he deny her the tiny bit of freedom to attend the fair by herself. Yet, the urge to scream brewed deep down inside. Soon, she would reach the point where she couldn't hold her ire inside any longer.

"Nothing has happened," she finally said in a soft voice and stared at an out-of-place thread on the worn Oriental carpet. "My beliefs sometimes don't run parallel to yours. There is no one right way to encourage people to the Lord." Perhaps she did herself a grave disservice by allowing the events of yesterday afternoon to run away with her imagination. The mystery Captain Storme represented wasn't for her. In fact, nothing in

Ipswich was, and she'd best reconcile herself to that fact.

"I've half a mind to forbid you from going to the fair this afternoon. It might encourage willful behavior." William once more perused his notes while cold disappointment sank into the pit of her stomach. "However, you've always been responsible and biddable. I suppose there's no harm, as long as you stay away from the fortune teller and anything else that smacks of dark magic and sin."

Is that what she'd become then? Biddable and a pawn for both her brother and the church? Annoyance twisted down her spine to obliterate the disappointment. The whole of her life she'd given over to what she'd considered good works in the Lord's name. How much actual living had she missed because of it? Was this the remainder of her destiny, to follow the decrees and wishes of others instead of her own?

The words of the fortune teller bubbled to the forefront of her mind. *Do not put stock in the opinions of others. Your life is your own.* How could Vadoma have known that was exactly what she—Elizabeth—struggled with right now? She narrowed her gaze. "Thank you for that *magnanimous* concession." The sarcasm in her tone was evident even to her own ears, and her heartbeat accelerated. Would he scold her for that and not curbing her tongue?

Shock rounded William's eyes as he looked at her. "However, it's Sunday. Perhaps the afternoon spent in reading the Bible and self-reflection would rid you of this sudden deplorable attitude. Women of the church should never show antagonistic spirit."

That spirt he detested seemed to have a mind of its own as it awakened, as if events from yesterday had somehow manipulated a lock upon her soul. "I rather think wishing to do something for myself isn't that, and neither is it selfish," she quickly added before he could respond. "I merely wish for an outing, to put fresh air into my lungs so that they'll continue to strengthen." It wasn't far from the truth.

"That *is* good thinking. You'll need every bit of vigor to survive the rigors of India."

She declined to comment on that. "I expect I'll return soon, for as you said, there is nothing much of interest to one such as me." The sourness of bile rose in the back of her throat. Elizabeth swallowed a few times. Suddenly, everything about her current life chafed. Current constraints were like a prison, designed of her own making and started with her parents. Surely this wasn't all she had to look forward to, not all life would offer.

To seek the life you desire, you must change your path and your thinking. Do something you've never done to reap the results you've only dreamed of.

How had one fleeting meeting with a fortune teller—as well as Captain Storme—caused such upheaval in her spirit? Heat flared in her cheeks, and she quickly turned to contemplate the scene in the garden once more. "By the by, I met a man in passing yesterday as we both observed a few animals. Do you know a Captain Storme?"

William snorted. "I know *of* him, certainly. He spends his time at one of the taverns, drinking and wagering, and is a rake by all accounts."

"Ah." Jealousy stabbed through her chest. Obviously, he wasn't a stranger to the opposite sex, so why did he want to tarry in her presence? She couldn't hold a candle to some of the women in the town. Neither did she have the experience. "Well, he was ever so polite during our brief conversation." And she couldn't stop thinking of the warm pressure of his lips on hers. Dear heavens, had anyone seen them in that embrace? Perhaps not if her brother hadn't mentioned it.

"Stay away from him and his ilk, Elizabeth. He's a man who chases scandal and sin. No doubt he's destined for hell and relishes that fact." He stood and took his sheaf of notes in hand. "One such as him can't be saved."

"Perhaps." Would he change his ways if the right motivation came along? The fact that he'd asked her to meet him today both sent dread and elation streaking down her spine. *Why* had he wanted the meeting? Surely it couldn't be as simple as him finding interest in her as a woman, but if that were true… A warm flutter moved in her belly. "I know you're anxious to be off." Elizabeth turned and moved toward the table to collect the tea things, merely to quiet her thoughts. "I shall see you at dinner." They customarily took the evening meal in a private dining room at the Great White Horse Hotel on Tavern Street. Afterward, William would sometimes conduct an impromptu preaching session until the proprietor asked them to leave.

"Very well." He nodded. "Remember to spread the Word while you're out. Idle hands make for the devil's work."

Was finding a bit of enjoyment and perhaps normal conversation with a sea captain considered damning in the eyes of the church? None of them knew anything for certain about the man or his soul.

"And remember to wear your spencer," her brother said on his way out of the parlor. "You're a godly woman, not a lightskirt."

"Oh, buggar off, William," she whispered, but categorically refused to run upstairs to fetch that item of clothing. For once in her life, she would do what she wanted. Only for the afternoon, then she'd take up the reins of her duty once more and savor the memories. Surely there was no danger of temptation in simply talking to the captain.

AN HOUR LATER, Elizabeth spotted Captain Storme standing beneath a large oak tree in the middle of the fair grounds. His arms were crossed at chest level and he leaned one of those broad shoulders against the stout trunk. The pose was inviting. She slid her gaze up and down his person. The sapphire blue jacket fit his form to perfection, as did the buff-colored breeches tucked into a pair of scuffed Hessian-style boots. Did the art of sailing keep him trim and muscled or did he indulge in some other form of exercise?

Merciful heavens, the man was a threat to her peace of mind. He was sin personified. Still, she advanced even as her pulse hammered hard in her ears and apprehension sat heavy in her belly. When she came close, she said, "Good afternoon, Captain Storme." Of course, her voice shook. No doubt she looked like a proper ninny, a girl just out of the schoolroom approaching the first young man she saw.

"Ah, Miss Hayhurst." A faint smile curved his sensuous lips, and her imagination gave way to flights of fancy that had her cheeks warming. "I had some doubt as to your keeping our assignation."

His choice of words had a wave of heat rolling over her. *Assignation* sent her mind skittering into all sorts of illicit activities a woman of the church should never linger over. "I said that I would." She clutched her hands together in front of her to quell their shaking. "Why did you wish to meet with me?" The area was too open. If William changed his mind and decided to visit the fair, he'd see her straight away.

"As I told you yesterday, I'm fascinated by you." His grin widened. Mischief twinkled in his eye. The eyepatch only added to his mystery and the arresting gorgeousness of his looks. Slowly, and with a leisure that rose gooseflesh on her arms, he studied her with intensity so she felt that perusal over her skin as if he'd touched her. "I appreciate the dress. It's quite an improvement over yesterday."

"Thank you." Heat infused her cheeks. "It's the most cheerful garment in my wardrobe."

"More's the pity. A woman like you should find herself bedecked in luxurious fabrics and fripperies." His gaze alighted on her bonnet. "Is that new?"

"No." Elizbeth's flush deepened. It was a plain bonnet, devoid of any ornamentation, for she'd removed many of the silk flowers and ribbons it had been decorated with, else William would never have allowed her to wear it. "A month ago, I was cleaning out a room in the house my brother rents. This was left behind, tucked away in a cupboard, and since it's a tad newer than mine, I appropriated the thing. It pained me to take the pretty ribbons and flowers off…" Her words trailed away when she caught him staring at her mouth.

Did he think about that kiss too, or stealing an additional one?

"That's too bad. No woman should feel the need to hide her personality for fear of what others might say." The captain pushed off the tree and then offered her his arm. "Perhaps you'll let me ply you with sweets and savories found throughout the fair."

How darling his response was, but it sent confusion swirling about her. Not trusting her words, she laid her gloved fingertips on his sleeve. "I could be convinced to sample some of those sugared nuts. They're a particular favorite of mine I'm not frequently allowed." It was both odd and wonderful at the same time to have a man wish to squire her about a public venue.

"I can arrange that." The captain took her hand and threaded it through his crooked elbow. "Much better, don't you think?"

Merciful heavens, she *couldn't* think, not when the action brought her so close to his side, and his manly scent wrapped around her. She knew next to nothing about him, but her senses threatened to cartwheel into chaos. "Will you tell me about yourself, Captain Storme?"

"Only if you promise to call me Brand."

"Brand? What an unusual name. I'm not sure I've heard that before." With every step she took, an invisible gossamer web wove around her, intent on binding her to this man, but why? What about him called to her?

"It's a fat lot better than my given name." He turned his head and winked. A faint flutter started in her lower belly that brought with it another round of gooseflesh even though the sun was as high and as hot as yesterday. "I was born Francis Hillenbrand Storme. As you can imagine, I felt the need to shorten that mess as soon as I attended school."

"I can see why." The thought of him as a boy had her smiling, but then doubts came sailing in to dash away the temporary happiness she'd found. "If this is to be our last meeting, why should it matter what I call you?"

He put his lips close to her ear. "Whoever said this was our last meeting?" The warmth of his breath skated over her cheek, and she gave into a tiny shiver. "I very much intend to see you as often as you'll allow."

"Oh!" Her heartbeat tapped out a frantic tattoo. "Then perhaps you should tell me how you came to land in the Navy. At least, to start with." There was so much she wanted to know about him, but his proximity caused the questions to fly out of her mind.

"I can think of better ways to introduce myself, but for you, I'll have to let talking satisfy me." When he winked again, a host of tingles went through her lower belly and buzzed at the base of her spine. In short order Brand procured the previously mentioned sugared nuts. Once the paper cone was put into her hand, he secured a glass of lemonade for her and a tankard of ale for himself. Then he led her across the meadow and to a stand of oak trees. "Shall we enjoy the shade? This spot looks as private as we'll get at a fair like this."

"That sounds lovely." Elizabeth promptly sat between a couple of large, exposed roots. Once she'd arranged her skirts over her folded legs, he handed her the glass of lemonade and then took up a space nearby, but he didn't sit. Oh no. The scandalous man lounged on his side, propped on an elbow as if he hadn't a care in the world, so very close to her legs. Heat trailed through her cheeks. Was this considered a sin, this talking to a man without others around, and in such repose? The rules were quite vague.

"I was in the Navy for ten years," he began, following the words with a deep swig from his tankard.

She wrinkled her nose against the alcoholic smell of his ale.

"Have you always had an affinity for the sea then?"

"No, but I learned to love it." His shrug was an elegant affair that pulled his jacket tight across his chest. "It was either join the Navy or the church, according to my father. I chose the lesser of the two evils."

How interesting. "Why were you in that position to begin with?"

His grin would become her undoing if she weren't careful and kept her wits about her. "Stories of my misdeeds in London reached my father's ears and he lost patience with me. Said I needed to make something of myself or else he'd cut me off." He shot her a wry glance. "I've a bit of a rebellious streak."

Oh, how she could relate! Hers was only just beginning to awaken. "Are you someone of import in the *ton?*" Never would she have guessed at such a pedigree for this man of mystery. "For why else would your parents care?"

Brand snorted. "I'm a third son of an earl. There is *nothing* important about me." A touch of bitterness lingered in his voice, and it tugged at her chest.

Shock filtered in her chest even as she knew that feeling all too well. He was connected to the *ton!* Dear heavens, she'd never known anyone high in society. "Everyone is important in the eyes of the Lord." Perhaps this was an opportunity to minister to him in a different way than her brother would.

"I have my doubts about that." He trained the full power of his grin on her, and Elizabeth caught her breath. Amusement flickered in his eye. It flirted with his lips. Goodness, but would he try for a second kiss today? Would she let him? "Don't waste time giving me a testimony, Lizzy. My soul is a lost cause. And frankly, I'd rather enjoy my life in the way I see fit instead of what some man of the cloth tells me is proper based on arbitrary rules."

He called me Lizzy. The moniker danced through her mind. A frisson of happiness wrapped about her. No one had ever called her anything except "miss" or "sister" before. The impropriety of it tightened her chest, but the imagined intimacy of it quickened her pulse. "I've not given you permission to use my name, let alone give you leave to shorten it."

He chuckled, and the rich sound reverberated in her chest. "May I have that permission?"

The man seemed so earnest that it would be a crime not to give in. "Of course." She bit her lower lip. "Do you attend church?"

"As a child, the family did when the whim took us. As an adult, I'm not as proper or stuffy as all that, but I do believe God is an undeniable part of the fabric of life." His grin faded in intensity. "I've seen too many things in my travels to believe that's not so. However, I think a man is capable of thanking God for his life while out in nature instead of sitting in a confining church listening to a self-righteous man expound on *his* views or lecturing the worshippers by putting fear in their hearts."

Those thoughts so closely mirrored her own recent musings that she couldn't help but lean a tick closer to him. What else did they have an affinity on? "It's easy to praise the Creator when doing something one enjoys, isn't it, surrounded by a glorious landscape?"

"Indeed, and now that the sea has become my mistress of sorts, I've found I can't be away from her for too long." The pleasant timber of his tones captivated her. "Being on the sea never fails to leave me grateful."

"Does it call to you too?" she asked in a soft voice. Oh, what must it feel like to meet with the sea and the open sky without worry.

"Aye, ever since the first time I stepped foot on a ship, I knew that it was exactly where I was meant to be." The skin at the corners of his eye crinkled as he renewed his grin. "There's no feeling like it." He took another sip of his ale. "I assumed I'd live out my life in the Navy and on the water, reveling in a command. But no matter how much my deeds and prowess were lauded in the Navy while I was active, England was fickle, and I ended up with a court martial that ruined my career perhaps more than the injury." Briefly, he touched his eyepatch with a finger.

"I'm sorry to hear that. Will you tell me about both of those episodes?" No doubt he'd lived an exciting life full of adventure and daring. "You're the most intriguing man I've ever met." His attention confused her, made her yearn for something she thought she could never have for herself. Perhaps it was silly and the ultimate folly, but she wanted to investigate why that was.

"Not today, but I will if you wish it some other time." He stole the cone of sugared nuts from her lax hand. Once he'd popped a few into his mouth and chewed, he met her gaze. "Have you a love for the water?"

Goodness, but if he kissed her now would she taste the sugar of the nuts on his lips? Elizabeth shoved the thought away. *Get hold of yourself.* "I've never had occasion to be introduced to it, but I feel a longing for the sea I can't explain." She'd not told those thoughts to anyone, so why now and with him?

"Ah. I think I can help with that."

"How? Do you live close by?"

"Aye." His grin turned decidedly rakish. "I have a set of rooms at the Great White Horse Hotel."

"Oh! William and I eat dinner there every evening."

"Ah. Pity I've never seen you else I'd have introduced myself sooner."

Heat blazed in her cheeks. "He demands a private dining room," she admitted softly.

"I see." For long seconds, Brand held her gaze, his speculative. "My sloop, the *Charlotte*, is in the harbor. Would you want to go sailing with me? At times I fish. In others, I ferry supplies up and down the coast for a handful of clients. And when my time is my own, I simply sail for the pure joy of it. Returning to Ipswich sunburned and hungry is the best sensation."

That meant he wasn't a layabout degenerate without a living, and the enthusiasm in his voice fired her own. "You're inviting me out on your boat?"

"I believe that's what I implied." He ate another nut, and

when she didn't say anything further, he added, "If you wish to come, I plan to fish tomorrow morning just after dawn, as long as it doesn't rain."

Oh dear. How could she manage to slip out of the house so early? "I'm not certain I can do that." Cold disappointment sank like a rock in her belly. She took a sip of the sweet and tart lemonade to hide her expression.

"I see." Brand shrugged. He then drained his tankard, the strong tendons of his neck working with each swallow.

Goodness, but she knew a powerful urge to press her lips to that neck and discover what that drink tasted like on him… *What is wrong with me?* Never had she thought such things before.

"Figure out the risk, Lizzy. Weigh it against all the exceptions, excuses, and your fears of what people might think as well as your preconceived notions. Then decide for yourself. I suspect you've had little freedom to do so in your life. Now is a good a time as any to change that." The captain rose to his feet. He brought her to a standing position with him, took her hand and placed a kiss upon the back of it. "Tomorrow, remember. Just when the sun is gilding the harbor, come meet me. I promise an adventure, or two if you're of a mind."

Before she could form another word, he'd taken his leave and soon vanished into the crowds. Elizabeth sagged against one of the oak trees. *Merciful heavens, he is quite potent.* Some of his words bordered on poetic. And clever man that he was, he'd given her only the verist bit of freedom, dangled it before her like a carrot to a donkey. She stared after him with a slack jaw. *What should I do now?*

CHAPTER FIVE

August 18, 1817

B RAND REVELED IN the relatively cool air of the summer morning, for all too soon the heat of the day would be upon them. Dawn was nearly awakened with a glimmer of fantastic pink and purple color just sitting at the horizon. It was one of his favorite times of the day. "Should be a nice day weather-wise," he commented to John Butler, who'd accompanied him to the harbor.

"That it will. Perfect for a seduction." His best friend's look was sly as John glanced his way. "I heard you met Miss Hayhurst yesterday at the fair."

"I did." Damn his friends who sought to keep a monitor on his progress of getting Miss Hayhurst into bed. "However, I only spent perhaps a half hour in her company."

"Whyever for? You can't sweet talk a woman if you're not with her."

He snorted. "The key to any successful liaison is to give them enough to tantalize and make them want more so they'll keep coming back." Seduction was a relatively simple accomplishment... *if* the woman in question knew anything about the opposite sex. In this case, Elizabeth was completely naïve, and given her response to his kiss two days ago, she was inexperienced in more ways than one. "It's my belief that Miss Hayhurst has been repressed in every manner a woman can be due to her upbringing and is now being manipulated by her brother." Of course, he didn't know that for certain, but it was fairly easy to discern.

And his chest tightened with indignation, for women were not put on this earth to be treated in such a manner.

A rumble came from John, a cross between a growl and a groan. "Not only do I not care for the clergyman, but I don't trust him."

"You and I agree on that." Brand adjusted the strap of a knapsack more comfortably on his shoulder and then climbed onto the deck of the *Charlotte*. "He might prove a stumbling block in my path." There was no way to predict what a religious zealot would do to keep his sister beneath his thumb. However, any opportunity to oppose the man was welcome.

"You're well-equipped to take on the fight, I suspect." John peeked over his shoulder. "Think she'll come?"

That is the plan, only perhaps not today. He couldn't keep from snickering. "There's a fair chance." If she didn't, it would make his path to winning a fat purse more difficult, but not impossible. Though, she certainly presented a challenge, for she hadn't fallen prey to the charm he'd already employed. Blushes aside, she hadn't lost her stiff reserve.

It only meant he'd need to try that much harder.

From his vantage point on the deck of the sloop, he could see both ends of the harbor. One side connected with a road that wound through the more expensive part of town where the wealthy, titled, and celebrated members of society resided. Townhouses and grand homes dotted the distance sitting regally in rows along the shore like satisfied and pampered cats. The road on the other side of the harbor meandered through lower to middle class neighborhoods where fishermen made their lives as well as those of merchants and everyone else who were vital to the heart and soul of an economy on the water.

And who should have taken her first step onto the wharf's decking just then? Elizabeth herself.

A pleased chuckle left Brand's throat. *She's actually decided to meet me.* Oh, yes, she was well on her way to being caught on his hook. Grudging admiration filled his chest for her daring at defying rules.

"I believe my quarry is here." He gestured with his head in her direction. "I'll check in with you fellows once I return. If all goes well today, first round's on me tonight."

"Awfully confident, aren't you?"

"Of course. There's no reason not to be." He would win the wager and have the physical satisfaction of bedding Elizabeth.

"I won't say no to your generosity." John glanced in that direction then returned his attention to Brand. "Keep a weather eye open, Captain. I look forward to hearing your report." As was his custom, he gave Brand a salute and then took his leave.

Let's hope I have something worthwhile to say. He kept himself busy by checking rigging and sails. By the time he finished, she'd arrived, pausing before his vessel, taking everything in with wide eyes. As soon as he glanced her way, she flashed him a grin that had him staggering back a step with shock. In the golden morning light, she was almost… beautiful. If only she weren't wearing a dreary, ill-fitting gray dress with a high bodice and long sleeves. At least she hadn't worn the ugly bonnet. "Good morning, Elizabeth."

"Good morning, Captain Storme, er, rather, Brand."

The sound of his name upon her lips gave him pause. Many women had said that word over his lifetime, but something about the way she seemed to hold it on her tongue before releasing it into the air caught him by surprise. "Would you like to come aboard?" Such nonsense he thought of. Immediately, he dismissed the musings. She was naught but a mark.

"Oh, yes. Please." She glanced over her shoulder. Apprehension lined her face. "Sooner rather than later."

"Very well." He offered her a hand, and when she put hers in his, Brand hauled her upward with enough force that she jostled against him, landing neatly into his loose embrace. When she uttered a tiny squeak, he grinned. "Are you worried?"

"About you?" she asked in a breathless voice as she peered at him, her palms firmly planted on his chest.

"Perhaps, but I meant do you think you were followed? You seem particularly concerned."

Elizabeth pushed out of his hold and put a few feet of space between them. "I'm not certain my brother believed my excuse."

"Which was what?"

"That I was heading out to minister and read to fisherman's children." A blush stained her cheeks and she glanced away. "I'm not that skilled in dissembling."

"Well, should you need pointers, I'm glad to assist." Brand scanned the wharf, but other than fishermen and merchants heading out to begin their day, there was no sign of the clergyman. "I think you're in the clear."

"Good." Her relief was palpable. She clasped her hands in front of her and gazed about the deck. "So, this is your boat."

"Ship, really." He waved a hand to encompass the whole of the vessel. "Welcome aboard the *Charlotte*."

"It's a nice name."

"Aye, given to honor a woman I used to know."

"Oh? A lost love?"

"No, rather a lady particularly skilled in carnal delights." Would that shock her right off his ship? What a nodcock he was to say it.

"I see. Well, you *are* a rogue, so that's to be expected." With a slight frown, she moved along the deck, touching a gloved hand to the sail, running a fingertip along the polished railing, investigating a coil of rope. "It's both large and small at the same time."

He hated that frown. Had he incurred her ire already? "Indeed." Brand worked at releasing the moorings that kept the ship docked in its berth. "This is a sloop. Five and thirty feet in length.

It features a single mast, which means there's one headsail in front of the mast, and one mainsail aft." While he spoke, he unfurled the sail and let it catch the wind. Slowly, the sloop eased away from the wharf. "Larger ships in this class were the preferred vessels of pirates due to their speed and ability to navigate in a mere eight feet of water. I imagine they still use them—if there are still any around."

"Now that sounds exciting." She tilted her head. Gone was the brief censure from before. "Is it difficult, this sailing?"

"Not once you have the gist." The urge to preen under her watchful eye assailed him, but he squelched it. She either approved of him or she didn't. "Give me a moment to navigate into the river and then you'll have my full attention." That's what the woman needed. Someone to pay her high compliments, devote copious amounts of time to her, kiss her soundly, and make her feel as if she mattered. She'd fallen between the cracks in life and occupied a gray space. No one deserved that, and in that revelation, he empathized with her, for that had happened to him as well. "Find a spot on the deck and make yourself comfortable. The bench on the starboard bow is especially nice for sightseeing." When she frowned, he chuckled. "The bow is the front of a ship. Starboard means the right side. Port means the left. If you mean to talk, you'll have to holler so I can hear."

"How fascinating." Elizabeth quickly moved down the deck, found the bench, and perched there, her attention fully on the water. "Do you sail this ship by yourself? It's big enough to fit a crew." Her lifted voice sounded no less lyrical, and he suspected it was the first time she'd ever talked in such a decibel.

"Most times I do unless I'm running cargo and supplies up the coast. My friend John Butler accompanies me on those trips. He used to be my first mate in the Navy." It was a trick to navigate the *Charlotte* through the narrow part of the River Orwell until he came to the wider open space of the waterway.

"I can't imagine what that freedom must feel like."

"It's quite like flying." If it were up to him, he'd gladly show her, but in order to win the wager, he'd initiate her into a different sort of soaring. Twenty minutes of navigating saw him into the meat of the River Orwell. "Are you feeling well?" Sometimes, folks didn't take to the water and experienced bouts of seasickness.

Elizabeth waved a hand, and he assumed she was fine. In fact, she'd left the bench and stood at the railing to better peer into the river.

He couldn't help a grin. She'd taken to sailing like a duck to water. That in itself was telling, for the handful of women he'd invited onto the sloop couldn't handle even the gentle roiling motion of the ship in its dock. Casting up one's accounts didn't usher in bed sport. In silence, he continued to guide the sloop through the barely stirring waves of the river. As the sun continued to rise, it sparkled on the surface and highlighted the greens and blues in the depths. The gentle breeze rippled his guest's skirting. For a tiny second, he was given a glimpse of the half boots she wore, and his grin faded. The woman needed someone to shower her with all the good things in life merely because she deserved them.

God, what would she look like transformed in the trappings of a lady?

That line of thought brought out a scowl. He had no business thinking of her in any other way than a means to five hundred pounds. Once he'd seduced her, he'd move on with his life, just as he did with any woman he took to bed. Never would he give her another thought. So why the devil did he feel the need to wax poetic about her hair, which she wore in a tight ugly knot? Ever since he'd first met her, he'd wanted to see those tresses hanging loose. Now, it bordered upon obsession, for he suspected her beauty would come to the forefront if she didn't insist on rigging herself out in drabness.

By the time the sloop cut through his favorite part of the river, a certain restlessness crept over Brand's skin. No other crafts were about, for most fishermen would go further toward the river's mouth where it opened into the North Sea if they were after deep water fish. The others would keep closer to the shallows and troll the waters with nets. Merchant vessels like his would choose the middle of the river for travel.

Quickly, he dropped anchor. From this vantage point, the marvel that was Ipswich couldn't be ignored. Hills nestled the harbor and surrounding area. At present, they were clothed in purple shadows while the rising sun glinted on the river. As the town came awake, so did the gulls and terns. In an hour, the harbor would crowd with boats. Calls and conversation would fill the air as people went about their workaday lives. He took in a deep breath and grinned. Yes, this was where he belonged.

For the moment.

Slowly, he prowled toward Elizabeth's location and then joined her at the railing. "This is one of my favorite spots. If my time isn't spoken for, I'll often drop anchor and fish by hook for a few hours or read for another few." He couldn't help a chuckle. "If I'm being honest, I'll fall asleep and won't waken until the sun shifts for its afternoon position."

She turned to look at him, questions in her blue eyes. "It's quite calming out here."

"Aye." Daring much, he took her arm and drew her toward the bench that had been secured to the decking. "A man can do much reflection on the water." When he encouraged her to sit beside him, she immediately stiffened. "Easy. I mean no harm." He'd need to go slowly with her. *Damnation.* So why go through with this wager? Yes, five hundred pounds was a veritable fortune, but Elizabeth represented the challenge of forbidden fruit in a way. Additionally, he was a randy bastard who wouldn't turn down the opportunity to bed any woman who was willing. Beyond that, she intrigued the hell out of him. For all her repression, he wanted to set her free to find her own path.

Everyone should have that chance.

"This is new to me," Elizabeth admitted in a soft voice. "I still don't understand why you sought me out."

"You had the look." Gently, slowly, he drew the fingers of one hand down her right arm while he laid his other along the back of the bench.

"What look?" She trembled and they transferred to him. Never had he known such an anxious woman in his company. How many meetings would it take for her to feel comfortable around him?

"The look that implores someone to set you free." He drew his fingers back up and then dared to tug at the ribbons beneath her chin. When she eyed him askance, he removed the headgear and placed it on the other side of him on the bench.

"I have no idea what you mean." Her eyes were wide with alarm and confusion.

"No doubt you don't, but I suspect you've felt in a prison of sorts lately." When she didn't answer, he plucked one of the combs from her hair.

A gasp escaped her. The fast flutter of her pulse in her neck indicated her alarm. "What are you doing?" She tried to retrieve the frippery, but he held it out of reach.

"Changing a viewpoint." With a grin at her scandalized expression, he methodically divested her of the other comb and a few hairpins. The brown mass tumbled about her back and shoulders; the breeze gave her a fresh, windblown appearance that did wonders for her complexion. "Ah, much better."

"Stop that." In an effort to retrieve a pin, Elizabeth's body slanted against his for a few seconds. Awareness of her swept over him as she frantically attempted to gather her locks into some semblance of order. "It isn't right for you to see my hair undone."

"Why not?" Brand took away the pin, deposited everything onto her bonnet and then turned more fully into her. When their knees knocked, hot desire streaked up his leg to lodge in his groin. He might be a bounder and a complete rotter, but he couldn't wait to see her spread on his bed without clothes, her body flushed and sated. "It completely transforms your looks."

"It's not proper." As she lifted a hand to tame the mass, he caught it in his. "Imagine what my brother will say if he finds out."

"I rather think it's none of your brother's business what you choose to do with your own life." He stared into her face until she blushed. God, how much did he like seeing her at sixes and sevens? With her hair wild about her shoulders, she could be a veritable siren if she glanced at him in a certain way. In short order, he divested her of the glove. It joined the bonnet. "My dear Elizabeth, you must accept the fact you are a vision and should enjoy having attention upon you."

"Women of the church shouldn't call attention to themselves." The words were a breathless affair, for he'd begun to trace her palm with a fingertip. "We're not as important as the work therein."

"Such gammon." Brand put his lips to the shell of her ear while drawing abstract designs on her palm. "Men only say that to keep females downtrodden and hidden. Why, if women could be their true selves in the church or elsewhere, a veritable revolution would occur." That was the truth. If the so-called fairer sex only knew the power they could wield, both singularly and together, the world would change, and quite rapidly for the better.

But they needed men to believe in them and support them. A tiny niggle of guilt went through Brand's chest, for he did neither. He used women for his own pleasure, even if he respected them. *Damnation*, why had a few meetings with this woman made him start thinking?

"What an interesting thing to say." She turned her head. "Keep on with that and I'll never want to leave this sloop." With each word, her lips brushed his.

The scent of apple blossoms teased his nose. That coupled with her loose hair and the tremors that racked her body sent blood rushing into his shaft. Despite the differences between them, he wanted this woman, plain and simple, wanted to initiate her into the world of carnal pleasures. Knowing he'd ruin her and send her back to the church played directly into the rake that he was. Would that encourage her to break from the invisible chains that held her?

"I'm told I'm an interesting man." He whispered the words that were designed to thrill. Slowly, he pulled back enough that he could caress her arm. Up and down, he moved his fingers, always coming to her hand to tease the sensitive skin there once more.

"That is quite true." The delicate tendons in her neck worked with a hard swallow as she watched him from half-lidded eyes. "You're as mysterious as the sea. I knew that as soon as I saw you."

When he trailed his fingertip along the inside of her wrist, the softest of moans escaped her. His damned prick twitched. "Ah, then I shouldn't disappoint your expectations." He'd give the contents of his coffers to know what she was thinking. With the wager sitting heavily in the back of his mind, he leaned close to her and pressed his lips to the side of her neck.

Another tiny moan issued from her, barely more than a sound, but it was confirmation that he'd found a crack in her maidenly armor, and it went straight to his stones. Too much more of this and he'd sport a raging cockstand. "Brand, this isn't a good idea."

"Why not?" He trailed his lips to the underside of her jaw. That satiny skin called to him much like the lure of the sea did. "We're both willing and able." When he touched the tip of his tongue to the fleshy part of her earlobe, she jerked away with an outraged gasp. Brand snaked an arm around her shoulders and pulled her close. "As I said before, your beauty has captivated me." What he wouldn't do for a quick peek at the slope of her breasts.

"I don't believe you, especially since you're quite the rake, if the rumors are true. No doubt you'd bed anyone in skirts." Yet she didn't squirm from his hold. If anything, she melted slightly into him.

"Damn the rumors." His chest tightened. For the first time in his adult life, he cursed his history that made her look down on him. "You're smart enough to make your own decisions regarding me. Just as I've done with you." This time, he caught her lobe between his lips and teased it with the tip of his tongue.

"Oh, dear." She shivered. "You'll corrupt me if I let you."

That was exactly the plan. "Will you?"

"I honestly don't know." A sigh followed the words and she shivered again. "What sort of decision have you made about me?"

Yes, she was intelligent if she persisted in keeping up a conversation instead of giving into curiosity or desire. "You are more suited for heaven while I'm fit for hell, yet here we are, on the cusp of something… highly interesting—together."

"Oh." A pink blush stained her cheeks. Elizabeth's eyes were dark as sapphire pools and her breathing had shallowed. With her hair down and dancing in the breeze, she appeared every inch undone, and damn if that didn't feed his lust. "I could teach you how to be good." She sighed when she slid a hand up to cup his cheek.

The soft touch surprised him, and what was more, he craved more of it. "Why bother when it's much more fun to be bad?" Brand stifled a groan as her gaze slipped to his mouth. "Would taking a tiny little fall with me be so horrid?"

"I'm beginning to wonder."

"Good. Keep on with that." He couldn't stand it any longer. Brand claimed her lips in a gentle, barely-there kiss. As much as he wished to devour her right there, now was not the time, and he certainly didn't want to spook her, but he needed something, a mere taste. The velvety softness of her mouth cradled his, and for one insane moment, he had the sensation of finding true north.

What a load of rubbish that is.

Elizabeth pulled away and broke their connection. She looked at him as if he'd opened the door to a fairyland she'd never seen before. "You are dangerous, Captain Storme, and if I were clever, I'd steer well away from you."

His laugh was too shaky for his liking. Firmly, he told himself that nothing mattered except winning that damned wager. The fact he found her company on his sloop pleasant or her delight infectious was immaterial. "If you want to continue down this path, will you meet me tomorrow?"

"Yes, but is our time together now ending so soon?" Disappointment threaded through her question. "I'd rather not return just yet."

A grin curved his lips. Oh, yes, she was interested. "It's not, but I wished to secure your promise before you grow too enamored of sailing and forgot all about me." He grabbed her hand, drew it to his lips, and kissed the back. "Where tomorrow, and when?"

"In the village." A fierce blush burned in her cheeks. "Just before noon."

"I'll do my level best."

"Good." Her hand shook in his. Her fearful anticipation was endearing. "My brother won't be suspicious of that, for I often spend time talking to the women there. It's a pleasant enough outing."

Suddenly, he was jealous of the time she spent with anyone else, but the emotion was so out of place that he tucked it away with everything else he refused to analyze or give life to. "Aren't you afraid you'll go to hell if you linger in my company?"

Elizabeth lifted a hand and tentatively brushed a lock of hair from his forehead. That tiny gesture tugged at his chest for all its intimacy that had nothing to do with carnal endeavors. "Perhaps, but I'm weighing the risks against the rewards." When she winked, Brand's lower jaw dropped. *This* was the same missionary's sister he'd met mere days ago? What else did she hide beneath that demure, frumpy façade? She stood. "Now, come. Point out the sights to me and give me a tour of your boat."

"Ship," he murmured and scrambled to his feet. None of the other women he'd brought on board had ever shown an interest in the craft or the scenery; they'd merely wanted him twisted in the sheets with them, feeding their need the same as him. Excitement shivered up his spine. "You're a conundrum, Lizzy. It's going to bedevil me for certain."

When she glanced over her shoulder at him with her hair lifted on the breeze, she had the look of a water sprite who's figured out her horizons have expanded. "What's life without an adventure you're unfamiliar with?"

"Indeed."

What the devil had he gotten himself into, and why couldn't he wait to find out what would happen next?

CHAPTER SIX

August 19, 1817

AT NOON, ELIZABETH walked about the fountain in the town square. The simple sculpture of a Greek goddess dumping out an urn of water couldn't hold her attention, for the whole of her being strained for the first glimpse of Brand.

Yesterday had been one of the best days of her life. She'd finally had the opportunity to sail upon the River Orwell. It had been everything she'd dreamed it might and more. The sensation of gliding upon the water in Brand's ship still managed to tickle her stomach. She'd stumbled perhaps a few times before she grew what he'd called her "sea legs." After that, she walked the deck despite the occasional pitching as if she'd been borne to it. He'd given her a brief tour, even of the cramped but cozy quarters in a cabin below that featured two narrow bunks, a low table, two polished wooden chairs and several cabinets she assumed contained bedclothes and other essentials that made life on the sea comfortable.

To say nothing of the joy she'd reaped of watching him manipulate the sails and navigate through the water as if it were as easy as cutting butter. The way what he'd called "the boom" swept over the deck when he changed directions and the sound of the wind filling the sail fabric had been one of the more exciting things she'd known. Beyond that, the views seen only from the water made her breathless and anxious to travel. Her body yearned to go farther where the river joined with the North Sea, to put the horizon before her and see only vast expanses of water.

Would he take her?

"Hello, Elizabeth." His rich tenor never failed to send goose-flesh over her skin and send delight skittering down her spine. "I trust you passed a good night?"

She spun about so fast the skirts of her navy dress flared slightly. He'd sneaked up on her from behind; of course he did. The clever man. "I did." Dear heavens, he was as well turned out today as he'd been every other time she'd seen him. Her heartbeat accelerated, for she hadn't become accustomed to his presence, and it was a tad exciting knowing he'd come merely to spend the afternoon with her. "I slept so well that I was late in rising this morning, much to my brother's annoyance."

A slow grin curved the perfection of Brand's lips, and she gave into a shiver. More than ever, she wanted a kiss from him. Yes, he'd stolen one yesterday on his sloop, but it had been all too brief to satisfy her curiosity. "If I may offer the truth, William can go hang. He has no right to keep you a veritable prisoner. You have a life to live."

Oh, he was charming to a fault, but truth shone in his eye, and that endeared him to her all more. "Thank you. I'm becoming rather addicted to these brief periods of freedoms." The faint tinkle of the water in the fountain behind her provided an idyllic backdrop. While villagers busily went about their errands through the town square, none of them paid her much mind. "Uh, what had you planned for this afternoon? There's a quaint tea shop not far from here if you wish for a repast."

I can't very well beg him to spirit me off to a shadowy doorway and have his wicked way with me, can I? How sinful that would be. But oh, she was exceedingly curious, for each time he touched her, caressed her skin like he'd done yesterday, gave her teasing gentle kisses, the need for more built within her.

Brand took her gloved hand. He brought it to his lips and kissed her middle knuckle before threading their fingers together. "I thought to stroll past the shops. If something should catch your eye, we'll investigate it."

"Oh? You don't mind doing something so... pedestrian?" She'd assumed a man used to action and adventure wouldn't deign wasting his time in such a manner.

"Unless I've missed my guess, it's what *you* enjoy doing, yes?" When she nodded, he continued. "Then it's what I'll enjoy doing, for I'll be with you." He tugged her away from the fountain and toward one side of the shop-lined cobblestone street. "Where do you wish to start?"

Her heart fluttered at his dedication. "There are a few seamstresses that have businesses along this stretch. Across the street is a milliner I particularly like. She makes wonderfully feminine creations. Next to her is a shop for gloves and fans, any accessories really, for both men and women." She smiled and looked into his face. His expression was intense as it always was, but no trace of boredom was detected. "I like to spend time ogling the goods in the windows and dreaming, for none of those items will ever be mine."

"Whyever not? Isn't that what ladies live for?" They reached the first shop and he paused, peering into the display window with her at the most stunning dress she'd ever seen.

Obviously, a gown intended for a high society event, the gold satin gleamed in the afternoon sunlight. A delicate overskirt of golden netting twinkled with tiny spangles. Puffed sleeves were trimmed with white tulle as was the scooped bodice that shimmered with the same spangles as the overskirt.

"Oh, my, isn't that the most gorgeous thing you've ever seen?" she breathed, temporarily forgetting Brand's presence. Elizabeth touched her gloved hand to the glass. "I can't imagine the lady this gown was meant for or what function she might wear it to." Those things were well beyond her ken.

Brand squeezed her fingers. "A ball or some other fancy dinner party. Perhaps even connected to the *ton*." He, too, stared at the gown. "It would look splendid on you, Lizzy," he said in a soft voice.

She snorted. "And where would I have to wear it? William only receives invitations to a few dinners and includes me out of pity. They're never anywhere with people high on the instep, though I'm sure he'd adore the chance to minister to the wealthy citizens of England." She shrugged. "I'm never more than an afterthought. Besides, my brother would never let me wear something that pretty."

A growl escaped the captain. Brand tightened his hold on her hand. "You are not an afterthought." He tapped the glass with a knuckle. "William is not your keeper, and if you wish to wear a gown like that, you should."

"To do what? Read to the poor children of Ipswich or bring baskets of bread to the indigent along the shore?" She shook her head. "No, Captain, such a life is not for me. To say nothing of the expense this gown would incur."

"It could be."

"How? You've seen the context of my existence."

"Perhaps you'll marry a man with connections." Emotions she couldn't identify graveled his voice, but he kept his attention on the shop window, so she only saw his face in profile, the eye patch prominent—another mystery.

"That assumes I'll meet such a man. The only one I know who is of the *ton* is you."

He grunted. "My best friend John is a baron's son."

A touch of mischief ran through her veins. "Perhaps you should introduce us."

"Not likely." The words blended with another growl. Why was he upset? Brand took her arm and moved her toward the next window. "Tell me about your childhood," he said, and this time his voice was more pleasantly modulated.

"Oh, there's not much to tell." She peeked into the window. Reticules and slippers were on display. The fancy embroidery work made her mind spin. "My parents were missionaries. Their favorite places to work were in Africa. I can only image what life there was like. William was a young child at the time. I hadn't been born."

"I am not now, nor will I ever be, interested in your brother." Brand put his lips to the shell of her ear. "I want to know about *you*, Lizzy."

A shiver danced down her spine. Warmth spread through her body from his proximity. "My parents, upon discovering they would bear another child—me—returned to England. They didn't wish to raise two children—and one an infant—so far away from home." She kept her attention on the window display. "They settled in Bedfordshire where my father secured a living. It was an idyllic life, I suppose, though a sparse one. We were quite poor, for the lord who was supposed to support Papa's vicarage was lax in his payments. We often survived solely on donations from the villagers."

"Damned fool peers," Brand whispered, but he moved her toward the next shop.

"I wouldn't know about that. No doubt the man had his reasons."

The captain cursed beneath his breath. "Yes, laziness."

"Suffice it to say, we got along well enough, but as William grew, my father saw talent in him, a fire for the Lord I suppose you could say. He funneled all his free time into my brother. I was left behind with Mama with nothing to do except learn domestic skills that would benefit a woman of the church and in keeping a home for my husband."

"Yet you remained unmarried." It wasn't a question.

"I was engaged once. Several years ago. William brought home a young man to dinner. Jacob was in the military, eager to fight for his country, and due to leave for the front in a few weeks. Papa basically arranged the match and the subsequent engagement, for I was painfully shy and awkward around the young men in the village."

"I'm glad to see you've outgrown that tendency." Humor threaded through his voice.

It pulled a smile from her as she looked at the few dresses on display in the shop window. These weren't as fine as the golden ball gown, but they were equally as pretty and well out of her pitiful budget, no doubt. "I am a work in progress. However, I do have moments where I want to pelt away from people and hide, for having all eyes on me is something I'm not accustomed to."

"Do you feel that way when you're with me?" The question, asked in a soft voice, sent a thrill into her lower belly. "You seemed quite confident while on my sloop yesterday."

Heat slapped at her cheeks. "At times I do, for your personality, your form, are large and commanding. You fill every space you occupy." Was that too much to share? "But as time goes on, the more I'm in your company, the easier it is for me. I think..." She caught her lower lip between her teeth as she thought over her words. "I think you give me the confidence I never found from my family."

"That's all to the good."

"Yes." Elizabeth shrugged. She studied a dress made of ivory muslin with dear little embroidered rosebuds along the bodice. "However, the war took Jacob's life the first battle he saw. He was a chaplain but anxious to defend England from evil. I never had the opportunity to spend much time with him, and he'd never even kissed me goodbye." Quick tears pricked at her eyelids. She blinked them away, for it wouldn't do to become a watering pot in the captain's presence or on a public street. "Shortly after that, my parents died in a fire when the church was struck by lightning. They perished making certain others got out before them." The memories tugged at her heart. Sadness rolled over her in wave after wave. A few tears fell to her cheeks despite her best intentions. "William is my sole family. I might not agree with his methods of Christianity, but he's all I have."

"Here." Brand pressed a handkerchief into her hand. "I apologize for making you relive maudlin memories."

"It's quite all right. At least I'll never forget the ones I've lost." She dabbed at her eyes and cheeks with the linen square. His familiar scent of citrus and sandalwood teased her nose. The handkerchief he'd previously given her lay carefully folded and hidden at the bottom of a drawer in her clothespress. Elizabeth tapped a gloved fingertip to the glass. "Every year on my birthday, I wished for a pretty gown, but I knew better than to ask my parents for such an irresponsible thing. It was pure vanity, of course, yet I couldn't help it. I thought that having a lovely dress might gain me notice and open a new path for me."

Silence brewed between them for long moments. "I understand what that feels like, that being overlooked and alone." When she glanced at him, a muscle in his cheek worked. The muscle in his arm beneath her fingers tightened. "My brothers took all the attention of my parents. Sometimes my cousins visited, and I had friends in them, but something happened between our fathers. I never saw them again. Once more I was forgotten. Still am."

The admission from him surprised her, for he'd not yet spoken freely of his past. "I'm so sorry. That must have hurt you deeply." Was that why he remained much a loner in life now, hidden away in Ipswich doing what he pleased?

"Oh, I've moved past it, especially after the stint in the Navy." He refused to look at her. "People leave. That's life. One grows accustomed to it."

In that moment, Elizabeth had an epiphany. Brand played the rake, refused to go home to London, had fleeting liaisons and few friends to avoid hurt—abandonment—to never find himself lonely again. He did all this to cast them off before they left, before he invested time and emotions in them, before he was left with devastation. Her heart went out to him.

"You're still hurting," she said in a low voice.

"Poppycock. I'm quite fine." He shook off her hand and put space between them. "I don't need attachments."

"Oh, Brand." She sighed and again wiped at her eyes. "You

haven't healed from anything in your life, have you?" He was naught but a disappointed little boy yearning for approval and attention from his parents, his superiors, his friends, his lovers.

He chopped a hand through the air. Lightning flashed in his gray eye. "Stop this gammon." His voice was graveled. Confusion filled his expression. "I enjoy my life as it is and need no one."

Empathy gave way to annoyance, for he'd slighted her with that statement. "Then why am I here? My presence is obviously moot if you're perfectly content." She retreated a step. The *clip clop* of horses' hooves pulling passing carriages reached her ears, a reminder they were in public and such behavior was frowned upon. But his dismissal rankled. Had he been toying with her this whole time? For what purpose? "I should go."

"Of course your presence isn't moot." Faint panic clouded his eye. When she frowned, Brand closed the distance and grabbed her hand. I'm sorry, Lizzy. Let me make things right. Each day I look forward to seeing you."

That mollified her slightly. "How?" She couldn't quite read the other emotions in his eye, but the panic confused her. What was he thinking?

"You'll see." The wicked grin had returned to his face, and before she could utter another word, he pulled her into the dressmaker's shop. As a reed-thin woman approached them, Brand's demeanor changed. "We need dresses and perhaps an elegant gown. Miss Hayhurst must believe she's deserving of such."

"Good afternoon, Captain Storme," the woman said with a curious look between them. "What brings you to my shop? It's been quite some time since I've last seen you."

"Stop this," Elizabeth hissed, her cheeks warm with embarrassment. Did his prior association with the shop keeper mean Brand often brought his mistresses there to pick out gifts for services rendered? *Oh, dear, I'll not live down the mortification.* If it was true, the dressmaker no doubt thought she was his newest conquest.

"Never," he whispered back. While the other woman looked on, he fisted the extra fabric at Elizabeth's back. "We need dresses that fit and flatter her form. This sack is an abomination and an insult, don't you think?"

"It certainly does nothing for her figure." The woman tugged on a tape measure that was draped about her neck. She stared over the tops of her half-moon spectacles as she walked around Elizabeth. "Her body will be easy to dress."

"That's what I figured as well." Brand's grin was as charming as she'd ever seen it. "How soon can a new wardrobe be made? From the inside out?"

"I understand. Let me think…"

Dear Lord, what is happening? Never say he meant to buy… undergarments? "Brand, don't!" But neither he nor the woman paid her mind. "This is highly improper."

He winked. "So it is."

The dressmaker continued to study Elizabeth. Finally, she stopped and met her gaze. "You're fortunate, Miss Hayhurst. One of my clients returned a large order the other day due to not liking the cut and colors of the clothes. I believe she was about your size." The woman beckoned. "Come. Let's try one on to see if you'll need alterations. You may call me Miss Danvers. I own this shop and these creations."

"But I…" Elizabeth's mind spun. Brand gave her a gentle shove with a nod. "I couldn't."

"You should," Miss Danvers encouraged with a faint smile as she whisked Elizabeth into a back room separated from the shop front by a curtain pulled across the doorway. "At least once in a woman's life, she should look splendid and feel the same."

"I don't have the coin to pay for anything in this shop." The protest fell on apparent deaf ears, for Miss Danvers assisted her out of the ill-fitting navy gown as well as the bonnet and then drew a dress of cheerful jonquil muslin over her head.

"I'm sure that won't be an issue. Captain Storme is good for the credit." Miss Danvers tugged and tweaked the fabric as she urged Elizabeth before a cheval glass. Sweet, dainty lace lined the hem and scooped bodice. "This one will require no alterations. That's wonderful, and a good sign for the others."

Despite the unorthodox happenings, Elizabeth peered at herself in the glass. "It's a pretty dress, to be sure, but where would I wear it?" Never had she owned such a garment in a bright color.

"Anywhere, everywhere?" Miss Danvers fussed with the hem. "So you're the one who has captured the captain's notice recently."

"I don't know about that." Another fierce blush heated her face, but her eyes were glued to the image in the glass. *Is that truly me?*

"Don't play coy, Miss Hayhurst. It's been quite the bit of gossip this week."

"Oh?" If that were true, had word of her hanging about Brand reached William's ears?

"Yes." Pleased with the drape of the skirts, Miss Danvers stood. "At times, the captain will chase a woman for a while, but he never lets anyone turn his head, and I don't recall him ever sticking with a female for two days in a row, let alone a week as he has with you."

How very interesting! Butterflies erupted in her belly. "He's never been in love then?"

"Goodness, no." Miss Danvers shook her head as she checked the fit of the sleeves. "The captain isn't that sort."

Then why had he made it a point to single her out? "Perhaps he could be." Elizabeth poked at her severe, plain bun of hair. With a grumble, she removed the pins and then rearranged the tresses, sweeping up the sides and securing them with the two tortoiseshell combs that had belonged to her mother. "In any event, Captain Storme and I are friends. Nothing more."

Except she'd never had a friend, or certainly never one who made her feel so special or a tiny bit wicked. And damn him, he was right about having her hair loose. She looked like a different woman with her hair flowing down her back while she was clad in the yellow dress. There was a sparkle in her eyes she'd not seen before.

"Ah." Miss Danvers appeared unconvinced. "I'd say this is a good sight better than the rag you wore in here." She flashed a pleased smile. "Shall I wrap the remainder of the order?" She gestured to a pile of dresses resting on a nearby table. "I'm glad my creations will be displayed on you. You do justice to them like my client never could."

Oh, the irony of that! Never had she lusted after anything before as much as she did those dresses. Vanity, envy, and jealousy welled into her chest, whispering to her, telling her to accept the largesse. Then common sense won out. "Oh, I don't think so, Miss Danvers." The cold disappointment that sat heavy in her stomach nearly brought tears into her eyes. "It's not proper."

The dressmaker cocked her head to one side and planted her hands on her narrow hips. "If a man wishes to shower you with gifts, let him, my dear. Once he leaves you, you'll still have the garments. Use them to make him jealous by catching a new man."

Elizabeth sighed. She turned away from her tempting reflection as she clutched the hairpins and his handkerchief in her hand. "I think I'd rather have the man instead of the finery." But was Brand angling for marriage? Why else would he have sought her out or spend time with her or even stolen a few fleeting kisses? Yes, he was a rake, but that was an inordinate amount of effort on his part.

Miss Danvers grunted. "Go out and show the captain the dress. Perhaps he will change your mind."

"Oh, I couldn't," Elizabeth whispered. "That's too intimate."

"My dear, you have much to learn about life." Miss Danvers ushered her through the dividing curtain. "Go on." She followed her into the larger room. "What do you think, Captain?"

There was no avoiding Brand's regard now. He strode across

the room from where he contemplated a tray of baubles. His eye widened. "Of all things holy on land and sea." Admiration lined his face as he touched a finger to her flowing hair. "As I've said before, you're beautiful." He took her free hand and led her more fully into the room where the sunlight pooled on the hardwood floor. "I adore this color on you. It brings so much life to your face, your eyes." Appreciation lingered in his voice.

The reaction warmed her from head to toe, and she lost a tiny piece of her heart to him in that moment. "Thank you, but these are fine clothes on a plain woman. Once they're removed, I'm still me."

"And the beauty I saw that first day." He brought her hand to his lips and kissed the back of it. "You work is exceptional, Miss Danvers. We'll take the lot, as well as the other things I mentioned, but Miss Hayhurst will wear this one out."

"Very good, Captain. Shall I bill you?"

"Ah, no. I'll pay you today."

A delighted smile curved Miss Danvers' lips. "I'll have them wrapped and boxed right away." The shop owner vanished behind the curtain.

Elizabeth forced a swallow to encourage moisture into her suddenly dry throat. The light fabric of the dress wisped about her legs and cooled her skin much better than the horrid linen she usually wore. "I'll be seen as a kept woman if I accept your generosity."

"Consider it a gift." He winked and continued to hold her hand. In fact, he drew her a tiny bit closer to himself. "I'm not bound for hell like you think, Lizzy. I do good works too, just not in the church or its name."

Another blush fired in her cheeks. At this rate, she'd perish in a blaze if he didn't stop. "You're a better man than you think." And she was such a ninny that she was falling for him due to his charm and attentions. "How will I explain all of this to my brother?" His rage and bruised ego would demand she throw the new clothes out.

"Tell him an anonymous donor outfitted you so that you can better serve the community." With a slight tug, he pulled her into his arms and pressed his lips to hers in a tender kiss that left her reeling and wanting more. "Nothing has given me greater pleasure than seeing you dressed as you should have been this whole time."

"Oh, Brand." Her voice broke and she once more dabbed at her moist eyes. "Thank you. No one has ever done something so nice for me."

"You're welcome." If he were as pleased as he'd said, why was there sadness and a touch of fear deep in his eye? Both were gone with a shake of his head. "After this, we'll go to the tea house you suggested. It will give me a chance to show you off and revel in the fact you're gracing my arm."

Tingles showered down Elizabeth's spine. Goodness, but the more time she spent with him, the deeper into sin she fell.

At the moment, she didn't mind the danger, for she rather liked the attention and belonging.

Dear Lord, please forgive me just this once.

CHAPTER SEVEN

August 21, 1817

IT HAD BEEN two days since he'd seen Elizabeth, but it couldn't have been avoided. Yesterday, he'd run supplies up the coast to a client after sending her a brief note explaining his absence. Cancelling or postponing the job wasn't possible, for he desperately needed the coin. Purchasing a whole new wardrobe for her had set him back nearly two hundred pounds. He hadn't minded the expense, for seeing the gratitude and joy in her eyes had been its own reward. However, it was funding that took away from his savings, which meant that unless he earned more coin or won the wager, the dream of buying a larger ship received a setback.

And he was adamant he wouldn't write to Drew and ask for an allowance. He'd either take control of his own life, or he'd return to London like a dog with his tail between his legs. If that happened, the freedoms he'd found in Ipswich would vanish like mist in the sun.

Besides, the vision of Elizabeth in that yellow dress wouldn't leave his mind. By the time they'd left the collection of shops, she'd acquired a matching bonnet and slippers to every dress and gown he'd purchased. To say nothing of undergarments, fans, gloves, stockings, and anything else her neglected heart had desired. It seemed where seduction was concerned, he'd spare no expense, fool that he was.

When he'd taken her for tea in a quaint café on the opposite side of the town square, there'd been a few admiring glances cast her way by men. It both pleased and irritated him. For the moment, she was with him, but for how long? Once he'd bedded her, she'd leave out of righteous indignation or high dudgeon.

Or else he'd send her away, for as he'd said before, he didn't need attachments, and if he broke the relationship, he'd never have cause to become emotionally connected and thereby hurt.

As he stepped into the public taproom of the hotel, his mates hailed him from a table tucked away in a shadowy corner. Brand raised a hand in greeting and then quickly made his way through the mess of tables, chairs, and patrons. No doubt they'd want an update.

Bastards. Didn't they realize seduction was an art and couldn't be rushed? Yes, he'd erroneously believed he could have cajoled her into bed within a week, but she was a special case. Elizabeth was an innocent and skittish. She wouldn't respond well to overt attention and he drew the line at forcing a woman. She might not be a lady by birth, but she deserved respect and everything good life could offer. Little by little, she was gaining confidence in herself and the world around her. His chest tightened with pride. *I did that for her.*

John was the first to speak when Brand sat down. "I've hardly seen you around the place these last few days." His inquisitive gaze roved over Brand's face. "All's well?"

"More or less." He accepted a tankard of ale from the buxom barmaid with a nod. To her, he said, "I'd like a cottage pie, if you please."

"I'd be happy to give you that and more, Captain." The purr of her voice shivered over his skin and had the hair at his nape quivering. Molly would be a quick conquest true enough, and would rid him of the restlessness and anxiety that kept his muscles bunched and tight. When was the last time that he'd gone so long without relieving the need in his prick?

He flashed what he hoped was a wicked grin and not a desperate expression. "Stick around, love, and I just might take you up on that." With a swat at her lush backside, he sent her on her way, and when his gaze connected with John's, he expelled an annoyed breath. "What?"

"I thought you were immersed in seducing Miss Hayhurst?" A note of censure blended with John's baritone.

"I am, so mind your business." He sounded like a grump even to his own ears, but he couldn't help it. Frustration was high in his inability to bed Elizabeth, and now that she'd been completely transformed, doubts had crept in. She deserved much more than a hurried tryst built on a wager as well as a lie; hell, she deserved to find a decent man, marry him, and have a wonderful life together.

Not be thrown away like so much rubbish once his need of her was finished.

George snorted. He scratched a few fingers through his scraggly beard. "Has the great Captain Storme won the wager yet?"

"I have not." Brand glared at him until his friend returned to eating his hamsteak. "She is proving a challenge I'd not anticipated."

"Isn't that what every woman is?" Philip smirked, which earned him a narrowed eye from Brand. "However, she's become a looker since taking up with you, Captain." A muscle in Brand's cheek twitched, but when he didn't prompt the other man, Philip continued. "I spied her yesterday trailing after her dastardly brother on their way to wharf. Wore a real nice dress that looked like summer. If you weren't trying to bed her, I might try my luck with her."

Hot anger stabbed through Brand's chest like a multitude of fire irons. "If you so much as talk to her without my permission, I will put a ball through your chest."

Philip's eyes rounded. He held up a hand, palm outward. "I said 'if,' Captain."

The ire with his friends was misplaced, but frustrated urges were a powerful foe. He took refuge in his tankard of beer, and gladly swallowed three mouthfuls before slamming the crockery onto the table. "I apologize."

An awkward silence descended among them. Finally, John cleared his throat. "Is your seduction not going well?"

"It's moving forward but at a glacier's pace." Briefly, he told them of his outings so far with Elizabeth. "I'm to meet her this afternoon with a picnic, which we'll take on one of the hills that overlook Ipswich." He shrugged. "God only knows how far I'll get with her today." Despite the wager he desperately wished to win, the woman interested him beyond having her spread her legs. Her life had been dismal and didn't look to improve, but she had a lively, intelligent mind and a mouth that would probably go tart if she'd ever forget the rigid rules that bound her. Plus, in clothing that actually fit her frame and showed off her gentle curves, she was quite the temptation. "There is only so much I can endure before I lose control."

Understanding lit John's eyes. "You have no idea how to be with a woman unless you're in bed with them." A slow grin curved his mouth. "This is a new experience for you, just as it is for her."

"What of it? I can't help it." The longer he sat with his fellows, the more irritable he became. "This is why I don't dally with virgins."

"No," John drew the word out. "You prefer an easier conquest, for if you have to work for it, you might develop an attachment."

It was insane how well his best friend knew him, and that insight coming hard on the heels of what Elizabeth had noticed in the dress shop picked at his brain like a buzzard with carrion. "I assumed she would have let down her guard by now."

George cleared his throat. All focus went to him. "I once had a skittish gal who was naïve about life. The trick to it is to share genuine bits of yourself with her so she'll trust you with her brain and her heart. Flattery only goes so far, as do chaste kisses." He shrugged and then took up his knife and fork again. "If you want a fast woman, go with the barmaid, but if you want a different sort of experience that means something else beyond pleasures of the flesh, continue with Miss Hayhurst. That five hundred pounds will be all the sweeter because of it."

John nodded. "And you might gain a friend. Lord knows you need more of them. Especially females who aren't impressed with your pedigree, title, or your skill at bed sport."

"I don't know about that." Relating to a woman outside of a carnal capacity seemed beyond his abilities at the moment. "It's difficult."

"Surely you don't wish every task to come with no effort?" John was as earnest now as he ever was. "When victory finally comes, you'll want it to be well earned." When Brand didn't answer, his friend sighed. "What the devil are you so afraid will happen if you put in the time to do the thing up properly?"

If he only knew.

Molly returned. Her hips swayed as she made her way through the room. Brand watched her, as did almost every other man in the tap room. When she reached their table, she set the cottage pie in front of him in such a manner that his arm brushed her breast. "Is there anything else you need, Captain Storme?" She laid a hand on his shoulder and gently squeezed.

Yes, there was only so much a man could take before he broke. "Perhaps there is." He shot back his chair and then grabbed the barmaid about the waist and hauled her into his lap, much to the entertainment of his mates. "Enough with your teasing." Brand nuzzled her neck, and when she giggled, his prick hardened.

"I'd wondered if you'd ever notice me." Molly's fingers were at his nape as she rubbed her ample bosom against his chest.

Those breasts were tempting, maddeningly so, but the image in his mind's eye was of Elizabeth standing before him in that damned yellow dress with her brown hair flowing freely down her back. Suddenly, the overblown barmaid in his lap wasn't as palatable as she was seconds ago. There was no challenge to her, for she'd give away her charms to any man who asked—or paid. Growling, he dumped her off his lap. "Perhaps another time."

With a pout, she flounced off, finding solace in another man's attention seconds later, which further soured Brand's mood.

When he felt the stares from his fellows, he grabbed a spoon and tucked into his meal. "What?" The word was twisted around yet another growl.

"Nothing." George shrugged. "It's just interesting, is all."

"What is?" He wasn't in the mood to have his friends pick apart his choices.

"A week ago, you would have ushered Molly upstairs in a heartbeat. Now, you act like she turns your stomach." He licked the gravy from a finger. "Seems like Miss Hayhurst is having an effect on you."

That was so far from the truth, it was laughable. Still, annoyance filled his chest. "Buggar off, George." This time when Brand shoved back his chair, he stood. "Enjoy the cottage pie, boys. My appetite's fled, and I'm promised elsewhere anyway." The hunger pains in his stomach protested the statement. He ignored them. The kitchen staff had better fill a basket with food for an army, and by Jove, he hoped Elizabeth wished to eat and do more than converse.

I'm on the edge as it is. Only burying himself deep in her honey-eyed heat would improve his frame of mind. For then he could win the wager and move on.

AT ONE O'CLOCK sharp, Brand met Elizabeth on the top of one of the lesser known hills overlooking Ipswich. He'd chosen this one for its lonely location and its lack of circumference, for he didn't wish to share the hill with anyone else. With a bare twenty feet of green space to play with, the hilltop couldn't accommodate a crowd, thus it remained unmolested. Already, she had a quilt that had seen better days spread over the ground. She sat on top, her focus on the town below, her knees pulled to her chest, her chin resting atop them, her plum-colored skirts flowing around her, looking for all the world like a princess held captive in a tall tower.

Of all things holy on land and sea. For one moment, he paused, basket in hand, to appreciate the picture she made. The new clothes and bonnet certainly helped her image, but there was something unique to her that gave him pause. What were her hopes and dreams for the future, and why the deuce did he want to help her achieve them?

What was more, he'd... missed her yesterday. God, what a bacon-brained idiot he was becoming. He shook his head and approached slowly. "Elizabeth."

When she turned her head and her gaze landed on him, her whole face brightened as if her body were lit from within. "Brand. I'm so glad to see you."

His chest tightened with unexpected pleasure. No one had ever shown such enthusiasm to be in his company before. Not since he was a little boy. "I apologize again for not keeping our appointment yesterday."

She changed position, and in doing so, he had a fleeting glimpse of a slender calf encased in an ivory stocking embroidered with delicate green vines. The sight of her small foot clad in a matching plum slipper sent tiny fires into his blood, for he desperately wished to explore that limb with his fingers and lips. "That's quite all right. I understood your reasoning."

"Good." And still, he stood like a nodcock at the edge of the quilt. Hesitation was unusual for him, so why the devil did it plague him now? "Uh, I brought lunch, as promised." He hefted the willow basket. A white linen serviette covered the contents. The tavern cook assured him that a lady would find the offering to her liking.

"I'm starving." Elizabeth rocked to her knees and beckoned him closer. The sun glimmered off the two tortoiseshell combs in her thick tresses, which he would take down at the first opportunity. "By the by, my brother had nothing to say about the new clothes once I told him of a mystery benefactor in the town." Her smile tugged him to the quilt, where he collapsed onto his knees and nearly upset the basket. "I gave the story a bit of embellishment by adding that the benefactor was always watching, and he might bestow additional blessings if William minded his manners."

Laughter escaped Brand's throat, for she was adorable in her enthusiasm. "Then you've learned how to tell a convincing lie?"

"Is it truly dissembling if part of it is true?" Happiness pooled in her lake blue eyes, and Brand wanted so much to dive in and lose himself.

He shook his head to clear such ridiculous thoughts. She was his target to win a wager, nothing more, for his life was perfect as it was without distractions or commitments. "Only time will tell." As he removed savories and sweets from the basket and handed them to her, he racked his brain for something erudite to say. "Ipswich is full of history through the ages. In the time of Queen Mary, Ipswich Martyrs were burnt at the stake on the Corn Hill for their Protestant beliefs." He gestured to a hill across the expanse from their current location. "In the early 1600s, Ipswich was a major center for emigration to New England in America. It was encouraged by the then Town Lecturer, Samuel Ward. His brother Nathaniel became the first minister of Ipswich, Massachusetts."

"So much of history is tangled up in religious beliefs and wars over such," she said in a soft voice. "I'd much rather people find the good in each other instead of fighting over the differences."

Brand nodded. "Ipswich was also one of the main ports of embarkation for puritans leaving England for the Massachusetts Bay Colony. To say nothing of the artists, writers, and other creative types who've settled on these shores because they enjoy the town's ambience." Pride for the town swelled his chest. "Even Lord and Lady Nelson have settled here. Nearly twenty years ago, he was appointed High Steward of the town. Lives in a huge townhouse in a plush neighborhood on the other side of the River Orwell."

"You certainly have a love for this area. I can hear it in your voice."

He shrugged. "It feels more like home than London ever did. If I can't be on my naval ship, I'll take Ipswich."

"I'm becoming rather fond of it myself. I certainly feel stronger since I've been here." When she flashed a smile—free of guile—Brand's breath caught. "I can only hope I won't fall victim to the lung ailment once winter returns."

"That's a long time off. You needn't worry about that. Besides, there is no winter in India." Why the devil was anxiety rising in his chest? He didn't care what she did with her life once he bedded her, right?

Some of the light died from her eyes and she glanced away from him. "Perhaps. I haven't decided if I'll go just yet. I suppose I should attempt to discover if there are positions I can fill here before the travel date approaches."

"If that is what you wish." Brand gave himself a stern shake. *Focus on the seduction, man! Put her at ease and at your advantage.* "You've told me about your childhood. Could I persuade you to share something from the days when you finished schooling as a young woman?"

"Like what?" She sniffed a plate containing savory beef hand pies.

What indeed? He'd never had cause to learn about any of the women he'd bedded. Brand shrugged, then reoriented himself so that he kept her on his right-hand side. "Perhaps a dream you had from that time in your life." As he reached for a slice of cheese, she did the same and their fingers brushed. Heat shot up his arm as if he'd been struck by lightning and the cheese fell from his hold.

Elizabeth chuckled. Amusement danced in her eyes and showed in her expression. What was it like to live free from the cares and concerns of life, or perhaps despite them? Suddenly, he wished she would teach him. "Here." She handed him the cheese then secured her own. "A dream from girlhood." Her clear blue gaze remained glued to him, and the bite of cheese he'd taken stuck in his throat. "Very well."

Brand fumbled in the basket for the flask of ale. He quickly manipulated the top and took a swig before he made a fool of himself in front of her by coughing that bit up.

"I suppose what I wanted above all things at that age was to dance with a dashing stranger. He'd wear formal dark clothes and I'd have on a beautiful flowing gown. We'd indulge in the exercise all night beneath the candlelight, then he would whisk me away to somewhere private, pay me compliments, and declare his undying love to me." A faint blush stained her cheeks. She looked away from him to tear a chunk of bread from the fresh-baked loaf. "It's naught but a silly dream made by a young girl, but…"

"Yes?" In his mind's eye, he could envision her gliding across a highly polished dance floor in the arms of a gentleman.

"Such things fade when one is grown." Elizabeth shrugged but a hint of sadness lingered in her expression.

"Not necessarily." He nibbled on some cold cut meat and bread. "Your dream wasn't to become a woman of the church or on the mission fields?"

"No." The blush intensified. "That was my parents' dream, as well as William's, but I want… more." Her eyes took on a faraway look. "I want to see the world, to immerse myself in other cultures, to help less fortunate or privileged peoples succeed or survive because…"

"Yes?" He was fairly hanging on her every word.

A tiny sigh escaped her. "I suspect there's not just one way of living, of worshipping, of thinking, regardless of what William or the church says." She slid her gaze back to his. "I want to find that out for myself."

Brand's respect for her as a person and a woman rose. "That is absolutely true, and an admirable wish. I felt the same way in the Navy. Traveling is one of the best opportunities to see the world and understand life is bigger than each of us." The vision in his mind shifted, and now instead of dancing, he saw her standing in the bow of his sloop, her hair loose and waving in the wind as he navigated the ship through the North Sea to points unknown.

Then he shook his head to clear the image. He didn't wish for a permanent attachment. Elizabeth was only here for a seduction. Nothing more. Once he'd accomplished that, it was over, and he could rejoin his life prior to meeting her.

That is the plan so stick with it. I don't need complications.

"Please tell me of the battle in which you lost your eye."

He swung his gaze to her, searching for the morbid curiosity so many others had shown, but there was nothing except compassion and interest. "Why?"

"Perhaps talking about it will help you heal."

"It was a long time ago. I'm fine." The growl in his voice told her to stay at a distance. "There is no purpose in talking about it, for it won't change the outcome." And it certainly wouldn't get her into his bed any quicker.

"Brand." Elizabeth laid a gentle hand on his knee. The touch sent streaks of need up his leg to lodge in his stones, and he shifted uncomfortably. "I'd like to hear your stories, to find out what has made you into the man you are today. And if, in the talking, you find you can release some of what you've been holding onto out of guilt or fear or whatever else, then I've done a small part to help your life improve."

For long moments he stared at her while he clutched the flask of ale in his hand. Every day that went by she was proving herself different than any other woman he'd known. She offered him a bit of peace. How long had it been since he'd had that? It was both nice and terrifying, for he didn't know how to handle a female like that. Finally, he nodded. "All right."

She nodded. A serene smile curved her lips. "Good."

"It was during Battle of Grand Port on the Isle de France in the Indian Ocean that my naval career ended." He took a swig from the flask then sealed the top and set it aside. "The French had squadrons of frigates in the water. They attacked us—the British Royal Navy. It was seven days of hell, and damn, seven years ago right now." He marveled at that. It seemed like yesterday. "We were ordered to blockade the port to prevent the bastard French from capturing the fort."

"Obviously, that didn't go well."

"Oh, it failed spectacularly." Brand chuckled, but there was no mirth in the sound. "Four of the five French ships broke past the blockade and took shelter in the protected anchorage. One could only access it through a complicated route between reefs and sandbanks. Their captains were skilled, I'll give them that. Our commander, Captain Pym, ordered us to pursue. We all knew our ships couldn't navigate the shallows, but we obeyed anyway. We were either trapped by the French or grounded in the sand."

"I've heard the French were merciless during the war. Did they destroy everything?" The concern and compassion in her face nearly broke him.

He quickly looked away. "Oh yes. After they were done firing on us with cannons—which we returned with gusto—we were forced to set fire to our ships that were grounded to prevent their use by the French. Men either drowned, were captured, or made it to land, where I assume they were taken prisoner or killed." He shrugged and closed his eye as memories washed over him. The scent of cannon fire and gunpowder clogged his nose. Screams of injured men and the annihilation of the wooden ships crashed in his ears. The heat of the blazing trapped ships warmed his skin as if he just passed them in the water. "I was the last in line and managed to reach the harbor, but the French squadron, led by Commodore Jacques Hamelin, intercepted. My ship was seized and boarded. Hand to hand combat ensued."

"Oh, Brand. I'm so sorry." When she touched a hand to his knee again, he nearly vaulted off the quilt.

His breathing hastened, but he couldn't look at her; he was lost in his mind. "I refused to let my ship be taken without a fight. Even though the odds weren't in my favor, I fought with everything I had in me. Man after man came after me. I dispatched them as best I could. Eventually I was left with my dagger, and the captain of the boarding party met me on the deck near the middle mast."

The fatigue in his muscles felt as real as it had back then. He flexed the fingers of his right hand like he still held the dagger slippery with blood. "My mates and I put up a good fight, but there were more French, and they weren't as exhausted as we were. My opponent was as fierce as any, and he was a bigger man. He slashed at me, kept me moving, pinned me against the railing. Eventually I dropped my weapon, and he went in for the kill. Thanks to my friend John Butler, who shoved me enough that the blow wasn't fatal, I received only a glancing slice. Unfortunately, it cut open my face and sliced so deeply into the eyeball that there was no saving it." The remembered pain of that moment filtered through him once more—the white-hot agony of the blade in his eye, the copious amounts of blood streaming down his face.

"Oh, Brand, I'm so sorry." She squeezed her fingers on his knee, bringing him back to the present.

"As am I. John saved me by pitching me into the sea. He followed." A shudder racked his body. "The sting of the salt water. Dear God, how that hurt. Eventually, we were picked up by English reinforcements, and the rest isn't relevant to this conversation." Emotions threatened to drown him in addition to the pain—grief, fear, horror, desolation, anger. In no way did he wish to unleash them or pull them out; it would be the end of him, so he tried to wrestle them back into the boxes in the back of his mind.

Yet it was becoming more difficult as time went on to ignore all that he'd been through.

Elizabeth moved dishes as she scooted close to him, put an arm about his shoulders. "Don't fight your instincts, Captain. You need to feel everything from your past, so you'll stop carrying it around, or at least lessen the load. Else it will fester."

Her hands on him, the dulcet sound of her voice, the delicate apple blossom scent of her grounded him into the moment. "I'm fine."

"You're not." She was so close her breath warmed the side of his neck. "You're tense and restless, looking for an outlet and an escape so you won't have to remember or feel." With gentle strokes, she encouraged the hair off his forehead. Everywhere she touched drove him mad with desire and need. "It won't make you weak to show your struggle."

For one tiny second, he almost let go, but then other memories from the past trod in to remind him why that was a bad idea. Brand snorted. "Not according to my father. He maintained that an Englishman should keep a stiff upper lip and face every challenge with a will of iron."

"Pardon me, Captain, but he was wrong." A hint of anger threaded through her voice, and it took him by surprise. Yes, there was fire burning in her soul and made her stronger than he'd ever be. "What of love, of joy, or grief? Every person has emotions. We run the gambit at any given time. It's what makes us human, broken, what helps us to salvation."

"Bah." He didn't wish to hear a sermon. "There is no such thing as love." Why did he insist on telling her that? He should be working to seduce her, not bear all his secrets. "I thought I had that once, but it dissolved as quickly as sugar in water. Never again."

"So jaded for a man so well-traveled," she whispered.

He couldn't bring himself to peer into her eyes for fear that he'd see pity. "With good reason."

"Tell me so I'll understand." Her fingers stilled at the side of his face.

"Not right now." He slid an arm about her waist. A gasp issued from her at his touch.

"Why not?" The inquiry was breathless.

"Because I intend to kiss you senseless." Brand cupped her cheek and claimed her lips, and this time the kiss wasn't chaste. She'd been right about the restless feelings. They stemmed directly from her, and his inability to land her in bed. All that would change, and soon.

The shiver that moved through her body transferred to him. It served to spur him onward. He drank from her lips, exploring, seeking, asking, and finally taking what he wanted from her. Elizabeth surrendered with a soft sigh. She wrapped her arms about his shoulders, and as she tried to mimic his advances, he chuckled. Oh, the woman was a complete novice, but he would teach her everything she'd need to know.

And still he played her mouth, sought to seek out her secrets, experience the taste of her. When he licked at the seam of her lips, she opened on another gasp of surprise. He touched his tongue to hers, watching her as she became acclimated to the new rhythm. Then her eyes fluttered closed and she lifted her chin which gave him a better angle to fence and chase.

The hint of lemonade on her tongue fed his need, as did the soft press of her body against his. Daring much, he skimmed a hand up her side, past her ribcage to cup her breast. When she shivered, he grinned and continued to ply her with questing kisses as he weighed the warm globe in his palm. Not too large or small, it was perfection in its size. His member throbbed with readiness, but she wasn't there yet. He tamped on the urge to throw her down and take her without finesse. She didn't deserve that.

Instead, he rubbed the pad of his thumb over her nipple until it hardened under the fabric of her dress. A curious mix of a gasp and a moan issued from her. Elizabeth wrenched away, breaking the kiss and their intimate connection.

Her eyes were wide and dark, full of confusion, fear, and longing; her lips were a deep rose and swollen from his attention.

"You must stop, else I'll drown in what you're doing."

"That is quite the point." But he chuckled and set her away. The hard points of her nipples were outlined beneath her clothing. She was nearly there. Bedding her was the next step, and he couldn't wait to lay her out naked. "Will I see you tomorrow?"

"Oh, yes. Please." The words fired his imagination and hardened his shaft to the point of pain, for he'd hear those same words from her in a vastly different capacity and soon. "Where?"

"I'll send notice. Unless it rains. I can't very well invite you to my rooms in the hotel, now can I?" Though if he were desperate enough…

"I suppose not, and William wouldn't be best pleased to have you turn up at the house." She smiled and put additional space between them. "Let's finish our lunch. I'm suddenly more ravenous than before."

You and I both, Lizzy. Dear God but he couldn't wait to thoroughly ruin her. And then what? He swallowed the guilt with another swig of beer. Her future wasn't his concern.

CHAPTER EIGHT

August 25, 1817

ELIZABETH BARELY HEARD her brother as he talked about his plans for the afternoon. The sunshine outside the parlor windows took all her attention. It had rained unceasingly for the past three days, which meant she hadn't seen Brand for the same. Despite her duties and obligations, the only thing occupying her mind was the captain and how his scandalous kisses had made her feel. Even now, after so much time, she swore his touch still lingered on her person.

However, the charming man had made certain that she knew he'd been thinking of her too, for on the second day apart, he'd sent over a small bouquet of summer flowers usually found for sale on handcarts along the wharf. The note had been brief but poignant: *Thinking of you. Counting down the minutes until we can be together again.* Those words would forever live in her heart from the romance of it all. William, in true brotherly style, had adamantly protested the floral tribute, demanding the name of the sender. She'd lied and said she didn't know, for there had been no name signed on the card.

"Are you listening, Elizabeth?" The annoyance in William's voice was pronounced.

"Hmm?" She directed her attention to her brother, but Brand

occupied her thoughts. Would he send for her this afternoon? Or should she take initiative and seek him out this time? "Did you say something?"

"Of course, I did." He poured another round of tea into his cup and then spread marmalade onto his toast. "I've been asking your opinion about a particular passage of this speech I'm giving this evening for the missionary society. You've said nothing."

"My apologies. I was woolgathering." She glanced at her half-full plate of breakfast goods, but her appetite had fled. It had been missing since she'd last seen Brand. What was he doing now? Was he anxious to see her?

"You've been doing so much of that lately I'm beginning to fear for your soul."

A laugh escaped her. "Slipping into pleasant thoughts is not going to send me to hell." Though, some of those kisses Brand had given her might. Why did such things feel so wonderful but mean such dire things?

"What has you in the clouds, Sister? I'll have the story right now, for you have responsibilities to attend." William tapped the table with a long forefinger. "Speak."

As if she were a dog trained to bark on command.

Where was the harm in being truthful? It might shock her brother into silence. "Over the past week or so, I've been spending time with one of the men in town." When William's eyebrows crept toward his slightly receding hairline, she rushed onward. "I truly believe said man is courting me." At least that's what it had felt like. Perhaps it was wishful thinking on her part, but Brand had been everything gentlemanly and charming. And outside of the kisses they'd shared and the ale he chose to drink in her company, he'd been more or less proper.

"Who would dare do such a thing without securing my permission?" William set his teacup down into its saucer with a decided *clink*.

Elizabeth pressed her lips together. "Captain Storme." She held up a hand when her brother's face began to purple. "Before you say anything, he's been a gentleman. We only spend perhaps an hour or two together each day."

"Without a chaperone." His tone implied that was the worst of all sins.

"I didn't feel we needed one, and I'm of an age that I know my own mind." She lowered her gaze to her plate. "Besides, it's not as if anyone else has noticed or has wanted to squire me about Ipswich."

"That man is a known rake!" The thunder in William's voice set her teeth on edge. When he slammed a fist onto the tabletop, cutlery crashed against china. "Furthermore, he is not for you. I believe I've already told you this." Lightning flashed in his blue eyes.

She waved away his ire as if it were an annoying gnat. "The captain is harmless. I doubt he has a nefarious thought in his head."

"Oh, Elizabeth." William shook his head. Shock and disgust warred for dominance in his expression. "I highly doubt that's true. Men like Captain Storme wish for one thing—taking a woman to bed. Their currency is scandal, and they dine out on sin. I'll wager he wants to deflower you. Please, have some sense in *your* head, and steer clear of him."

Indignation rose hot and heavy within her chest. "Is it too much to think I might have value outside of your world or that of the church?" Was that all she was, then? "Can you not fathom that a man might have seen something interesting in me?" Brand certainly had, for hadn't he said that from their very first meeting?

"Yes, if it was any other man in Ipswich I might agree with you, but Captain Storme is not a good person. Neither is he a godly man."

"You don't know that." Neither did she, but it was something she meant to find out. "Perhaps he is exactly who I need and has been sent by God."

"I'm not convinced our savior would send you *that man*. It's akin to putting a lamb into a pen with a wolf." William pinned her with an intense stare—the look he employed on listeners when he wanted them to follow his dictates. "Stay away from him, Elizabeth. The church is your place, and you'd do well to remember that."

"So, just like that, I don't a have a future." She snapped her fingers as the annoyance built. "I've grown tired of you dictating to me how to live my own life. The church only uses me as you do, to further your causes, to do things you consider far beneath your station."

"Elizabeth Anne!" William appeared so aghast from her words that he dropped his knife. It bounced off the table and clattered upon the hardwood floor. His mouth opened and closed like a caught trout. It took several seconds for him to regain the powers of speech. "Ministering within the evangelical movement has been your calling for years."

"No, it's yours. You only assumed I wanted to do the same."

He curled a hand into a fist and talked over her as if she hadn't responded. "Why would you wish to toss it away by throwing your lot in with a man with no discretion and little to recommend him?"

Was that true? Brand had mentioned in passing the wish to build a shipping company, but he'd done nothing more than that. Yes, he owned a sloop, yet without an income, how would he continue to rent his rooms? She narrowed her eyes on William. Did any of that matter when there was love in the offing? "I haven't tossed away anything. I'm simply stating that you and I are going down different paths. There is nothing wrong with that."

Finally, her words sank in, for his expression softened, as did the look in his eyes. "You don't enjoy the work you do in conjunction for the church?"

"It's good and satisfying, of course, but it's not where my heart lies," she admitted in a small voice. "I've known that for a while now, even before I met Captain Storme, so don't turn this around and say he's pulled me away from those duties."

"What do you wish to do instead?" William gazed at her as if she'd suddenly grown a second head. Apparently, he couldn't think of a world beyond the church or converting folks with his brand of intimidation.

"At present, I'm not certain, but I'm confident the Lord will show me where I need to go." Despite everything, she retained her faith that everything would come to light when and where it was always meant to. There was a certain peace in her soul about it.

"I see." William drummed the fingers of one hand against the delicate china teacup, over and over and over. The rhythm would drive her mad before long. "You are my only family, Elizabeth, and I am yours. I might be many things, but I don't want you hurt by the terrible choices you're making."

The last of her patience evaporated. She uttered an unladylike curse beneath her breath. "How do you know they're terrible? Do you see me in peril or shame?"

"No, but—"

"How do you know this isn't exactly where I need to be right now?" Her brother's inability to keep an open mind or see a different viewpoint had a megrim looming behind her eyes.

"I don't, but I honestly don't believe God would want this for you."

"Want what? To find happiness? To find confidence? To see what I can do for myself outside the shadow of the church? There are many opportunities to do good works beyond your narrow limitations."

"The protectiveness, I think you mean," he countered. "There is a reason why godly women are to remain hidden and obedient." William whipped the linen serviette from his lap and threw it upon the table. "I don't appreciate this new outspoken attitude you've acquired."

"Oh, I expect not, for then I won't remain the docile servant you've enjoyed for years." A feeling of lightheadedness had come over her, quite like she thought being drunk might be. Oh, had she gone too far this time? She was beyond caring. "How is it that you, a self-proclaimed man of the cloth, can go about town wherever he wishes, yet I must cover myself and remain behind church walls or in this house? You have the freedom to visit the taverns for a drink or two, but if I wished to imbibe, that smacks of sinning."

Now that the invisible filter over her mouth had broken, the words came out in a torrent, words she'd held back for years. "In fact, I've seen with my own eyes that you've tarried with women in the town square, accepted gifts from them, yet if I should go to a fair with a man, I'm thought of as little better than a harlot and need my soul prayed for. I'm weary of your prejudicial standards. Godly rules should apply to all or no one."

"Enough!" William planted both palms on the table and leaned over it, staring her down. Elizabeth shrank into her chair. Guilt and fear twisted along her spine. For years she'd let her brother intimidate her, and the habit of letting him have his way for the sake of peace was a difficult habit to break. "If you wish to spread your wings and find your way outside of the tasks I've set before you, I take no offense and will welcome you back with open arms to forgive your streak of wayward independence once you've failed. However, I forbid you to keep company with the captain, for I won't have you spreading your *legs* for him."

The daring part of her brain ran away with the thought. *Then it's perfectly acceptable to let a different man make the beast with two backs?* Hysterical laughter bubbled in her throat, but she quickly swallowed down the urge to release it. "How dare you." She sprang to her feet so quickly that her straight-backed wooden chair toppled over with a satisfying crash. Heat filled her cheeks. Anger at her brother battled with the unrelenting need to be with Brand and find comfort in his arms. "I can—no, *will*—make my own decisions."

"Not if you believe your path lies in playing doxy to a glorified fisherman who left the Navy in disgrace."

"That's not true."

"Who can say, for much of what we hear is false." Ire flashed in his eyes. "You will lock yourself in your room with no other occupation than reading your Bible and reflecting on what you've done."

"I will not!" He was not her keeper, and neither was she a prisoner. Shock plowed into her so hard she took a few steps backward. That was exactly what the ennui she'd felt these past months was—feeling trapped and stuck, much like a prisoner, constantly under watchful, judgmental eyes and those who sought to subdue her spirit. "I realize it's beyond your limited comprehension, but I have thoughts and dreams, William, and I mean to pursue them until I've found where it is that I belong."

"None of those things will see you into heaven, and isn't that our ultimate goal?"

"I thought it was to live a life filled with joy, and to shine the light of God from within so that we bear witness of something that others will want. Only then can we minister out of love." She allowed a small smile, for she'd won the battle. "There is more than one way to lead others to salvation."

He looked down his nose at her. "I have an appointment. When I return, I'm going to drag you to prayer meeting tonight and demand the elders lay hands on you. Obviously, this rebellion of yours stems from the presence of a demon. Once it's expelled, you'll return to the sister I knew before this week." Without another word, he quit the room.

"Like hell I will."

Oh, good heavens! Was cursing out loud supposed to feel so good? Elizabeth's grin widened as she stared at his empty place at the table. Even as she shook from reaction and fear, anticipation buzzed down her spine. The fact that William violently opposed Captain Storme as a possible beau meant he must have some redeeming qualities. And there was no better way to discover if that were true than to find out for herself. If those kisses from the other day were any indication, the tumble into sin wouldn't be so bad, especially if he would ask for her hand at the end. Had not their prior meetings been leading to exactly that?

Then everything would be right and tidy before God, and her new life would finally begin.

SHE WAITED A few hours after William's departure before building the courage to leave the house herself. Dressed in the cheerful jonquil dress, bonnet and slippers from the other day, she quickly made her way through the town, stopping frequently to look over her shoulder in the event that her brother had her followed, until she reached Tavern Street. It was the same route she walked each evening with her brother for dinner at the Great White Horse Hotel, and since she hadn't had word from Brand yet, this was where she'd start her search for him.

As she stared at the front façade of the historic building, a sense of calm enveloped her. She might not know how or why, but she was adamant that her future lay with Captain Storme. How she arrived at the end result didn't matter as long as she did.

Or else I'm the most naïve goose of a woman Ipswich has ever seen. And if that were the case, it meant William was right. A shiver racked her shoulders. That couldn't be allowed to happen, for as much a horrible loser he was, he was an even more obnoxious winner. He would hold her failure over her head for years regardless of whether she'd sought forgiveness for it. *No.* She gave her head a firm shake. *This is my path; I'm certain of it. For good or for ill, I'm walking it and will have no regrets.*

After taking a deep breath and letting it ease out from between her lips, Elizabeth entered the building. A corridor forked both left and right. She waved to the man behind the smooth, wooden counter that belonged to the hotel where guests received their rooms and keys, which is where the left branch would take her. But then she followed the right branching corridor. The rich scents of food and the buzz of conversation reached her. Trepidation circled through her belly like a snake, but that was only because this was her first time coming here alone. Once she'd pushed open a door at the end of the hall, she entered the common tap room.

Sturdy oak tables and straight-backed wooden chairs littered the floor. The dim interior and exposed beams along the ceiling gave the room a feeling of prior generations. No one paid her much attention, for which she was glad. A quick scan didn't immediately bring the captain to light. Misgivings fired down her spine. Had she made a mistake? Perhaps he'd had a sailing commitment this afternoon.

A barmaid ambled in her direction. With her blonde curly hair and half her bosom on display, she was no doubt a crowd favorite in the tap room. "Are you lost, Miss Hayhurst?" Amusement twinkled in her brown eyes.

"Ah, no. I'm looking for Captain Storme. Is he here?" The only other option was inquiring of the concierge of the hotel.

"It's one o'clock. He and his mates take luncheon in private dining room number one every day." The barmaid gestured with her head at a door that led to another narrow corridor. "Do you want me to fetch him? I never turn down a chance to be with him."

Elizabeth frowned. She was well aware where the private dining rooms where located. "How often do you talk with the captain?"

The other woman shrugged as she balanced a wooden tray filled with dirty dishes. "Depends, but he's not exactly keen on talking when I'm around, if you know what I mean." She winked. "I have my duties, miss."

Did that mean that woman was a favorite of Brand's? Hot jealousy stabbed through her chest. It was such a foreign emotion that it stole her breath for a second. Had he been entertaining that barmaid while spending time with her? The possibility of it strengthened her resolve. If she wanted to change her fate and find her purpose, she needed to go after it herself. It wouldn't simply come to her.

With her spine ramrod straight, Elizabeth marched through the room. She wrenched open the door and proceeded along the dimly lit corridor until she arrived at the first door at the end of the hall. William always requested room number four. The door was open, allowing the sound of male laughter to filter to her location. Her throat went dry. This was the height of improper, even she knew that, but she refused to let her brother win, and she'd be darned if the only thing in her life was what he decreed.

Hoping whoever was in that room wouldn't see how badly her hands shook, Elizabeth stood just inside the doorway. Four men occupied the round table, one of them the captain. Sunlight filled the room. Immediately, all sound ceased when her presence was detected. Her nerves felt strung too tight, but she cleared her throat. "I'd like to speak with Captain Storme for a moment." Drat the fact that her voice broke at the last second.

"Miss Hayhurst." Surprise rang in Brand's tone as he scrambled to his feet along with the other men. He tossed a few playing cards to the tabletop. "What the devil are you doing here?" Pleasure lined his expression before concern banished it as he came toward her, looking for all the world like scandal and sin with his relaxed cravat and his disheveled hair. "Are you well?"

"Yes. Please don't worry." Merely seeing him, hearing his voice after days apart put her at ease. She kept her tone low, for she didn't know those other men. "I wanted to see you."

"Why?"

"I…" Oh, how embarrassing! The weight of the men's stares smacked into her despite the breadth of Brand's shoulders. In the barest of whispers, she said, "I missed you."

Emotions darkened his eye, but she couldn't read them. "Is that right?" His lips curved into the devil's own grin. "I can honestly say that I've missed you too."

Flutters filled her belly. Anxiety crawled over her skin. "I didn't hear from you."

His shrug was an elegant affair. "I had a supply run and only returned not a quarter of an hour before, but I'd planned on calling for you."

She nodded. "I apologize for interrupting but…" Fear of the unknown kept her captive. Never had she been brave enough to assume control of her own life. "Will you take me sailing this afternoon?" she all but blurted in the same low voice as before.

"Of course." His eyebrows shot upward, but interest and deviltry lined his expression. "Should I bring anything in particular on this outing?"

Dear heavens, if the heat in her cheeks intensified any more, she'd expire on the spot. "A bottle of brandy and… just you." Her heartbeat raced. Did other women think they might expire by being so bold? "That's all I need." She cocked an eyebrow to be certain he understood the request.

His lower jaw dropped open as he stared. "Are you certain?"

"Yes." The word barely squeaked out from her tight throat. "I've thought of nothing else the past few days."

Brand rubbed a hand along his cheek and jaw where a shadow of stubble had formed. Then he nodded. "Meet me on the wharf in an hour at the *Charlotte*. I'll be there."

Relief coursed down her spine. "Thank you." Every ounce of courage she'd managed to summon dissipated. She turned on her heel and fled. *Dear Lord, I've just propositioned a man!*

If that didn't send her straight to hell, what she'd do next with the captain surely would, but that risk was more than worth it, for she had faith he'd marry her. He was an honorable sort, wasn't he? Surely, she'd feel it if he weren't.

CHAPTER NINE

BRAND'S MIND REELED. Anticipation streaked down his spine to lodge into his shaft as he turned toward his fellows, who stared at him with varying degrees of interest and envy. "Boys, I'll have to ask that you excuse me from our customary game. I believe I'll win our wager this afternoon." For there'd been no mistaking the invitation in her eyes when she'd asked him to come sailing. What had driven her to seek him out at the tavern?

"You're a damned lucky dog, Captain," George said. A trace of admiration lingered in his expression as he scratched his fingers through his shaggy beard. "She's not the frumpy, ugly thing we've always seen."

"No she is not," he replied with a grin. Faint pride filled his chest at knowing that he'd been the one to encourage her out of that shell. "I hope to give you an update soon. Best have your accounting affairs in order." Once he won the five hundred pounds, he meant to put out inquiries around the harbor regarding ships for sale, specifically in a schooner-sized vessel.

John nodded. "Good fortune to you, Captain. We had every faith in your abilities."

"Thank you." Brand took his leave. He quickly made his way to his rooms, where he tidied himself up, shaved, combed his hair, and collected an envelope from his bedside table drawer where he kept a supply of lambskin sheaths. One could continue being a successful rake only if one didn't impregnate the women one bedded.

Why did she want brandy though? Looking forward to discovering why, he left his rooms, stopping by the tavern on his way out for the spirits.

Twenty minutes later, he arrived at the wharf and the slip where the *Charlotte* was moored. Elizabeth waited, staring up at the sloop, her hands clasped, anxiety clear in her expression even in profile. Damn but that yellow color brightened not only her person but also the immediate area. She was quite like a lighthouse beacon or the North Star, and part of him loathed the fact that he was about to ruin the hell out of her for no other reason than to win a wager.

Shoving the thought away, Brand cleared his throat. "I'm glad to see you've come, Elizabeth. Are you having second thoughts?" He hoped not, for he'd been primed and ready for this moment seemingly for days.

She started and turned toward him. Already, a blush stained her cheeks. "I have not, but I am wondering how clever the decision is."

There was no time to soothe skittish nerves. He grinned. "Well, come aboard. If you'd like, we'll talk for a while before doing other things. Perhaps that will set you at ease." Climbing onto the sloop, he offered her his free hand and then hauled her up, releasing her only when she'd found her footing on deck. "I brought the brandy as requested. France's finest, I'll have you know."

Elizabeth glanced at the bottle he held. "Good." With a tentative hand, she appropriated the bottle from him then flicked her gaze to his face. Apprehension clouded her eyes, about the liquor or impending bed sport, he couldn't say. "I *am* curious about this."

So was he, for she wasn't the type of woman to readily drink away her troubles. "Where did you wish to sail? I'm yours to command." Once he'd won the wager, he wouldn't need to put so much effort into charming a woman, for Elizabeth would be gone from his life. He frowned, despite still needing to keep in her good graces until the deed was done. A part of him rebelled, for the past week or so hadn't felt as exhausting as he'd assumed, doing the pretty with a female.

"Somewhere well away from Ipswich. At the moment, I want to put space between myself and my brother." She drifted to the railing, her posture stiff and taut. "I'm so furious at him I can hardly speak."

"Aye." Some of Brand's enthusiasm dimmed, for while she was in a temper, she wouldn't want to be intimate. *Damn it all.* "Let me get the *Charlotte* underway then you can tell me what the bastard has done."

"Yes, he *is* quite the bastard," she said in a low voice as if worried someone might overhear her say the word.

He kept his own counsel while releasing ropes, letting out the sail and readying for departure. Every beat of his pulse urged him to get on with it, for there was five hundred pounds in the offing. Yet the sane part of him wanted to go slowly with her. If he came on strong, urging her into something she wasn't ready for, she'd spook and demand that he return her to the harbor.

As he guided his ship into the River Orwell and around the other vessels that dotted the water, he kept one eye on her. Those brilliant yellow skirts made her look like a tropical bird who'd perched for a few seconds on his deck. Ever since he'd entered the wager and pursued her, he'd looked forward to seeing her. What would his days be like once she was gone, and no doubt despising him for what he was about to do?

Like he'd done with so many other ponderances and emotions he didn't have the capacity or courage to own or examine, Brand shoved those thoughts to the back of his mind, but that didn't lessen the pressure in his chest. Since she wasn't inclined to talk and had taken to pacing the deck with the brandy bottle clutched beneath her arm, he let her be. The breeze today was more insistent than the last time Elizabeth had visited the sloop. It rippled through her skirting and clawed at her bonnet ribbons. He couldn't help but grin, for soon he would encourage both those items from her form.

Finally, he reached a spot far enough away from Ipswich's harbor that would satisfy his guest. The early afternoon sun sat high in a blue sky dotted with puffy white clouds. It glimmered on the green-blue water like a million diamonds. Nary a fishing vessel was in sight, for everyone working the river had no doubt already found their perfect spots earlier. "This is as good a place as any," he shouted to her while he dropped anchor. In the distance, the mouth of the river emptied into the North Sea. The water there appeared a deeper blue and it called to him. What he wouldn't give to traverse that sea without a destination in mind for the sheer joy of sailing.

Would Elizabeth wish to accompany him? He'd come to rather enjoy her companionship.

A snort escaped. Of course she wouldn't. No after she found herself ruined and discovered he'd only lain with her for a wager. *God, I'm a prick.* But then, he'd never claimed he was a good man.

She didn't turn away from the railing, so he joined her. "Look." Elizabeth pointed to the pale shape of a fish swimming just beneath the water's surface. "What is it?"

Brand peered down and chuckled. "A sea bass. Probably a good foot in size. The Orwell is teeming with all sorts of bass. Easier to catch here than in the sea where the water's deeper and they can hide better."

"It's wonderful." She glanced at him. Excitement danced in her eyes. "I've never seen a fish in its natural habitat before."

"You'll find that that water has many secrets and that each one is fascinating." Brand drew her across the deck and encouraged her sit in on the bench. When he settled beside her, he took the bottle of brandy from her hand. "Now, tell me why you're out of sorts with your brother."

Immediately, the joy in her expression vanished beneath a thundercloud of annoyance and ire. "He assumes I have no worth in life unless I'm toiling away for the church or doing the same for him." She tilted her chin up in defiance. "The man ordered me to stay in my room today and think over my poor decisions this past week." When she scoffed, her eyes snapped. "Told me to stay away from you, and that if I didn't, he'd have the church elders banish the demon inside me that has made me rebellious."

Brand didn't know what to say. His lower jaw dropped open as he stared. "A demon." It wasn't a question.

"That's how he explains my sudden confidence and courage." She shrugged. Her lips were set in a hard line, but when she looked at him again, some of the aggravation faded. "It's not a demon that's encouraged my behavior."

"No?" Though he yearned to find out if she knew the cause, wanted to hear it.

"No." When she smiled, he forgot how to breathe properly, for the full force of that gesture had the power to knock him off his seat. "It's been you, Brand."

"How so?"

"You saw me when I was all but invisible. You continued to meet with me even though you know my brother." Her smile faded slightly. "You've gone out of your way to court me when no one else would. That alone has buoyed my spirit and encouraged me to start finding my place in the world."

Heat crept up the back of his neck, for her praise tightened the knots in his stomach. He was nothing but a blackguard and would corrupt this innocent without regret, all for the sum of five hundred pounds. "I don't know about that. You're placing too much importance on me, and I'm not that altruistic a fellow." Hell, for far too long he'd only thought about himself. Still did and wasn't inclined to change.

"Hush, you."

"It's true. I'm not the hero you think."

"You're enough of one to warrant that moniker with me." The longer she stared at him, the more uncomfortable he became. "William needs to realize I'm entitled to live my own life, to find my place in the world, even if it's not the same as his."

"Quite right."

"He also needs to understand I don't see the world the same as he does, and there's nothing wrong with that."

"Absolutely, there isn't." With every statement uttered, her voice sounded stronger. Brand's respect for her grew.

"I have a feeling it will be a long process and bring a fight with each step." She released the ribbon beneath her chin and removed her bonnet with a sigh. When she placed it on the bench beside her, the wind caught it and swept it to the decking. Elizabeth didn't notice, for the whole of her focus was on his face. "Should we toast to the new life I'm moving into?"

"Uh, sure." The silly widgeon didn't realize one didn't toast with liquor, but he wouldn't dissuade her. After removing the cork in the bottle's top, he slightly lifted it. "Here's to future endeavors." He took a swig from the bottle and let the burn of the alcohol slide down his throat before offering it to her. "Careful you don't over-imbibe your first time out."

"I promise." With care, Elizabeth lifted the bottle to her lips. She took a delicate sip. Immediately, she coughed and sputtered. Moisture pooled in her eyes. "You men make it look so easy and elegant, but this is a vile drink."

"Only because you're not accustomed to it." There was something wild and arousing about watching a proper female drink from a brandy bottle. "Try again." Besides, the liquor would relax her for things to come.

As she held his gaze, she once more lifted the bottle to her lips. Then she took a healthy gulp. Again, she coughed and gave the bottle back to him. Her eyes streamed. "Goodness, it burns, but once that's faded, there's a certain... smooth loveliness to it."

"And I'm certain I'll land in hell if you start taking a liking to booze." He took another swig for courage and then recorked the bottle. "You're unlike any woman I've ever known." That was God's honest truth. Once he'd set the bottle on the deck, he turned toward her, their knees crashing together. Full blown lust streaked through his insides.

It was time.

"Is that a good thing?" Apprehension clouded her bluer than blue eyes.

"Absolutely." Best to continue with the flattery until he'd obtained his goal. Brand took her hands and slowly removed her gloves. They fell to the deck with the veriest of whispers. "You make me want to be a better man." Another truth, and this one stabbed through his chest leaving surprise in its wake.

"That makes me so happy." She trembled, and for the space of one heartbeat, he considered not going through with the wager, but then the urgent need hardening his shaft scattered that thought.

"Good." One by one, he plucked the pins and combs from her hair. As he tucked them into the interior pocket of his jacket, she shook out her tresses and they flowed about her back and shoulders in the most erotic of waterfalls. "Ah, Lizzy. I'm a fortunate man indeed that you've chosen me," he murmured as he slid his arms about her and pulled her close. Again, that wasn't far from the truth, but oh how she would rage once the wager became known.

Elizabeth planted a palm against his chest, holding him off when he would have kissed her. She found his gaze with hers. "Before we go farther, can you promise that you haven't bedded the blonde barmaid at the tavern?" A trace of insecurity flitted through her expressive eyes. "I have the feeling she's angling for your attentions."

If only you knew. Despite the renewed heat that crawled up the back of his neck, Brand nodded. "I've not bedded her." She didn't need to know that he'd thought about it.

"I knew you were better than that." With a happy sigh, she pressed herself into his embrace, and when her lips found his, she shivered and went pliant in his arms.

No, he was a bastard and a snake, but he shoved self-recrimination from his mind to better concentrate on kissing her senseless. The sharp taste of brandy on her tongue spurred him onward. He plundered her mouth, explored every centimeter of her soft lips until she was breathless, and she restlessly plucked at his cravat.

"Would you rather move below to the cabin?" The delicate scent of her teased his nose, and made him more reckless than usual.

"Not just yet." She nipped and nibbled a path beneath his jaw, and the hesitancy of her movements only increased his ardor. Her inexperience fanned the fires popping his blood. "However, I do want to explore your chest. I've…" The blush renewed in her cheeks. "I've thought of that since the other day."

A tremor moved through his shaft. She thought of being intimate with him? "That's easily done." Brand eased back. It took all of thirty seconds to divest himself of the jacket and waistcoat. They joined her bonnet and gloves on the deck. When he reached for his cravat, she was there ahead of him, tugging at the length of cloth until the ends came loose and danced in the breeze.

"Much better." Elizabeth slid her palms up his chest and pressed her lips to the skin bared by the gaping placket of his fine linen shirt. "You're so different from me." Before he knew it, she'd pulled the tails from his breeches. The moment she laid her bare palm to his chest beneath the garment, he hissed as need circled through his belly.

Damnation, but he couldn't wait to feel her hands on other parts of his body. Her caresses hadn't been erotic in nature, but they'd stoked fires that couldn't be doused. Too much more of that innocent play and he'd spend before he was ready. "Perhaps I should guide you in this, hmm?" Before she could say anything, he resituated himself on the bench and hauled her into his lap with her back to his chest, her legs dangling over the sides of his.

"What are you doing?" Concern threaded through her tones as she turned her head to look at him. "This isn't proper, Brand. Let me off."

Her protest increased his desire. There was something about

being able to teach this woman, usher her into carnal pleasures, that he couldn't glean from liaisons with other women. "Not a chance. You'll enjoy this."

Her swallow was audible. "I might not have personal knowledge, but I don't think this is how it goes."

Oh, how delightfully naïve she was. "Shh." He slid his lips down the soft column of her neck. "There are many ways one can achieve release. But first, we're going to play." When he nuzzled the spot where her neck met her shoulder, the shiver that worked its way through her body transferred to him.

"Like we did the other day on the hill?" Elizabeth lifted her chin to provide him greater access.

"Better." He needed to go slowly, for as much as she was enjoying herself now, her muscles were still tensed, ready for flight. "If at any time you feel uncomfortable, tell me and I'll cease immediately." As he spoke, he drew his fingers up and down the inside of her left arm. When gooseflesh popped on her skin, he gave the same treatment to her right. Oh, yes, this would be such fun. "Do you like that?"

"Yes." A whisper propelled the word into being. She relaxed backward against his chest. "It makes me feel both naughty and excited."

"Then I'm doing it correctly."

"But this, doing *this*, is a sin. God won't like it." Her voice was small and soft.

"Honestly, I'm not sure God even concerns himself with every couple that's indulging in pleasure all in this same moment." But he paused. "Do you wish to continue?"

"Yes." The breathlessness of the reply confirmed her intent.

For several minutes, he caressed her arms, the side of her neck, glanced his fingers along the bodice of her dress, pausing every so often to let her acclimate to his ministrations. "All is well?" he murmured then gently bit her earlobe.

"Oh, yes. It's lovely."

"How about this?" Daring much, Brand dipped a finger beneath her bodice. He did nothing more than stroke that digit over the swell of her breast.

"No." With a slight shake of her head, she deterred his hand.

"All right, but are you sure?"

A moment of silence, then, "No…"

"Then let's try that again." He did, and when she uttered a soft sigh, he grinned. "Good." He kissed her shoulder, nibbled a path up to her nape and kissed the fragrant skin there. Then he withdrew his finger and eased his hand beneath her bodice to cup that fleshy globe. "Does this feel like a sin, Lizzy?" he whispered against the shell of her ear.

"I…"

"Such pleasure is God-given."

"William says it's from the devil in order to trap Christians and make them stray from the path of righteousness."

By sheer willpower, Brand bit back the retort he sorely wanted to make. Instead, he said, "Then William is doing it wrong." The warmth of her skin sank into him as he molded that mound to fit his palm. Only then did he brush her nipple ever so gently with a finger, and he waited.

"Oh!" Elizabeth sat up so quickly her head bumped against his chin. "I'm sorry. You took me by surprise."

"Think nothing of it." He ignored the slight pain but brushed his finger over that tip again, encouraging it to tighten. His mouth watered, for he could almost feel the pebbled skin on his tongue. "Shall I continue?"

"Yes, please."

That tiny little plea went straight to his shaft and he clenched his teeth against the urgency. Reminding himself to use care in the handling her, he tugged down her bodice until her glorious breasts were bared to the sun and his gaze. Thank God there weren't other vessels nearby, for he didn't want any other man to look upon her charms. They were for him alone… at least in this moment.

"Brand?" Worry rang in her tone. Again, her body tensed.

"Easy, now. Relax and enjoy what I'm doing." He kept his voice light and soothing as if coaxing a skittish animal out of hiding. As he murmured empty endearments, he took her breasts in his hands, gently kneading them, holding them, smashing them together to better see the dark rosy tips harden into aroused buds. Damn, but he wanted to taste them, tease those nipples with his tongue, and he would soon.

Elizabeth once more reclined against him with a sigh. With a tight grin and a tighter control on his shaft, Brand rubbed his palms along those straining tips. They hardened further. She squirmed on his lap, which did nothing to relieve the ache in his shaft. He took her breasts in hand once more. This time, he rolled the buds starting at their base and eased his way upward until he worried the nipple itself.

"Mercy," she breathed. The utterance mixed with a moan. "We shouldn't."

There was only so much a man could endure, but he did. "Would you like for me to stop?" If she said so, he would, for he wasn't in the habit of forcing women against their will.

"No. I want to know what this—everything—feels like." She lifted a hand and wrapped it around his nape.

"God, you're so responsive." He adored women like that. As her back arched and put her breasts more firmly into his care, Brand drank in the sight of her. "Tell me where you want me to touch you, Lizzy," he whispered into her ear.

"Anywhere," she managed to croak while pressing her free hand to his and encouraging him to continue his torment. "Everywhere."

"Aye." The next few minutes were filled with him discovering just how reactive she was by experimenting with different levels of friction and play at her breasts. Every sound she uttered from the back of her throat brought him closer to the edge. Already, his member pressed painfully against his breeches, stoked and primed when she squirmed on his lap. Suddenly, he needed more of her. "I'm going to turn you around to face me."

"Why?" She squealed when he jostled her from his legs only to lift her up and resituate her so that she straddled his lap. Her skirting bunched between them.

"So I can kiss you and have better access." This time he made love to her mouth with determination, hoped to give her a taste of what was to come. Brand chased her tongue with his, bossed it until they fenced and fought for dominance. Oh, she was a quick study, but she was still an innocent and had no idea about relations between a man and a woman. Would that they both were naked with skin pressed against skin, but there was no time for that now.

A bit of his control slipped as he dragged his lips down the column of her throat to close them around a nipple.

"Oh, my!" Elizabeth shot upward on his lap, which only thrust that breast deeper into his mouth. "This is…" She panted. "I never thought… William said only harlots acted this way." A muffled scream burst from her when he suckled that pebbled nub.

"William is quite misguided about relations between men and women, and I most certainly don't wish to talk about him right now." Brand ignored the pulsing insistence in his prick. He continued to tease the nipple with his tongue and teeth while he shoved a hand beneath the yards of skirting. The thought of her splayed thighs drove him mad. Had they been on a bed in private, he would have worked her over with his mouth, but this would have to do. Quickly, he found her sex that was slick with arousal. He slid his fingers through her feminine curls, encouraged the tiny bundle of nerves out of hiding.

"What are you doing?" Fear rolled through her tone. It clouded her eyes, battling with the dark desire in those sapphire depths.

"Showing you that coupling doesn't mean what you've been taught."

"It's not natural, not proper."

He snorted. "I'll wager it is, since intercourse is as old as time, but no, it probably isn't proper. That's why it's so damned fun." As he claimed her lips in a kiss, he rubbed his fingertip over that nubbin, using varying degrees of friction.

"Merciful heavens." She gasped and wriggled from his attentions. "I can't… This is too wicked…" A moan escaped and she pressed her fingers to her lips. "I'm falling…"

"Keep going, for the landing is more than worth it." Over and over, he stroked that bud. With his free hand, he pinched and rolled one of her nipples. "Come for me, Lizzy. Dive over the edge into bliss like you've never known," he encouraged in a soft, crooning voice. God, if he didn't bury himself into her heat soon, all this effort would be for naught.

"I don't understand." Panic set up in her voice.

"Shh. We'll get there." Brand renewed his efforts to bring her to completion, but it had no effect. He eased a finger into her passage, and Elizabeth nearly bucked off his lap. The tiny sounds of pleasure she made, the moans that left her throat, the way she blindly gyrated her hips seeking release worked at his own undoing. Need slammed through his shaft. Desire tingled in his stones, tightening them. He gritted his teeth. Soon… In and out he slid, priming her, and always came back to circle that swollen button, yet she didn't fall.

Why?

To hell with it. He couldn't wait any longer. His shaft pulsed with warning and he fumbled with the buttons of his frontfalls. "Elizabeth, please tell me you're ready." Lust graveled his voice. The urge to spend raised gooseflesh over his skin.

"For what?" Her head lolled onto her shoulder, her eyes half-lidded, her cheeks and chest flushed.

"Flying." *God, I'm so hard.* He renewed his efforts on her nubbin. "Hurry, Lizzy."

"I don't know what that means." She opened her eyes and met his gaze. Tears made those blue depths luminous. "What am I doing wrong? You're waiting for something to happen, and I don't know what that is." The delicate tendons of her throat worked with a hard swallow. "I can see it in your eye."

He paused at the last button on his breeches. *What an arse I am. I'm worse than a cad. Of course she doesn't understand. This is all new.* The tears were off-putting, but he was determined to regain her attention. "Never mind. I'll explain later." Brand kissed her, harder than he'd intended. "This will be unorthodox but still good."

"Oh!" Her spine straightened as he continued to pump his fingers into her. Though she moaned and squirmed from his attentions, she never found release. "Brand, help me do what you need." She touched one of her nipples, pinched it and threw back her head.

"Of all things holy on land or sea." That was the most erotic thing he'd seen. Before he could stop it, his length pulsed. He shot his wad, coming hard in his breeches. "Damn it." He withdrew his hand from between her thighs to rub it against himself, finishing the job. His release wasn't as spectacular as he'd hoped, and he certainly hadn't won the wager. The heat of embarrassment crept up his neck and spread through his chest as he uttered a groan of completion.

How long had it been since he'd spent in his breeches like a green boy?

Elizabeth frowned. Worry creased her forehead. "Are we finished?"

More than she knew. "For tonight it seems. I, uh, lost control and came prematurely before I could join with you." Cold frustration circled through his insides. This afternoon hadn't remotely satisfied him, nor had it calmed his desire for her.

To say nothing of sending her to the heights of passion.

"I'm so sorry." A tear fell to her cheek. "I'm not experienced like the other women you've been with. I should have done more to pleasure you." Another crystalline drop fell. "I couldn't even manage to be ruined properly, and now it's over." The tears came faster, and she glanced away from him, a blush in her cheeks.

Well, damn. "Hush. It wasn't you fault. Never think that." The sight of her distress and tears brought him low. Concern tightened his chest. Brand wrapped his arms around her and held her close. "Please don't cry. Sometimes these things are like this, especially first times." He stroked her back, hoping to soothe and quiet her, and in the process, he realized he liked it. There was nothing carnal about the embrace. Shock moved through him, from the roots of his hair to his toes.

When was the last time he'd let himself connect with a woman like this? More to the point, why the deuce did it feel... nice?

"No, it was me. My mind was too cluttered with what everyone would think of me after I became a fallen woman." Her words were muffled against his shoulder.

"Perhaps, but what do *you* think of you? That's all that matters."

"That I really want to be ruined." She raised her head and met his gaze. "By you. There has to be more to life than keeping a house, reading a Bible, or trying to convert sinners." Truth and longing reflected in her eyes. "Don't you think?"

"Oh, yes." Despite the situation, Brand chuckled. She was so adorable in her distress, and she'd alluded to a next time. His spirits rose. "By the by, Lizzy, you are now a sinner. What you let me do, where my hands and mouth have been... You're more or less ruined even though we didn't lie together."

"I know." Never had he seen a glummer expression from the woman in his arms. "I wish the sin had been... more amazing for the crime."

He laughed outright at that. Genuine laughter that came from the gut and temporarily kept his own failings and shortcomings at bay. "You wonderful thing." Holding her close once more, he said, "Just you wait. I'll ruin you as much as your heart desires. You'll see." Content to remain with her pressed against him in scandalous repose, he sighed.

Though he might have lost the wager, the challenge of bedding Elizabeth remained.

CHAPTER TEN

ELIZABETH UTTERED A sigh when Brand secured the last rope and the *Charlotte* bobbed in her slip. "Thank you for a wonderful afternoon." No matter how much she might have wished otherwise, the day had to come to an end.

"Truly, it was my pleasure." The captain jumped down onto the wharf. Then he turned and lifted a hand. "Careful now. It's a bit slippery."

All around them boats and ships of varying sizes were coming home for the evening. No doubt the fishermen and merchants were hungry for their nightly meals and the chance to relax weary bones after a long day on the water.

When she put her hand into his and he assisted her down, she squealed. For one heart-stopping moment, she was weightless, but then he caught her in his arms and held her close for a second longer than propriety might allow. She felt… different somehow, as if she weren't the same woman who'd boarded the sloop hours ago. Why though? *Something* had changed, at least for her. She was now a wild thing after having connected with nature and the sea, feeling the wind in her hair and the sun on her face. There had been laughter exchanged between her and Brand. And his touch, his lips, on her body had certainly ushered greater enjoyment into the outing.

How long had it been since she'd conducted herself with such abandon without fear of the consequences or the judgment from the church?

Then Brand released her and stepped away. Immediately, she missed the warmth of him, the solid manliness of his presence. "Shall I escort you home?"

"I'd like to say yes, but William will no doubt be waiting for me, and…" Her words trailed off, for what else was there to say?

"And he doesn't care much for me," Brand continued for her. A wicked smile curved his sensual lips. "That's all to the good, for I don't like him either."

An unladylike snort escaped her. "Hush, you." She smiled at a few fishermen walking the wharf. Some nodded while others threw her looks of confusion. All of them greeted Brand with friendliness and respect. "Well, I should go, but I'm grateful for the afternoon. I can't tell you the last time I enjoyed myself or felt so… free."

"I understand." Desire darkened the gray depths of his eye while he looked at her. "Until our next meeting."

She nodded, and in desperation blurted, "When?"

"Day after tomorrow. I have a few supply runs to complete tomorrow that will occupy my time."

Cold disappointment snaked through her insides. Two days seemed so long, but she nodded. "I can't wait."

"Good. Meet me here around noon. I'll take you sailing again since you seem to have an affinity for the water. Perhaps it's time you learn to swim." He stepped closer and gently tugged on a lock of her hair. "The flush of sun on your skin is enormously erotic. I can't wait to see what you'll look like completely wet." The accompanying wink sent her imagination flying into dark, wicked places.

Heat jumped into her cheeks. "You are quite the rogue, Captain."

"Aye." He made a shooing motion with his hands. "Go, lest the sinless William come searching for you and calls me out in a duel regarding your virtue."

She rolled her eyes. "Which remains untouched so there is no need for his fury." But she fled with the sound of his laughter ringing in her ears.

ELIZABETH OPENED THE front door to her house with a fair amount of trepidation. She hadn't wanted to return home, but here she was, for there was nothing else for her to do.

Her stomach growled as she entered the townhouse and softly closed the door behind her. Knots pulled in her belly. It was almost dinner time. William would be pacing the floor in a temper wondering where she was, for he detested tardiness. Of course, they would go to the tavern as they always did. Would Captain Storme's cronies still be hanging about their private dining room? Heat fired in her cheeks. Had her appearance there earlier in the day and Brand's subsequent absence give them a clue as to what had happened aboard the *Charlotte*? Perhaps more to the point, would he brag about what he'd done to her?

Good heavens. I never assumed his friends might know.

Barely had she passed the parlor when William called her. "Elizabeth, I would like to see you, please."

A tremor of unease shivered down her spine. As she turned about, she put a hand to her hair. *Drat!* She'd forgotten to set it to rights, and Brand had the pins and combs. Worry increased, and she hastily finger-combed her hair and used the strands themselves to secure the mass into a low chignon on the back of her neck. It would have to do. Smoothing her hands along the front of her dress—now hopelessly wrinkled—Elizabeth entered the parlor.

"Hello, William. I trust your meeting went well?" Perhaps the best way to proceed was to pretend nothing untoward had happened.

"It did. Thank you." He sat in a winged-back chair upholstered in the same mauve color as the rest of the room. One ankle rested on a knee. His fingers were steepled beneath his chin. Displeasure filled his eyes. "I believe I told you to remain here while I was out."

Not this again. "And I believe *I* told *you* that I could make my own decisions." A pleasant drowsiness had swept over her from the sun. How delightful it had been to breathe in the air and feel the warmth on her skin instead of passing those hours hidden away in the house.

"That very well may be true, but those decisions are wrong and have put your immortal soul into danger." He stared at her with a look akin to disgust. "Where have you been?" He swept his gaze up and down her person. "You're windblown, sunburned, and stinking of sin."

Did he mean that literally or figuratively? "I spent some time on the water today. It's the perfect weather for it." She'd stick to the truth as much as possible. "Captain Storme was gracious enough to take me out on his sloop. He taught me how to fish." That was also true, for once they'd finally stirred from the romantic embrace they'd shared after the failed ruination, he'd been ever so helpful and eager to please with promises of teaching her how to swim and sail later. After that, she'd been content to sit in the sun regardless of her complexion and enjoy a couple of hours on the river while he gave her a tour of the harbor.

A knock rained upon the front door, but neither she nor her brother paid it much mind, for the housekeeper, Mrs. Friedmont, would attend to the visitor.

"Again, you sought him out after I forbid it." William leaned forward and planted his feet on the floor. "Why must you continue to antagonize me? We've been in Ipswich for nearly a year, and in that time, you've been the perfect sister of the church. Now, I fear for your soul."

Elizabeth pressed her hands to her cheeks. Oh, dear, she'd left her gloves—to say nothing of her bonnet—behind on Brand's ship. "Perhaps I didn't have cause to enjoy myself here until now." She certainly hadn't knowledge of Captain Storme. If they'd met earlier, she could hardly imagine what her life would have been like.

"Keeping company with a rogue and creating scandal is not how you should enjoy yourself."

"What scandal?"

"You know what you've done."

"Nothing. I've done nothing." Except let Brand touch places on her body only a husband should. She fought off a blush. Even now, delicious tingles meandered through her lower belly. Thinking about what he'd done to her tightened her nipples. To hide her reaction, Elizabeth crossed her arms over her breasts. "But if you have other news regarding that, please tell me so I may set the record straight." *I'm done letting you bully me.*

"Stop that. Women who are committed to keeping themselves above the dreck in the world shouldn't engage in arguing." He narrowed his eyes. "You are guilty by association merely by being seen with him."

"Is my name being gossiped about?" She arched an eyebrow. "Furthermore, if it is, why are you listening to such vitriol to begin with? That's not something a godly man should do."

"Do not think to engage is semantics with me, Elizabeth." He shook a long forefinger. "Regardless, I realize that I can't lock you in your room."

"I'm glad you've come to your senses." Had the sin with Brand been worth the potential lecture that would come if William ever found out? She bit her bottom lip to prevent a grin. Yes, it was. During those hours with the captain, she'd felt wanted for the first time in her life. Surely God would excuse that.

William cleared his throat, scattering her thoughts. "However, I have made arrangements to curb this wild bent of yours."

Please don't tell me you've arranged an engagement. "Oh?"

"Yes. I've gotten word of a ship departing from London on September first for India. Since I'm anxious to be off, I've made a transfer of our passage from the ship that will leave Ipswich on the fifteen of September.”

“You have.” It wasn’t a question. Shock weakened her knees while hot panic filled her chest. “You’re leaving in seven days.” She clutched the edge of a small round table to keep from collapsing to the floor.

“I am, as are you, for your soul is in jeopardy here. In this way, I can be assured you’re living for the Lord as solemnly and seriously as you should.”

And I’ll return to being a prisoner. Six days to spend with Brand. The adventure she craved would end well before she’d hoped. It wasn’t enough time for him to realize that he should ask for her hand, nor did it give her an opportunity to know what lying completely with a man would feel like. “What if I don’t want to accompany you any longer?”

“Have you other plans then?”

“No.” The word came out in a whisper. Tears crowded her throat. As much as she’d adored spending time with Brand, he hadn’t spoken of a possible future with her, so what exactly was she doing? *Have I made a terrible mistake? Does he only want me to assuage his need?*

“Ah. You have no choice but to come with me as we’ve planned. Frankly, this will be good for you.” His stern expression softened by an increment. “All will come about right. You and I are family, and we’ll do the Lord’s work in India. I suspect we won’t have much time for other interests.” A fanatical light gleamed in his eyes. “Now, go make yourself presentable. It’s past time for dinner.”

“Right. Dinner.” How could he expect her to eat and converse when the whole of her world was crashing down about her feet?

In a daze, Elizabeth exited the parlor and drifted upstairs to her small bedchamber without cognizant thought that she did so. The housekeeper was just exiting the room with her arms full of dirty linens. “Oh, I beg your pardon.” Elizabeth gave her a wan smile. "I didn't see you." Mrs. Friedmont came twice a week to assist with chores and laundry, and it was one of the bright spots of Elizabeth's day to talk with her, for the housekeeper reminded her of her own mother.

"It's no bother, dear." Her forehead wrinkled with the same concern that laced her voice. "Are you quite well? You're by far too pale under the sun you got today and look ready to weep."

That's exactly what she felt like. Not having any more strengthen to remain on her feet, Elizabeth sank onto a straight-backed wooden chair at a tiny desk. Not much correspondence waited for her attention, for who would bother writing? "Oh, Mrs. Friedmont, I rather think I've made a mess of things." With William's desire to depart England earlier, there was no chance that she and Brand could deepen their relationship enough that he'd ask for her hand. What was more, the one time she wished to give herself to a man hadn't ended in the splendid bliss she had hoped. There would probably never be another chance.

"Life is often like that before everything works out." The matronly housekeeper gathered the linens into one hand and patted Elizabeth's head with the other. "Don't worry so, dear. It'll sour your looks."

She snorted. "For what? I'm hardly a part of society, and if William has his way, I'll be whisked away just as I'd started putting down roots." Yes, that sounded rather splendid. To have a home and a sense of belonging in Ipswich, where the sea called, and the air was clean and clear. Never had she felt stronger or more hopeful...

Until this evening.

"Yes, your brother informed me of his plans when I came in." The other woman clicked her tongue. "I don't have the answers for you. However, I do know that it's not all glum."

"How can you?"

A twinkled appeared in her dark eyes. "When you were talking with Mr. Hayhurst, a letter was delivered for you." She nodded toward the nightstand. "I placed it there for you." She lowered her voice. "Took charge of it myself, for I didn't think your brother would be pleased. The flowers are a sweet touch, so don't give up hope, miss." With a wink, she bustled toward the door once more. "I must run. My man will be wanting his dinner."

"Thank you, Mrs. Friedmont." Curiosity buzzed at the base of Elizabeth's spine. She left the chair to stumble across the floor. As she sat upon the edge of her bed, she lifted a nosegay of a few violets and two miniature summer daisies to her nose. They'd been tied with a purple satin ribbon. A small envelope waited on the nightstand, her name scrawled with a heavy hand.

After setting the nosegay down, she opened the envelope and slipped a scrap of paper from it.

Dearest Elizabeth,

Thank you for spending the afternoon with me. I've not appreciated a day more and look forward to seeing you again soon. What is between us certainly isn't over.

Yours, Brand

"Oh, my goodness." That was the most romantic missive she'd ever received. She pressed the note to her chest while heat blazed in her cheeks. Perhaps there was hope indeed. Quickly, she tucked the note and the envelope into her Bible lest William find it, then she moved to her washstand.

Dear God, please let Brand's regard be true; I could fall for him with little effort.

CHAPTER ELEVEN

August 26, 1817

B RAND DIDN'T BOTHER to cover a yawn as he entered the private dining room that he and his fellows reserved each day for dinner. He'd made his supply runs, which had taken too many blessed hours. If he'd had a bigger ship, he could make one trip weekly instead of doing the jobs every day. But that was a dream. Now all he wanted was a pint or two and to talk with his friends and to dig into a nice serving of roast beef. If the feeling of restlessness would fade, that would be all to the good, but the truth of the matter was, he was just plain randy. Not being able to claim Elizabeth's body yesterday kept him on the edge of frustration and his shaft hard. If things didn't improve in that quarter, he'd be forced to take himself in hand.

Damn, but he wanted her. Inability to bed her aside, she was an interesting person who viewed the world as if everything were a miracle as it opened for her.

George was the first to glance up as Brand joined them at the table. "Is there news, Captain?" His expression was sly. Of course he would go right for the meat of the matter.

The other men studied him with degrees of interest.

Philip nodded, his grin wide as if he suddenly remembered the wager. "Yes, have you succeeded in bedding the missionary's sister?" His fork was paused midway to his mouth. "From the way she looked yesterday, I'd say you had an easy time of it."

If only he knew. As three pairs of eyes bored into him, Brand sighed. He rubbed a hand over the side of his face. "Uh, yes and no." There was no better way to phrase it.

"What the devil does that mean?" John frowned. He scoured Brand's face with his gaze. "You either seduced her into your bed or you didn't."

Heat crept up the back of Brand's neck. "It's not that simple." As he leaned back in his chair, he told them bits and pieces of his afternoon with Elizabeth yesterday. In the telling, he wished to leave some of the details to himself. It was difficult to explain what had occurred after he'd attempted to pleasure her with his fingers. Not to mention they'd tease him mercilessly for holding her in his arms for much longer than he should have.

I'm not that sort of man. I don't cuddle with them or show tender concern for them or try to soothe their emotional distress. I bed them and leave them satisfied.

Until the advent of Elizabeth.

All three of his friends gaped at him with varying degrees of shock lining their expressions. The bite of cottage pie on Philip's fork fell to the tabletop with a soft *plop!*

"You didn't bed her." There was no question George's voice as he continued to stare.

"Not in the traditional sense." The remembrance of having Elizabeth on his lap was as powerfully arousing now as it had been when he'd experienced it. Brand shifted in his chair, but his engorged length didn't find relief. Her perfect nipples, the heat of her when he'd penetrated her with his fingers, the tiny moans she made all worked to drive him insane. "However, we *were* intimate."

In more ways than the obvious.

"That's proper rubbish, Captain." Philip shook his head. Disappointment clouded his eyes. "What you did doesn't count toward winning the wager unless you coupled with her."

"Hold on. I don't know if that's exactly true." John held up a hand. "The captain *did* do the job. In a roundabout way, I suppose." He glanced around the table. "I say we count that as winning the wager, for I imagine it took a fair amount of convincing and seduction to bring Miss Hayhurst to that pass."

Both Philip and George voiced a noisy protest.

John pounded a fist on the tabletop. "Hear me out, mates." He looked at Brand and back to the others. "We can either pay out our share to the captain or…"

"Or?" Brand asked with anticipation streaking down his spine. The whole business almost turned his stomach, for he didn't want to cut his association with Elizabeth over the ill-advised wager.

"Or…" John's grin was this side of sly. Speculation gleamed in his eyes, which meant certain trouble for Brand. "Or we can extend the wager."

"How?" He didn't like the sound of that.

John and George exchanged a speaking glance that conveyed a message Brand couldn't understand. Then, Philip nodded slowly. "Go ahead," he told John.

"The three of us have pooled our resources." John sobered. He looked at Brand like the soul of an account manager. "So, instead of paying you out the winnings of five hundred pounds, we have recently purchased a schooner that went for sale just this week."

"What? When?" Surprise punched Brand in the chest. "Why didn't you ask me to go in on it?" A trace of hurt followed, for he'd thought they were fast friends.

John chuckled. "The four of us will be forming a shipping outfit. Import and export business, so with your sloop and the new schooner, we can double the work and the profit." He flashed a grin. "We wouldn't have left you out, Brand."

"Well, that's better." If his voice was a tad gruff, he ignored it. "But you're right. Forming a partnership sounds like a capital idea." It was something tangible and solid that might attract the right woman—

"You've been preoccupied, Captain," George said in a soothing voice with nothing but honesty in his eyes. The statement interrupted Brand's thoughts. "And from the looks of things, you still are."

"The devil you say." Brand scoffed. "Such nonsense. Miss Hayhurst has been a diversion, a way to win five hundred pounds. Nothing more."

Wasn't she?

"Hmm." John frowned. He tapped a fingernail against his tankard of beer. "I'm not so certain. You're… different."

"How so? I'm quite the same man I was all along." What poppycock was his best friend attempting to put forth?

"Many little ways." John leveled a speculative gaze on him then shrugged. "In any event, the three of us are willing to offer you the schooner—since you'll head up the shipping company— on the condition that you can make Miss Hayhurst fall in love with you." A twinkle appeared in the man's eyes that sent cold foreboding down his spine.

"What?" Brand shook his head. He couldn't believe the cheek of his friend. "I haven't properly bedded her yet. Now this?" What did the three of them play at? How much of a commitment would such a thing require of him?

"Come now, Captain." George leered and waggled his bushy eyebrows. "Do so quickly. Women like Miss Hayhurst confuse being bedded and love all the time."

"*Then* we'll sign over ownership of the schooner to you," Philip added. "After that, our shipping outfit can get properly underway and we can set about to make our fortunes."

"Exactly." John nodded, but he didn't lose his frown. "With the schooner, you'll have the means to sail farther, acquire goods for our business and deliver them to more customers, plus find the adventure you crave. Philip means to keep the books. George and I can sail with you and be the face of the company." He inclined an eyebrow. "It's been our dream since leaving the Navy, as you know."

"I do, of course, and I believe I was the one who put forth the idea once upon a time." He rubbed his chin. "It's a fantastic opportunity, to be sure." To have a schooner, the very size ship he'd lusted over for nigh onto two years. It would give him the chance to show his family that he wasn't good-for-nothing or a bounder. "I suppose I *could* make Elizabeth fall in love with me…" Yet, it smacked of deception. She was still an innocent in every way that mattered. Doing this went beyond winning a wager. He'd break her heart. His chest tightened.

What care I about that? Wasn't the plan to bed her and leave her?

"Now you're thinking like a businessman." John grinned, but it didn't reach his eyes. "Does that mean you're willing to take on the modified wager?"

It was on the tip of Brand's tongue to agree, but a warning flared in his gut. Immediately, he was suspicious of the plan. "Why do you want me to do this so badly?"

"Why not?" John shrugged. "Pursuing Miss Hayhurst has seemed to make you, if not happy, then less lonely. Don't try to deny that," he added when Brand opened his mouth to protest. "Why not continue the wager and see where it leads?"

Of all things holy on land and sea! "Damnation, John." He kept his voice low. Fury rang in those tones. He shoved back from the table and to his feet so fast the chair toppled. It crashed against the floor with a raucous clatter. "You wish to *match* me with the woman! You wrapped it into a dare you know I can't refuse."

The three men exchanged perplexing glances, for his outburst had nothing to do with them and everything to do with his own insecurities.

George waved a hand as if the conversation at hand wasn't life changing. "Listen to what we've told you, Captain. *She's* to fall, not *you*. There is no danger to your person."

"Quite so." Philip drained his tankard. "Besides, you've avoided such disasters for all these years. There's no harm to you now."

"Unless you wish for the same," John added, his face carefully blank. "Unless you wish to make that descent yourself."

Except he'd have to spend even more time in Elizabeth's company and pretend he was enamored of her. Brand didn't know how he felt about that. His chest ached from too many emotions he couldn't put to words. In her he'd found a companion who liked much of the same things he did, who he enjoyed as company on his sloop, who he looked forward to seeing which each outing. In a perfect world, she *might* be a candidate for romance, *if* he were searching for one, and *if* he could overlook her horrid brother.

But love? Him falling in love? Absolutely not! He refused on principle. That wasn't his style. A man in that state would need to upend his whole life and change nearly everything he was because the parson's mousetrap demanded it.

Because *she* would want him to.

I'm not certain I can change.

The buxom barmaid entered the room with four tankards of beer on her wooden tray. All the frustration from the past few days collided with the exhilaration of perhaps owning a schooner and the annoyance at needing to further seduce an innocent woman to make a perfect storm of lust and need within him. After Molly served the men, Brand closed the distance between them, caught her into his arms, and then kissed her hard. Her tray dropped to the floor with a dull thud.

No, he wasn't ready to change. Not for anyone, and certainly not for a woman with caramel-colored hair and who gained freckles over the bridge of her nose when in the sun too long. He released the barmaid, who stumbled, unsteady on her feet. "There's more where that came from, if you're willing." The best thing to do was put Miss Hayhurst from his mind, for nothing good would come of dwelling on a woman so unattainably... *good* that the light which shone from within her acted as a damned beacon to his soul.

She can help me be... more, be... better.

Molly looked him over, and her grin was decidedly wicked.

"Always, when it comes to you, Captain." She retrieved her tray, giving him an unobstructed peek at her copious cleavage, and then sauntered from the room.

Ignoring the curious glances from his mates, Brand stifled a groan. *I'm losing my damned mind.* The way to chase a certain woman from his thoughts was to bed another one. He loped from the room and caught the barmaid in the hall. "Come here." Emotion graveled his voice. He gripped her hips, planted her rear on a narrow table that rested flush against the wall, and he once more kissed her without any sort of tenderness or care. Her tray lay trapped between them. The feel of her lips against his was different than the kisses he'd shared with Elizabeth. Though she was experienced and knew exactly how to quickly arouse him, her exploring hands weren't Elizabeth's, who touched him with a timidity that drove him wild and close to the edge almost immediately.

Botheration! He needed Elizabeth to cease haunting him.

Renewing his kiss with Molly, he fondled her breast, and she slipped a hand to cup his throbbing equipage, but the sounds she made weren't the moans of sweet surprise that Elizabeth's had been. *Damn, damn, damn.* Murmured voices down the hall reached his ears, breaking his concentration. He turned his head and opened his eyes, glancing along the corridor. *Bloody hell!* Elizabeth and her brother were being shown into a private dining room at the end of the hall.

The urge to assert himself, cling to the life he'd lived and valued before meeting Lizzy died a swift death.

Suddenly, the barmaid's charms held no sway. A wave of disgust poured over him enough to cause him to step away from her. He wiped his mouth on his sleeve as the pair at the hall's end entered the dining room.

Thank God she didn't see me.

With his mind reeling and the need for repentance riding down his spine, Brand peered at Molly. "I beg your pardon." He took another step backward as confusion wrapped around him.

What the devil is happening to me?

Her eyes were bright, her lips kiss-swollen, but annoyance lined her face. "You need only to say the word and I'll gladly warm your bed, Captain." Her gaze dipped to the front of his breeches. In a blatant display, she licked her lips. "I'll do anything you ask or can imagine."

Heat, swift and sure, went through his hard member. "I'm quite well without your attentions. Thank you." The thought of her in his bed was no longer pleasing. He wanted Elizabeth, naked and writhing, beneath him, *her* hair spread over his pillows, *her* apple blossom scent clinging to his sheets instead of Molly's cloying scent of roses, *her* lips on his.

Dear God. Never had he put so much effort into seducing a woman as he had with Elizabeth, and never had he cared to learn so much about one as well. He enjoyed hearing about her life and her dreams. No, she'd hadn't fawned over him like the others, which made the chase that much more intriguing. Why was he investing the time, letting thoughts of her overtake his sanity, when all he needed to do was finish the seduction and win the wager?

The barmaid pouted as she hopped off the table. "If you change your mind..."

"I won't. That I can promise." *At this point, I don't even know my own mind.* He shoved a hand through his hair as the man he was battled with the man he wished to be.

"It's that meek woman, isn't it?" Molly asked, narrowing her eyes. "You fancy her over me, because I'm *bad* and she's good."

"I... I honestly never looked at it that way." Did his subconscious think that? "I'm not a saint either." Too bad all of Ipswich knew that, too. Did his past bother Elizabeth? He hadn't thought to inquire. If it did, what then?

"Well, if you want more experience in the sheets instead of her who'll just lie there, come find me. You'd be a fat lot better in the sack than the skinny missionary, that's what," Molly grumbled. She held the tray against her chest. "For all his talk of damnation and hell, he's rough and cruel in bed. Got the bruises to prove it. And he doesn't pay full price."

"What?" Brand's eyebrows shot upward. Anger burned through his chest. Regardless of Molly's station in life, she didn't deserve to have any man beat her. "You've… serviced Mr. Hayhurst?" Now *that* was news worth hearing. And he'd tuck that bit away for future leverage if needed.

"Since he came to Ipswich. Regular, like clockwork. Usually once a week when his sister is on her daily walk." She shrugged. "Coin is coin. I don't mind where it comes from, especially when rent's due." Then she walked down the hall toward the door leading to the tavern.

"Now what to do about that?" he whispered to himself with his hands on his hips. All too soon, his ruminations were interrupted when John joined him in the corridor.

"Your tastes have suddenly changed?"

"Perhaps."

"Interesting." John snorted. "For the past few months, you've angled to get the barmaid alone. Now you act like she's poison."

Brand glanced at his best friend in time to catch the knowing light in his eyes. "What difference does it make to you?" He didn't like not knowing himself, didn't care for the upheaval Elizabeth had caused within his being, didn't enjoy the thoughts that he might have an interest in her beyond taking her to bed.

"Does this mean you'll take up the wager?" Speculation shadowed his face. "How bad could continuing in Miss Hayhurst's company be?"

How bad? It could very well change his life, and that terrified him. "Yes, damn it. But how will you know I haven't lied?"

"Secure a lock of her hair as a memento. Then we'll know."

"Fine." He shoved a hand through *his* hair. "Are you happy?"

John shrugged. "Are you?"

Hell if I know. "Buggar you all," he growled, and without another word, Brand left the area, bound for his room as he navigated the confusing, twisting corridors of the hotel.

What the devil was he to do? The proposed modified wager was a game sure enough, but someone would be hurt at the end. And he suspected it might be him, because he was in danger of becoming the biggest bacon-brained idiot.

Over a woman.

CHAPTER TWELVE

August 27, 1817

ELIZABETH BLEW OUT a breath of frustration. She pulled out the knot Brand had tasked her to tie while they sailed the River Orwell.

"Patience, Lizzy. It won't go any quicker if you're annoyed." Amusement threaded through his voice as he adjusted the sail. "Duck, love."

She'd barely done as instructed before the boom swung across the deck. The fickle wind filled the sail which allowed the sloop to change directions. Ever since he'd found her on her walk around noon and invited her to go sailing with him, she'd allowed the nautical world to catch her up in it and give her an escape. For two hours the captain had taught her the basics about sailing, and she reveled in the new knowledge.

Except about knot tying.

"Explain these to me again. My mind has them muddled," she asked with a peek at Brand. Flutters filled her belly, for here in his element, he was magnificent.

Without his jacket and waistcoat, and as the breeze rippled through his loose lawn shirt causing the placket to gape, he was the perfect image of a pirate. His silver-shot midnight hair ruffled and disheveled, his eyepatch speaking to mystery and wicked delights, it was no wonder she had trouble tying knots when he guided the craft like the mischievous rogue that he was.

"The most useful knot aboard any sort of sailing vessel is the bowline. It forms a fixed noose at the end of a line that can't run or slip. We mostly use it to secure sheets to the clew of a headsail."

Oh, drat. What was a clew again? She pressed her lips together and thought over all the terms he'd taught her. Ah yes, the corner of a sail. "Right. Proceed."

He flashed her a smile that scattered her thoughts and had her twisting the rope in her hands into a mess. "Two bowlines can also be used to connect two lines. The advantage of a bowline is that no matter how tight it grows after being employed, it can always be easily untied."

"I understand that type of knot. It's like magic."

Rich laughter emanated from him. "Not magic, but close enough." When he glanced at her, tingles danced down her spine. Longing for something she couldn't name set up deep inside her. "Which one is proving your downfall?"

"This dratted stopper knot." She held up her hand. Rope was tangled around her fingers and not in the tidy formation he'd shown her.

"Silly widget." Brand secured his line. He dropped anchor near a cove on the far side of Ipswich that lent itself to collecting the wind and more shallow waters that kept both fishermen and townsfolk away. Then he joined her on the coil of rope and took up a line himself. "Watch."

"I watched you demonstrate it before," she said with some annoyance. Why couldn't she master this one thing?

"To keep a line from pulling through a block or rope clutch, a knot should be tied in the end of it."

"I know!" She shook out the mess and held up her piece of rope.

"The easiest way to tie a true stopper knot is by using your hand as a form." He wriggled his fingers with his palm facing her.

"Just loop the end of the line twice around your palm, tuck the working end under the two loops, and then pull the loops off your hand."

"Why is this so difficult?" she asked of the rope. Another huff of frustration left her, and she sorted the rope again, to do the knot over.

"Go slow and don't force it." Brand held up his hand. "Working back to front, pass the working end twice around your open palm." His voice was soothing and respectful. "After you have two full wraps, pass the working end under the wraps on your palm away from your thumb. Then use the end to pull the knot tight as it slips off your hand." As he talked, he tied his knot and let the whole thing dangle before her eyes. "Now you."

Elizabeth did as instructed. The knotted end of the rope fell off her palm just as he said it would. "I tied it!" She kept looking at her handiwork. "I finally learned it."

"Now do it again."

"So mean, Captain." But she unraveled the knot. When she completed the task a second time, the knowledge came quicker, and she was able to hold up the properly knotted rope with more confidence. "Ha!"

"With a few more lessons, you'll be a fit sailor." He winked. "Tell me what aft means."

"The back of the ship."

"And port?"

"The left side when facing the bow."

"Good." He tugged the rope from her hands and laid both it and his on the deck. "What does windward mean?"

"Ooh." She scrunched up her nose. "The direction the wind is blowing. Which is opposite of leeward." Nautical talk was a veritable language all its own.

"You have been a rapt pupil." Pleasure rumbled in his voice as he snaked an arm about her waist. "I'll need to provide harder quizzes in future."

"Surely, not more knots." Frissons of both alarm and need

skittered over her skin.

"One last question for today. How does the rudder on my sloop work?" Then he scattered her concentration by pressing his lips to the underside of her jaw and nibbled a particularly sensitive spot there.

A shiver raced down her spine. "Um…" She couldn't think with him so near and smelling so delicious. "It's a flat piece of wood."

"Mmmhmm." He slid his lips along the side of her neck while caressing a hand up and down her ribcage.

Oh, dear. Awareness of him intensified. "Larger boats—ships—control the rudder by a wheel, while smaller vessels have a steering mechanism directly aft." A shaky breath escaped her when he teased the hollow of her throat with his tongue. "That is what the sloop has."

"Aye. You have quite the affinity for learning."

Elizabeth placed a palm on his solid chest and slid it upward. When his gaze found hers, another round of flutters erupted in her belly. "It's all so exciting, this life that you lead." Beyond that, she adored the feeling of freedom found on the water, loved being with him in any capacity, and the times he called her by a nickname were the ones she'd treasure always. Part of her wondered if it was a sin to enjoy her days with him, while the other part worried because she had so few left. "Now I know why you prefer the water."

"Just wait until you meet the sea." He resumed nibbling her skin. While he followed the scooped bodice, he pressed baby-fine kisses to the tops of her breasts.

She'd melt into his arms if he kept on with his ministrations. With a hand, she cupped his cheek and forced his chin up until he looked into her face. "Tell me about your family. I wish to know as much as I can about you, while I can."

Insecurity briefly flashed in his eye, gone with his next blink. "You don't need to hear about them." Brand pulled her closer into his embrace. "Not right now when we can find many other uses for our mouths."

"Oh!" She gave into a full body shiver at the delights his words conjured, but she pushed him away and held him at arm's length. "I won't let you distract me, Brand Storme. Talk first then we'll play." Cold sadness pooled in her stomach. "I only have a handful of days with you."

He frowned. "What do you mean?"

"William switched departure dates. We leave England on September first instead of fifteen days later."

Shock lined his expression as his eye widened in surprise. "There's four days left."

"I know." Silly tears crowded her throat. "I told him I didn't want to go, but he said without solid plans, I couldn't stay." Would that prompt the captain to say something about a possible future together?

"Four days together." Why did panic flare deep in his eye?

"It's disheartening, I know, but we'll have to make the best of it." Yet, that wouldn't sustain her in the lonely years in India. "William means to match me with an Englishman there, for then he won't bear the responsibility of me any longer." And she would never see Brand again, let alone perhaps find a life with him. When tears welled in her throat, she quickly swallowed to stave them off.

"Your brother." He clenched his jaw so tight a muscle ticked in his cheek. "He's not as good as you think."

"What do you mean?"

Brand shook his head. "It's premature to reveal my knowledge."

What did that mean, and why did he look as if he wanted to call out her brother? "Then tell me of your family."

"Fine." His voice softened. "You're quite a troublesome bit of baggage."

"Better that than one having no personality or backbone." *Oh, dear.* Should she have said that? When she glanced at him, he wore a wide grin. "Unless you prefer your women docile and submissive. I've had a lifetime to learn how." Was that truly her flirting with the captain?

His eye darkened with desire. "I prefer my women spirited with a sense of adventure." Brand once more tugged her close. He slid a hand down her back and at her buttock, he pinched a cheek. When she squealed, he snorted. "Are you that sort of woman, Lizzy?"

Was she? A week ago, the answer would most certainly have been no. But now? She met Brand's gaze, nearly drowned in that stormy pool. Now, she had no idea who she was as a woman or a follower of the Lord. Somehow, the answer to that question lay with Brand. "I hope to discover that soon." Why did she feel such a connection to this man after a short time? There was no answer to that question either.

"I'd be happy to help you find out." He slid a hand around her nape and slowly reeled her toward him.

"No. You're distracting me again." Elizabeth struggled out of his hold to her feet. She stumbled out of the rope coil and moved to the starboard bow railing and leaned her forearms upon it. Being close to him blanketed her ability to think clearly, but she *would* have her answers. "Why do you dislike talking about your family?"

Eventually, Brand joined her at the railing. "I'm not one to dwell on the past." He took up a similar stance to hers, their shoulders touching. "They only think to order me about in much the same way that William does you."

"Understandable." Once again, they had things in common. "But they are your family, Brand, not an event you survived that you're trying to forget."

He snorted. "Says you."

She lifted her head to the breeze coming off the river. All too soon this freedom would vanish, and she'd be back in the prison she'd only just escaped.

"Ha! I'd forget them if I could. They certainly have done so with me." A trace of bitterness threaded through his voice. For long moments he stared at the water, then, with a sigh, he spoke again. "Drew is my oldest brother; the new earl. He's arrogant and pompous, thinks his way is the best and the only way to do something. Demands all of us follow his rules and his idea of what the Storme family should be, but his temper is off-putting. He was Father's favorite."

Elizabeth's heart went out to Brand, but she didn't wish to touch him for fear he'd go silent again.

"Finn is the brother who's the closest to me. We used to be best friends. He's got a head for business, but I always thought he'd be a poet for all his romanticism, even if he'll deny that." A chuckle escaped him, but he didn't spare her a glance. "He was the sensitive one, the brother who tried to keep the peace between Drew and I, between Father and Drew, between Father and me, but for all that Finn is, he didn't understand my wanderlust or my need to remain on the sea. Mother coddled and spoiled him more than Drew or me." A muscle twitched in his cheek. "In the end, when Finn joined the military, Father was beyond proud, yet when I joined the Navy, it was because of Father's ultimatum. I had nothing but consternation and embarrassment from him by the time I left home." His Adam's apple bobbed. "I never saw Father again."

"I'm so sorry, Brand."

He shook his head, still refusing to look at her. "He never knew what I became in the Navy, how respected or lauded I was." Emotion she couldn't name graveled his voice. "After Father died, no one cared that I was in the wind or that I'd been injured. And they knew nothing of my court martial unless they read about it in the papers. I rather have the feeling that unless I'm in London, I don't matter."

"How sad." Elizabeth frowned at the water. "Regardless, you need them still."

"Why?" He cleared his throat, and the emotion he labored under had passed. "I have a new family here in Ipswich, one who doesn't hassle me about what's expected of me or is proper. It's quite different in every way, so why would I need the family who gave up on me?"

"I don't believe they have," she said slowly. "Your family has been thrown into turmoil with your father's death and are only just figuring out the new normal." A shaky sigh escaped her. "I envy you the family, even if yours is broken, and I envy you the friends. Yes, it's a sin to do so, but I can't help how I feel." Tears clogged her throat. She attempted to swallow them. "That's something I've never managed." When she turned her head to look at him, his gaze collided with her, so intense and stormy that she caught her breath. "I've never fit in with others." Something about the captain demanded she give him all her secrets.

"Neither have I, and perhaps that's the best thing about me." Brand covered her hand with his on the railing. "People like us, we have to walk our paths alone, for we're different. Folks don't understand us or what drives us, so they ignore us."

She'd not had someone in her life think in the same way that she did. "Yes, but it's a lonely existence."

"At times." Emotion clouded his eye that she couldn't read, but it sent flutters into her belly. "But in others, it really isn't. Life is what we make it." As was his wont, he coaxed the combs and pins from her hair. She'd stopped fighting him on that, for he would have his way. They fell to the decking with tiny *pings*. "We discover others like us, and they become our surrogate family who fulfil us like our blood relatives never could. There is nothing wrong with that."

Did he mean for her or for him? And was he inferring that was what she'd become to him? She didn't dare ask for fear she'd misunderstood. "At least you have a new family. I have William, and he is lost to his own ambitions." She shrugged. "We were never close due to the gap in our ages."

A frown tugged at the corners of his mouth. "Yet you intend to follow him to India." It wasn't a question. "Why?"

"What else *can* I do? There is no place for me here." That was the most horrid part. After everything she'd experienced since meeting Brand, no matter how much her eyes had been opened to certain things, her life hadn't changed. Not really. "I honestly have no recourse." Despite the fact she still looked into his face and waited, he said nothing. "No reason to stay," she added in a barely audible whisper.

Longing pooled briefly in his eye, gone with his next blink. "Choose your own path, Lizzy. Don't let someone else's expectations of you ruin the wonderful you can accomplish." He moved then, caught her face between his palms and stared into her eyes. Such passion blazed in his that she forgot to breathe.

"What are you trying to say?" Her heartbeat accelerated. Would this be the moment he declared himself?

"Find the courage to say no to your brother and do something for yourself because *you* deserve it, because *you* wish it."

The plea was so earnest and genuine her heart trembled. Her spirit ceased to flag under the renewal and intent. "I promise I shall try." But she had only four days to accomplish a miracle, and Brand still hadn't taken the hint.

"Good." He closed the slight distance between them and brought his lips crashing down on hers.

With a sigh, Elizabeth let herself become lost in the glory that was kissing Brand. She clutched his shoulders and gave herself over to the sheer wonder of knowing that he wanted her. She kissed him back, gaining confidence, and explored his mouth as much as he did to her. Oh, his lips were a delight! Soft but firm at the same time, they cradled hers with gentleness even as a sense of urgency sank into her as he explored, asked, posed a question to her she wanted so much to answer.

Over and over, she took from him, matched his pace and rhythm, and when she tentatively slipped her tongue into his mouth, he gasped and immediately deepened the kiss with enough passion that her toes curled. Awareness of him fired through her blood; need pulsed into every nerve ending. He was hot and strong and real, and God help her, she wanted him in every way a woman could want a man.

For long moments they communed without words. No longer did she put stock in what anyone would think of her if they saw her. In Brand's arms, freedom and opportunity intertwined, made her dream impossible things, and fed the longing deep her in soul. So caught up was she in the drugging passion that swirled around her that Elizabeth tugged at the placket of his shirt, so great was the need to touch his skin. When she slipped her fingers beneath the fabric, he groaned and tightened his embrace. A thick cord hanging about his neck triggered her curiosity, for she'd seen it before but had forgotten to ask about it.

Eventually, the need to breathe pulled her from his wicked and highly distracting mouth. She gently tugged on the necklace while she struggled to regulate her rapid heartbeat. "What is this?" As she moved aside the shirt fabric, she nodded. "It's a compass."

"Yes." He took it from her fingers and stared at it. The small, round bauble set in brass had seen its fair share of battering. "I've had it since I was a boy of ten. My uncle gave it to me for my birthday that year." A note of fondness had crept into his voice. "Life was chaotic at times and lonely at others as I passed the years." When he released the compass, it thudded gently against his chest. "This stayed constant and always points north." His voice dropped. "It never disappointed me."

"Is the compass significant in some way?" To her, it seemed an ordinary tool for a man comfortable upon the sea.

A faint wash of red color infused his neck. "I like to think it will always guide me home when I need the reminder."

"How sweet." She met his gaze. Longing and a certain wistfulness gleamed at the back of his eye. What was it he truly wished from life? "Is it pointing to London?" Whether he believed it or not, he needed to repair relations with his family.

"I'm not certain anymore. I've grown rather fond of wandering."

"I can understand that. The hours spent on your sloop have been nothing short of magnificent. To travel the world, visit new places… So much freedom." She caught her bottom lip between her teeth and shivered when his regard dropped to her mouth. "What happens when you settle down? Surely you'll want to give up such a life." But oh, how wonderful it would be if he didn't. Married to an adventurous sort of man. Imagine such an existence!

"If I fall into the parson's mousetrap, I suppose my life will be over." He frowned. "I can't give up the sea, not even for a woman."

Her budding dreams for a future died in that moment. From his own admission he wasn't the marrying kind. "How truly sad." She turned her head and regarded the water once more so he wouldn't see the cold disappointment flooding her person. "I like to think life would then begin again once marriage vows are taken, but in a different way."

"How so?" Curiosity threaded through those two words.

"Each stage of life is a new beginning. There are new people to meet, new tasks to learn, new roads to travel. I've only trod one path, but I'm anxious to find another, and then another, and so on until my life is filled with memories and experiences. That's what makes living worthwhile."

Brand remained silent for long moments. He cursed beneath his breath. Then, he laid a palm against her cheek and moved her head until their gazes connected. "How does that make you feel knowing this is where you are, and those paths might not open for you?" The whispered words held such emotion that the same blazed in his eye, but she couldn't read it.

"Trapped." Her own whisper was forced through a tight throat. "Frightened, as if I'll never know the life I should live due to following William's." She swallowed down the fear, the uncertainty, and lifted her chin. "Despite what seems impossible right now, I have faith I'll find my way."

"What if you don't?"

"Then I'll keep waiting. God knows when the timing is right. I'll merely need to practice patience." With a shrug, she gave him a wobbly smile. "Like you said, it's past time I should have found my own path, so that is what I'll do."

"We never know what we're capable of until we try and take that first, anxious step."

"Yes." She brushed a shock of hair off his forehead. "Will you pray with me, help me ask God what I should do next?"

A flush appeared on Brand's neck that spread upward into his face. His mouth worked like a caught fish, but finally, he nodded. "I… I suppose I can if it will help you."

Joy filled her chest. "It has always given me a sense of peace and happiness, just as being with you does." Had she said too much?

"Oh." Guilt stamped across his face, followed by a profound sadness she couldn't understand, but he took her hand. His shook as he held hers. Why was he so nervous? Or perhaps he was afraid. *Poor man.* "Whatever you need, I'll endeavor to make it yours." Why did his voice sound rough and graveled?

She dismissed it as nerves. "Thank you." Then she closed her eyes. Perhaps all he needed was someone to believe in him without conditions, and then perhaps he'd realize that he rather enjoyed having her around. "Heavenly Father…"

CHAPTER THIRTEEN

August 28, 1817

THE DAY HAD been long and tedious, filled with multiple supply runs up and down the coast with very little breeze, which meant progress had been slow. Now, perhaps half an hour until sunset, Brand was running late to meet Elizabeth. They'd agreed to take in the evening air and watch the tide come in on one of the isolated stretches of beach in the less populated areas of Ipswich, and if he didn't hurry, he'd be the reason she'd wear a worried frown.

Somehow, Elizabeth and the thought of displeasure didn't go together. He always wished to keep her in smiles and sunshine, yet... he was well on his way to winning that blasted schooner. The name currently emblazoned upon its hull was the *Idle Thoughts*, but if it were his, he would gladly rename it to... something else.

Something he had no right to, but perhaps she would always smile when she saw it.

Bah! That would mean she'd only stay in his life under his false pretenses. He shook his head as he followed the footpath that would eventually lead to the beach. It wound through the harbor and through a few clusters of homes and wooded areas, but it was pleasant enough. Yes, he could have sailed the sloop there, but being on the water hadn't brought him the same joy as it usually did, and besides, the walk would help to clear his thoughts.

Of her.

Would she fall in love with him? He recalled the look in her eyes yesterday when he'd consented to pray with her and when he'd kissed her. A shudder of need went down his spine. Oh yes, she already was. A wash of hot self-loathing smacked into him heavy enough that he might drown in it. And then what? He'd leave her once the schooner was his? Sour bile hit the back of his throat. The days he'd spent in Elizabeth's company had been idyllic, and she'd taken to life as a sailor in stride. She had a knack for it. How many women had he known that would have done that? Most merely wished for a possible tryst. None of them had ever willingly learned the art of sailing or knot tying.

And none had inquired about his past, his family, or anything personal about him beyond how he might service them with his prick.

Except Elizabeth. She genuinely enjoyed being with him for his own sake.

God, I'm scum. Nay, I'm worse than scum. I'm the stuff scum feeds upon and then spits out after finding it unpalatable.

The fact that his own conscience was taking him to task worried the hell out of him, for it meant he was more attached to Elizabeth than he ought to be. How the devil had that happened? Then cold disappointment mixed with sheer panic in the pit of his belly, and not because he might lose the wager if she discovered his deception prematurely. He only had three more days with her. Three! And he still hadn't managed to bed her, but now he wanted to couple with her, not in an effort to try and win the wager, but because he genuinely wished to be with her, to see her face light with delight, to teach her the ultimate way a man could show a woman how much he cared—

With the devil is wrong with me? What had happened to the life he'd previously adored and excelled at? The freedom of taking any woman he pleased to bed and then not having to do the pretty with them afterward? The sensation of standing on rapidly shifting sand assailed him, and he angrily shook his head. *I refuse to fall for the same scam I'm running on her. I'm not developing feelings for her!*

"Captain Storme!"

He started at the hail and glanced over his shoulder. A fellow ran toward him with an envelope clutched in one hand. The naval uniform in blue with silver buttons sent a wave of nostalgia over him. "Yes?"

"I'm glad I caught up to you." The man rocked to a halt when he reached Brand's location. "I'm Lord Nelson's private secretary, and yours is the last invitation I needed to deliver. Lord Nelson insisted they be given in person." He held out the ivory envelope. *Captain Brand Storme* was scrawled across the front in a heavy, elegant hand.

"An invitation to what?" Though he'd been a part of Ipswich society for the past handful of years and was quite popular in some circles, he'd not rubbed elbows with the upper crust.

"Lord Nelson's annual ball. In two days' time." The younger man shoved the envelope into Brand's hand. "He wishes for you to join him this year."

"Why?" Brand couldn't fathom a reason.

"Who can say?" The man shrugged. "However, he did mention that everyone invited was either high on the instep or an up and comer in society, so consider yourself fortunate you've been noticed." He cocked his head to the side. "Shall I tell him you'll accept?"

What if I don't wish to be noticed by society? No doubt word of the affair would find its way to London and remind his family that he needed to come home. But then a new thought occurred. Here was a chance to solidify Elizabeth's affections and for her to have an opportunity to wear the ballgown he'd bought her that seemingly long-ago day when they'd browsed the shops. "May I bring a companion?"

"Of course."

Slowly, Brand nodded. "Good, then you may tell Lord Nelson I accept with my thanks and gratitude." If nothing else, he could give Elizabeth the dance she'd always dreamed of.

"Jolly good." The man saluted him. "I shall do so indeed. Enjoy your evening, Captain."

"Thank you." As the secretary returned up the path he'd come, Brand tucked the invitation into the interior pocket of his jacket. An invitation to what was considered by some the biggest social event in Ipswich of the year. How interesting. What had he done to warrant the notice of Lord Nelson after all these years? The only thing he'd done differently in his life was befriend a lonely missionary's sister…

Of all things holy on land or sea. Did that mean he appeared respectable now that it seemed he was courting a decent woman? His chest tightened with anxiety while another wave of self-loathing swamped him. Everything he did from here on out would only serve to heap coals of her anger upon him.

Damn.

Not having anything else to do, Brand continued down the path. The heat of the day was fading the longer the sun set. The last handful of days with Elizabeth had been too idyllic and relaxed. She looked at each day as a gift instead of a steppingstone to something else. Could she teach him how to do that? How to court gratitude for everything in his life?

As soon as he set foot into the cove, he spied her, and his heart squeezed. She sat on the sun-warmed sand *sans* slippers and stockings, her feet half buried, her knees drawn up and her chin perched upon them. Those garments plus her bonnet lay on the sand beside her. Her hair was loose with a yellow ribbon holding it away from her face, and the yellow dress he'd seen twice before on her caught his attention. Perhaps it was a favorite, or perhaps it reminded her of sunshine, for that's the first thing he thought of when he saw her in it. She was truly the personification of summer.

I need more of that in my life.

"Elizabeth." Would he ever become accustomed to seeing her without some sort of reaction? His chest tight, he approached her and reveled in the crash of the waves against the shore as much as he did the picture she made.

She turned her head. Pleasure lit her eyes. "Brand!"

How did she do it? How did she manage to convey such delight each time they met? He was nothing special. Hell, he was a cad for what he intended to do, how he still planned on manipulating her.

With his stomach in knots, Brand joined her, dropping to the sand of the shallow cove beside her. "You're as beautiful as always in that dress."

"Thank you." She ducked her head. A faint blush infused her cheeks. "I like the cheerful color."

"So do I." And, damn him, he enjoyed her company far too much. It gave him pleasure to know she appreciated a gift from him which was different than what he felt upon bedding a woman. Not knowing what to do, he reclined back on his elbows as the sun began its trek toward the horizon. "Would you like me to tell you a tale of the sea?"

"Oh, that sounds lovely." When she smiled at him, twin threads of wonder and dread twisted down his spine.

"Do you have any requests?"

"Since my knowledge of anything having to do with the sea is minimal, I'll let you choose."

"Very well." He racked his brain for some of the more tame stories he'd heard over the course of his stint in the navy. "This one comes from Scotland. In folklore, selkies are gentle, shapeshifting creatures who live their lives as seals while in the water and shed their skin to become human on land. As the stories go, once on land, men often steal a selkie's seal-skin. They refuse to give it back unless the woman marries him. The selkies are frequently equated with mermaids because in Gaelic stories they are associated with *maighdeann-mhara*, or 'maid of the sea.'"

"How intriguing. Are the women happy in their forced marriages?" Elizabeth's eyes were wide and full of curiosity, the irises a deep sapphire in the rapidly fading light.

"Perhaps some were, if they managed to find love along the way." Brand remained silent for a time as he watched the water. "Unfortunately, selkie legends usually end in tragedy; the folktales all agree about that. No matter how many years have passed within the marriage, the man's selkie wife continues to long for the sea. He might have made her gloriously happy in the time they'd spent together, but the yearning never goes away."

"Oh, no." Elizabeth pressed the fingers of one hand to her lips. "She leaves, doesn't she?"

"I'm afraid she does. Either the man is worried sick over her and gives the seal-skin back to her, or she finds it on her own, but once she has it, she transforms and joyfully goes to the water, leaving her children with their human father."

To his surprise, tears sparkled in Elizabeth's eyes. "Does she ever return? Surely she can't turn her back on love—both for her husband and her children—no matter how strongly the sea calls to her."

"I don't know, for I've never met a selkie." It was adorable how much she let herself get caught up in what was naught but a fairy story. "But perhaps there is always an exception to everything in life."

She nodded. "I'd like to think there is and that some of them return and learn to balance both sides of themselves because nothing is more powerful in this world than love."

"Ah, Lizzy." The woman was both hopelessly naïve and wonderfully wise. Without his consent of even his knowledge, a tiny piece of his heart flew into her more than capable hands. When had the wall around that organ been breached? He had no idea, neither did he know when she'd found her way beneath it. "Would that you someday find all that you believe in," he said in a barely audible voice even as knots of disgust for himself pulled in his belly.

"I think I am," she responded in an equally low tone as she looked at him with a certain soft expression that gave away more of her feelings than she probably knew.

Oh, God. Brand glanced away before she could spy the truth in his eye. "Would you like to hear another tale?"

"Does it have a happy ending?"

"Only you can make that assessment, but generally tales and legends are designed as a warning, not an encouragement to follow in their footsteps."

"Well, if I had the creation of them, they would." But she nodded. "Tell me something about mermaids. I've always been curious of them."

"Such a classic tale." Despite his feelings and the subject matter not spoken, Brand grinned. "Let's see. Oh, here's one that hails from Ireland." He took a moment to recall the story. When he'd been a young man in the Navy, many a night spent on watch on deck he'd kept vigil with his mates while they'd spun the tales for him. "In Irish lore, a merrow is what they call a mermaid, but they need a bit of magic in order for them to live beneath the water. So, they don a hat called a *cohuleen druith*. Female merrows have long green hair. They're like a traditional siren in that they're extremely beautiful, even if they're the half-human fish of mythology."

"Isn't it funny how women in fairy stories are *always* beautiful?" Elizabeth's laugh went straight to his groin. "I suppose the tales would make less of an impact if the women were hags, but it certainly leaves out a huge segment of the female population, doesn't it?"

"I've never thought about it that way, for beauty is subjective and personal to the beholder."

Her eyebrows rose. "How intelligent of you to say."

As much as he wished to preen under her praise, he tamped the urge. If he spent too much time peering into her eyes, he'd want to dive into the cool pools and lose himself... Quickly, he gave his head a slight shake. "Male merrows, however, are considered hideous and frightening, more fish than man. They are never said to be handsome. They are also cruel. Which is the reason that many merrow women sought out relationships with human men."

"Because love is the driving force of all life." The dreamy, sing-song sound of her tones sent awareness sailing over him. "Love doesn't see differences."

Oh, how he wanted to believe her! "Yes, well..." He swallowed around the ball of emotion lodged in his throat. "Their offspring ran the risk of having scales and webbing between their fingers, which would make them pariahs in both human and mer society. As with the selkies, the love of the sea is always in a merrow's blood. They often tire of their life on land and wish to return to the sea—with or without their human family."

"That's horrible." Elizabeth shook her head. The faint scent of apple blossoms drifted to his nose. "I'd like to think they could have worked everything out with their human husbands. Perhaps moving close to the sea, or at least a large body of water that might make the longing a bit... less."

"Would you upend your life, do whatever you could, to make someone... different feel less so?" he asked in a quiet voice.

"Of course I would. What a silly question." Elizabeth glanced at him with speculation. "As I said previously, love doesn't see differences, and if it does, it seeks to understand them. It fills the divides, the holes, and brings people closer, lets a couple find strength in those things that were meant to divide them."

"That's a rather nice way to look at it." She made him see things so differently than was his wont that it stole his breath, caught him up in a vortex of confusion.

"I think so." The smile she gave him dazzled him and worked to further scatter his ability to think straight. She caressed the side of his face, drew a fingertip along the edge of his eye patch, and he trembled from both need an acute anxiety. "Brand?"

"Yes?" He took shallow breaths, for he suspected what she'd ask.

"May I see the space where your eye used to be?" There was no guile or pity in her expression, only concern and perhaps a trace of curiosity.

"I'd rather you not." He eased into a sitting position as his pulse rushed hard through his veins. "The surgeon sewed the socket closed in a rush. The wound has since healed but is a bit sunken. To say nothing of the scars left behind by the slash of that dagger. It's not something a woman should behold." The fact she'd even asked left him reeling and feeling a bit out to sea. No one of his acquaintance—male or female—had ever done so.

"It's an integral part of you. There is no shame in that." Her pout almost had him on his knees before her, begging her for anything—everything. "Please let me see."

How did he think he could deny her? "Don't say I didn't warn you." Would this be the moment he lost her? At least if that were so, he wouldn't need to tell her about the wager... *Bah! This is why having anything to do with a woman beyond the physical is a bad idea.* With a shaking hand, he slowly removed the eye patch. Though he steeled himself for her reaction, the truth of the matter didn't disappoint. As she stared in horror, her attention riveted to his empty eye socket, his stomach bottomed out. The urge to cast up his accounts grew strong. He fought through it even as cold disillusionment washed over him. "You're disgusted." It wasn't a question.

Of course, she'd be like all the rest.

The tendons of her throat worked with a hard swallow. "It's shocking, yes." To her credit, she didn't look away or give him empty platitudes. "But given time, I will seldom notice."

Liar! "I don't need this." Brand scrambled to his feet as his lungs labored to draw breath. "I thought you'd be different." How stupid he'd been to extend trust to another woman. "You're exactly like *her.*" What had he thought? Women didn't want a broken or disfigured man. He stormed away from her, his boots kicking up sand as he retreated. "This is why I never wanted a relationship, never wanted to—"

"Brand, stop!" Elizabeth soon caught him up. Her hand on his arm nearly snapped him in two. "Anyone would be shocked at first. Even you must admit that."

In a small corner of his mind, he knew she was right. When he'd first beheld himself in mirrors after he'd been patched up, the image staring back was shocking. Gruesome, even. "I…"

Though his body was taut and tight from the emotions coursing through him, she turned him about to face her. Concern lined her face. Compassion clouded her eyes. Her chin quivered from the effort of holding back emotion. The last of the sun's dying rays backlit her and gave the brief appearance of an angel. "None of that means you disgust me."

"I know what I saw in your eyes." He wouldn't give quarter, not when he was so vulnerable in his insecurity.

"No, you saw what you *wanted* to see, what you *expected* to see." Her focus never left his face. Not once did she shy away from including the empty socket in her regard. "I'm sorry the last woman in your life behaved with something less than courage and kindness, but love doesn't do that."

He couldn't let down his guard, for what if she didn't want anything else to do with him even after those words? "I loved her," he admitted in a tight voice. *Walk away, you fool, before she can hurt you.*

"I believe you." Elizabeth squeezed his arm, and he almost died a thousand deaths to know she still stood before him without duplicity. His chest ached. While he… he had done nothing *except* deceive her, was doing it even now, all to win a wager. "However, she didn't love you back. For if she had, your looks or handicap wouldn't have mattered. She would have loved you for you."

Oh, God. How was it that this woman, innocent in almost every way of the world, had the power to see him undone? But he strained to hear the words of approval, of acceptance, from her. Needed them. "It took me a long time to realize that."

"Yet you continue to push people away because of her, so

you can leave first and keep your heart intact." When she lifted her hand to caress the side of his face, he flinched. She soothed him with gentle strokes of her fingers and a soft tsk of her tongue. "This is you, Brand. Don't let it embarrass you, and never think yourself less." When he didn't answer, she continued. "The wound is your history, a mark in time that means you survived the war for a purpose."

"But I…"

Tears pooled in her eyes. As she drew her touch along the scars from the dagger as well as the surgery, he gasped. It was both heaven and hell. No one had ever dared before. "I'm glad you're here today to bear witness to that time, but never, not for one second think I don't value you because of this injury." A hard note had crept into her voice. Her eyes snapped blue lightning. "I am *not* that woman from your past, so it is roundly unfair of you to paint us with the same brush."

Finally, he found his voice, for she'd given him that tiny glimmer of strength. "Oh, that is readily apparent." Quickly, he replaced the eyepatch, watching her all the while. Some of the pressure within his chest lightened. "Thank you."

"I only speak the truth." She searched his face, for God only knew what, but he suddenly hoped she found it.

I want to be worthy of her. Yet, he never would be as long as he courted her only to make her fall in love with him for a damned ship.

"Why have you not considered a glass eye?"

His spirits immediately plummeted. At least if he were angry with her, that deflected the loathing from himself. "Is that the only way you can stomach being in my presence?"

"Of course not." She frowned. "I'm merely curious."

He had to learn to temper his reaction. Not everyone was like him—a horrible person. "I find the patch is more rakish and suits me better."

"Fair enough." Elizabeth shrugged. "I like you just as you are, but you might be twice as handsome with a glass eye."

"Given time or enough reason, I'll inquire to a much-lauded glass blower in London. Mr. Cecil Carrington's shop is full of exquisite and unique things. Perhaps he could fashion something for me."

"No hurry." She smiled and it reflected in her eyes. "I've grown rather attached to the patch."

"Oh." The sudden sensation of falling assailed him, and Brand began to panic. None of this was in the plan. Him having feelings for this woman had not been part of the bargain. Yet here he was, staring stupidly at her as if he had no brain. Not having the words to respond to her, he wrapped a hand about her nape and brought her to him. Her arms went easily around his shoulders. "I'm so glad I met you at that fair," he murmured and then claimed her lips in a kiss so intense he hoped it conveyed what he wanted to say but didn't have the courage to even admit to himself.

Elizabeth matched and mimicked his overtures until he was the one who wrenched away before he tossed her down, right there on the sand and claimed her body. She murmured a protest. "Why did you stop?"

"If I don't, I'll have to plunge into the sea to cool my ardor." His honesty surprised him, for wasn't bedding her what he'd angled for as soon as he'd met her? Now, suddenly, he wanted… more, and he wished her first time to be somewhat special. With a shaky breath, he stepped away. "Also, I've been invited to a rout at Lord Nelson's home in two days. Would you accompany me?"

"How wonderful!" She clasped her hands together as her eyes lit with excitement. "I'd be ever so pleased. And I can wear the exquisite gown you gave me."

Brand continued his descent into apparent madness, for this one little thing made her so happy that he craved doing something that would keep her forever in such a state. "Good." He shoved a hand through his hair and blew out a breath. "Now, I'm going to escort you home, because if I don't, you'll think me the biggest rake in Ipswich."

"Aren't you?" She winked as she left his side to retrieve her belongings.

"Perhaps." Yet... he suddenly didn't want that moniker any longer. *What the devil is happening to me?* He was only with her to win a wager, nothing more.

Right? He didn't know any longer, and what was more, he continued to fall.

CHAPTER FOURTEEN

August 30, 1817

Elizabeth paced the confines of the small parlor as she wrung her hands. Her nerves felt strung too tight, but alternately, tingles of anticipation zipped up and down her spine. Never in her life had she been so anxious or excited. In moments, Brand would arrive. He'd promised to escort her to Lord Nelson's home in style but hadn't had more details than that.

"I should forbid you from going tonight," William grumbled from his place in the chair.

The sound of his voice snapped her from her musings. She came to a halt by the window which looked out onto the street. "You can, of course, but I won't obey."

"No, I didn't think you would. Ever since you've met *that man*, you've changed."

"For the better, I hope." A small grin curved her mouth, and she couldn't stop it. Spending time with the captain had given her confidence she hadn't known she possessed. She'd also developed a backbone while her mind had expanded past the narrow views she'd had before the advent of Brand.

"That remains to be seen. It doesn't matter. All too soon we'll be gone from here and you can forget the captain." William huffed. "However, I'm going to let you go, for this unprecedented access to the wealthy of Ipswich is exactly what we need to spread the Gospel or perhaps even garner donations to help fund our upcoming trip."

Ah, and there was the truth of the matter. He wanted the coin. Elizabeth bit her bottom lip to keep from blurting out a response she might regret later. So, she declined to answer. "You could try being happy for me."

"What is there to rejoice about? He'll no doubt ruin you… if he hasn't already." The pause was obviously her chance to deny the charge, but she declined on that too. He sighed. "Why can't you see the man is a bounder?"

"Why can't you see he's as human as the rest of us and trying? Deep down inside, he's a good person." She didn't need to hear Brand's confession to know that. It was reflected in everything he did or said.

William snorted. "When you fall—and you will—I hope you'll remember to repent clearly and openly, for he'll drag you down in the muck with him."

"And you'll be there to forever remind me you've forgiven me." That was what William did. He couldn't just talk about a misdeed once. Oh no, he had to trot out her shortcomings every chance he got, with the reminder that he'd forgiven her. No one deserved that in their lives.

"That is my right."

"Your right can go hang," she said, and then was immediately contrite. "Please trust me enough to know I can make my own decisions. For better or for worse, they're mine alone, and I've had precious little of that in my life."

"I'm more concerned with your eternal soul than your decisions."

"Of course you are." Elizabeth shook her head. "But where's the fun in that?"

"You shouldn't be seeking entertainment or fleeting pleasures, Sister. Your purpose in this life is to live for the Creator and draw others into the fold."

"Where they'll learn that everything is a drudgery and they'll never be allowed to do anything that brings a smile again?" Where had that thought come from? More to the point, why had she spoken it aloud?

"It seems like the devil has been your constant companion, Elizabeth."

"I'm not that naïve or careless."

Her palms inside the elbow-length gloves were sweaty. She ran her hands down the front of her gown and once more sent up a prayer of thanks for Brand's largesse. It was the most wonderful piece of clothing she'd ever owned let alone donned. The ballgown of turquoise satin was the exact color she imagined the sea must be. White ribbons trimmed the low bodice and the short, gathered sleeves. Tiny clear beads and white seed pearls were scattered over the skirt and twinkled with each movement. Fine silk stockings and lawn underthings made her feel like royalty while matching satin slippers completed the ensemble.

Then her breathing hitched. An open carriage pulled by a dappled gray horse came to a halt at the curb in front of the townhouse. Brand manipulated the reins, and oh he was magnificent in dark evening clothes! A top hat sat at a rakish angle on his head; his wild hair had been tamed and combed, but he was still every inch the devilish ship captain, and her heart raced at the handsome picture he made with the beginnings to twilight as a backdrop.

"Captain Storme is here." Exhilaration bled into her voice. She spun away from the window and then had to remind herself not to pelt through the room. On her way past William's chair, she dropped a kiss upon his cheek. "I'll probably be late in coming home, so please don't feel the need to wait on me."

"Elizabeth, stop." He grabbed her wrist, holding her with a vice-like grip. His eyes were hard and cold as he met her gaze. "Deporting yourself like the world and dressed as a lightskirt is a certain way to usher in sin. Do not relax your guard tonight. You are not the same as the people you'll mingle with, and that world is not your future."

Some of joy bubbling through her chest died. She yanked her hand from his hold. "How could I forget exactly what my future is? You've told me enough times I don't have one."

"We live for the world beyond this one, sister."

"I know." Blinking away quick tears, she made her way to the door. "Let me have this one night to experience things that make a woman feel wanted and needed. It's not that much to ask before I put all of this away and leave for India with you."

Not waiting for his reply, she exited the room. A pat of her hair confirmed that her homemade attempt at sweeping up her tresses still held. No doubt it would pale in comparison to the ladies she'd see tonight, but there was nothing for it. By the time she opened the front door, Brand had come up the short walkway.

His eye widened with surprise and pleasure as he raked his gaze up and down her person. "Of all things holy on land or sea," he whispered, admiration evident in the tone. "You're beautiful, Elizabeth, and you look like the sea personified."

"Thank you." She followed him to the waiting carriage. "That makes me feel better. William said I was dressed like a lightskirt," she admitted in a small voice. Then she remembered she'd forgotten her fan. "Perhaps I should go back inside and grab something to cover myself. I'm showing too much décolletage—"

"No." So much authority rode in that one word that a shiver went down her spine. As Brand handed her into the carriage, he said, "Your brother is, quite frankly, a nodcock of the first order. He wouldn't know a good thing if she came up and smacked him." Seconds later, he came around and then climbed into the vehicle beside her. The close confines of the carriage meant his shoulder and leg brushed hers as he settled on the bench. "Why would you wish to cover such a wonderful form? If God has indeed given you those looks, be proud of them. You're going to make the other ladies jealous."

A queer little tremble went through her heart. "Hush, you."

Heat infused her cheeks as he set the horse into motion. She kept her hands tightly clasped in her lap. "I appreciate your regard all the same."

"I'm only speaking the truth." He took one of her hands and brought it to his lips, kissing her middle knuckle. Emotion clouded his eye that she couldn't quite read. "Any man who tells you something differently tonight is a bald-faced liar and doesn't deserve your time."

"I'm so nervous. I've never been in society before."

"Stick close to me and you'll be fine."

The excitement William's comment had stolen came rushing back. "Is this your carriage?" She could barely sit still as they rattled along the cobblestone street toward the wealthy section of Ipswich nestled in the hills.

"Not at all." He chuckled, and the sound resonated within her chest. "I borrowed it from the innkeeper. Traded a case of brandy for the privilege of bringing you to the admiral's ball in style." He glanced at her and shot her a grin that brimmed with wickedness. "After all, how often does a simple sailor have the opportunity to squire such a beautiful woman about?"

"I suspect you're not a simple anything, Brand Storme." More heat infused her cheeks. "Such flattery."

"Again, the truth." Confusion lined his expression. His mouth worked, but then he shook his head. "However, my friend John will put my sloop in the harbor on that side of town should we wish for a sail afterward. He'll return the carriage to its owner, so I won't need to in the middle of the night after escorting you home." He guided the horse to one side of the road and then tugged on the reins.

"What are you doing?" Elizabeth frowned. Had he changed his mind in bringing her to such an exclusive society event?

"Your toilette is not yet finished," he whispered and delved a hand into the interior pocket of his jacket.

"I don't understand." Had she forgotten something essential due to ignorance?

"A neck as graceful and elegant as your needs to be adorned." He withdrew a necklace of fine silver filagree. The glimmer of opals winked in the setting sunlight. Eight in total, they were no more than half an inch in diameter, but they glowed with a life of their own. "I bought this for you a few days ago in anticipation of an appropriate time to gift it to you."

"I couldn't."

"I wish you would."

Tentatively, she touched a gloved fingertip to one of the stones. Thin veins of blue, green, and pink crossed through the milky interior. "You've already given me so much."

"It's not nearly enough, I suspect." A certain fondness reflected in his eye that had hope blooming in her chest. "Let me do this. Turn." When she twisted on the bench, a shuddering sigh left his throat. With gentle fingers, he settled the piece around her neck and fumbled with the fastening at her nape. The warmth of his breath on her skin sent awareness shivering through her. "Opals have always been associated with love and passion. Wearing one of these stones is said to bring loyalty and faithfulness."

Joy danced in her heart. "You've certainly been that since I've met you." She turned back around and found his gaze. "I couldn't be more thrilled you're with me." Would that she had a mirror to see how the bauble looked on her.

Guilt and despair fought for dominance in his expression, gone when he shook his head. "You deserve every good thing in life, Lizzy. Never forget that." He bussed her cheek and then took up the reins once more. "God, I'm so damned fortunate tonight." The surprise and shock in his tones gave her pause. Was it possible he was truly seeing her as a woman he might need in his life for the first time?

Tamping on her hope and excitement, Elizabeth smiled. "Oh, Brand." A tiny piece of her heart flew into his keeping. "There is no one quite like you in this world, and I'm glad of that."

TWO HOURS PASSED at Lord and Lady Nelson's grand townhouse in next to no time. Elizabeth hadn't a moment to catch her breath, for she'd been introduced to so many people she couldn't remember their names. Brand was as charming as she'd ever seen him, and many of the men knew of him, either from the Navy or from his life in London and his family connections. The buzz of conversation and the laughter filling the rooms was so foreign to her that she couldn't decide where to look or what to pay attention to.

Never had she seen such wealth. From the décor filling the townhouse to the clothing and jewels each lady had donned to the champagne circulating through the rooms on silver trays by servants in satin livery, everywhere she looked excess and luxury met her eyes. It was certainly a far cry from her humble beginnings and even how she lived now.

And it made her exceedingly uncomfortable. As much as she adored the feel of her new clothes against her skin and the coolness of the silver around her neck, this wasn't her life. William's words rang in her ears. Should she attempt to minister to these people, tell them the trappings that money bought wouldn't insure a path to heaven?

Then Brand was there, concern etched on his brow. "I can almost hear you thinking, and it's not my words you're ruminating upon."

"No, they're not. William wants me to minister to these people."

"Then he can come do the work. You are here to dance and have fun."

"Perhaps." Elizabeth pasted on a smile but didn't know how successful it appeared. Pangs of guilt bounced through her gut. Was it fair that she ignored his entreaty when calling people to the Lord had been her life since before she could remember? "I can't help it. This," she gestured to encompass the large ballroom she currently stood in, "is all so… lavish. It's a bit intimidating."

"It is, rather." He nodded and lifted a hand in greeting to a gentleman who called his name. A woman blatantly winked as she passed him. Clearly, Brand was no stranger to society life. "I can understand your wariness. It's not how I would choose to live either, even if a little extra coin does make one's existence that much easier."

At the last moment, she recalled he was familiar with this world, for he was an earl's son. Her spirits plummeted. Regardless that he'd chosen to make a life in Ipswich doing odd jobs and fishing, he would eventually need to return to London and take up the reins of that life again. "There's such a difference between these people and me," she whispered. Once his interest in her faded, he would no doubt move on to another woman—a lady with a title—and marry well.

"None of that." He took her upper arm in a light grip and guided her onto the polished marble floor. "Essentially, everyone is the same. People generally wish for good in each other."

"None of what?" When she realized he intended to engage in a dance the string quartet was preparing for, panic took hold of her stomach.

"Comparison. It will tear a body's soul to shreds in half a minute if you let it, and it steals one's dreams. I can see it in your face, and you're thinking you're not enough."

"I… How can you possibly know that?"

"Because I often have thoughts along those lines." For an instant, his expression sobered. "I've felt exactly that way before, that I'm not enough for anywhere I've landed." He shrugged. "You either come to terms with the person you are, or you don't and will be forever miserable. The choice is yours."

She stared at him. "I struggle with that all the time." When she held her bottom lip between her teeth and his gaze dropped to her mouth, she shivered with a need she didn't quite understand but sorely wished to. "I'm not good enough for this life, neither am I perfect enough for the life William wants for me."

"Pish posh. You are perfect enough for me." Brand waggled his eyebrows. All trace of the serious conversation was gone. "I suppose I should have asked if you'd like to waltz."

It was a moot point now as other couples filled the empty spaces on the floor. Knots formed in her belly. "I'm not certain I remember the steps. It's been an age since Mama taught me, and even longer since William forbade it after my parents died. At least in the case of my parents, dancing wasn't considered a sin and was an acceptable form of exercise."

"William has some nerve in dictating what you should do with your time when he—" He cut off his words before the sentence was finished. With another shake of his head, his grin was back. "Then you and I shall make a scene together, for I haven't danced since before I joined the Navy." In short order he assumed the position with her. The press of his fingers at the small of her back sent tingles down her spine. "I promise not to step on your toes."

Oh, he was such a dear man!

"I also *don't* promise that I won't take as many liberties as I can during the dance. I am, after all, a rake."

"Now that I know you better, I rather think you're not." His lighthearted teasing was infectious, and soon she laughed at another of his jokes as the musicians began the song and Brand set them both into motion. She tightened her fingers in his when her first trip around the ballroom nearly ended in disaster as she forgot the steps or the timing or both. But he murmured encouraging words into her ear, and she transferred her attention to his face.

Then everything fell into place. Soon she glided over the floor, her steps flowing and matching his, her skirts swishing about her legs. With each turn, Brand reeled her a tiny bit closer to his body until her breasts brushed his chest and their thighs nearly touched.

"I knew you could do it." He grinned and the delicate skin at the corner of his eye crinkled. "In fact, with your determination and spirit, you will conquer any obstacles you might encounter."

Heat once more filled her cheeks. "If you keep on with that, I might swoon at your feet from the blatant attention."

"Ah, then that would allow me the opportunity to whisk you away to revive you." His eye darkened to the hue of storm clouds swollen with rain. "Or at the very least steal a kiss."

Foreign need tingled deep in her core and she caught her breath. "You don't have to steal one, for I'll give you it freely."

"All the better." His scent of sandalwood and citrus teased her nose and worked to weave a spell of enchantment about her. It was all too easy to pretend she belonged in this world and that the man waltzing her about the floor was hers for an eternity instead of mere days. "If I didn't know better, I'd say Lord Nelson was angling to lead you out for the next set."

She missed a step in surprise. "Surely not."

"You've made a sensation." Brand nodded. Pride reflected in his eye and expression. "Shall I let him, or should I play the selfish suitor and deny him?" The look he bestowed upon her spoke of jealousy, and she hoarded that to her heart like the victory it was. He already thought of her as his.

In that second, Elizabeth made a decision solely for herself. "Brand?" Feeling reckless, she gave him what she hoped was a suggestive glance.

"Hmm?" On the next turn, he took full advantage and pulled her close, holding her hand between their chests.

The romance of it tugged at her heartstrings and sent her head into the clouds. "Could we please leave early?" She could hardly think with him so close and her heart beating so fast surely he must hear it.

He frowned. "Are you not enjoying yourself?"

"I am, greatly, especially while dancing, but..." *Oh, dear heavens.* Her cheeks burned with embarrassment. Did other women have this problem? "I'd rather find myself alone with you, perhaps on your sloop for a different sort of... entertainment." *Please say you know the direction of my thoughts.*

"Ah." His eye widened in astonishment. Then it was his turn to miss a step. "Are you certain?"

"Yes."

"You are referring to…"

"Yes." It was adorable how flustered he'd suddenly become. Never had she been so sure of anything. "I think it's time."

Finally, he nodded. "Aye. We'll take a discreet exit once the dance ends."

"Good." This decision would change the course of her life. For good or for ill, she would accept whatever consequence or responsibility came of it, for all she wanted in this moment was Brand. At least she could have that before she left England. Quick tears jumped into her eyes. She tried to blink them away, but he saw her distress anyway.

"What's wrong?" he whispered as the music ended and each couple drifted to a halt. Polite applause circled through the room. "Why the tears? Have I done something amiss?"

"No." She swallowed down the ball of emotion in her throat. "What a ninny I am." With her fingers on his sleeve, she let him lead her from the floor, and then out a side door that passed a few other rooms where cards had been set up. "I have two more days with you, and then…" Oh, she couldn't finish the sentence. It was too sad.

And tragically unfair.

How had she fallen so hard and fast for this man in such a short period of time?

"I understand." His muscles beneath her fingers went taut. He quickened his pace. "I think Lord and Lady Nelson will excuse my bad manners if we don't give our excuses, don't you?"

Elizabeth had no idea, for the inner workings of high society were beyond her. *Oh, dear. If Brand declares himself and offers marriage, is this the sort of life I'll need to live?* She didn't know if she could do it without his connections and peers finding her lacking. Ipswich was a rather cozy place, but London? The thought of the capital, crowded and large, sent chills down her spine. Then another idea occurred to pour more heat into her already flaming cheeks. "Will everyone know the reason we're leaving early?"

"That's doubtful. And even if they saw us, they won't know our destination." Once they'd left the house and began walking the road that circled the harbor, he spoke again. "I want you to know I don't take your decision lightly."

"You're a gentleman through and through."

He snorted. "I've said it before. I'm not a good man. Now who is seeing only what they want?"

"I'm not wrong." But what did he mean? It wasn't the first time he'd said that. What worried him that kept prompting the words?

Their flight through the cooling summer's darkness was both thrilling and fraught with anxiety. After tonight, she wouldn't be the same. Fornication was a huge sin and could possibly see her cast out of the church. Would she be fit to minister to the needy in India? Or worse yet, what if, once Brand bedded her, he didn't want her any longer? Where would that leave her? And there was one more worry to consider. What if this coupling resulted in a pregnancy? Could she raise a child alone and abroad? Or would William, obnoxious prick that he was, leave her and condemn her in Ipswich with no recourse?

I've never been so confused before. There were no answers, but that didn't lessen her need to be with Brand, especially knowing her time with him was so limited. Her faith in him as a gentleman didn't waver, but if she found herself increasing, would he do the honorable thing? And if he did, could she willingly trap him in a marriage he didn't want, for he wasn't in love with her.

I wish I knew what the right thing was for me to do. Do I dare leap before I look?

"Don't worry. Everything will come out right," he murmured as they found the *Charlotte* in one of the slips.

A minute later, Brand lifted her onto the sloop. When he joined her, he took her immediately into his arms and treated her to a series of long, drugging kisses that had her senses reeling and her traitorous body reacting to his touch.

And fallen sinner that she was, she wanted him.

"There is nothing I love more than kissing you on my ship." He threaded his hands into her hair. Pins and combs were removed to ping on the decking. As her tresses tumbled down her back, he gazed at her as if he'd never seen anything so marvelous. "Ah, Lizzy. What am I to do with you?" he asked so softly, she wasn't certain if he was talking to her.

"Well, you can kiss me again to start," she shot back while a cloud of recklessness swirled about her.

"I like how you think." Tenderly, he drew her into his embrace, watching her the whole time that he lowered his mouth to hers.

Even more gently, he moved his lips over hers as he tangled his fingers in her tresses and slowly tilted back her head. When her throat was exposed, he nibbled and licked a sensual path beneath her jaw and then downward to tease the hollow behind her collarbones, and finally sought to drive her mad by trailing feather weighted kisses over the slopes of her breasts above the gown's bodice.

"Brand," the word was propelled by need as she clung to his lapels.

His eye darkened to that of a storm-tossed, cloudy sea. "Come with me." He took her hand, led her to a hatch and guided her down a short wooden ladder into the only cabin of the vessel. Two narrow bunks occupied the low-ceilinged room, one on each side and encased in an impressive wooden frame. A small circular table was secured to the floor between them. A stout wooden chair that matched the bed framework rested at the far end near a few portholes, a book lay abandoned on its surface. "This is where I sleep and unwind when out on longer trips that mean I can't immediately return home." The top of his head brushed the ceiling, and most of the time, he was obliged to slightly stoop.

"It's wonderfully cozy." In her mind's eye, she saw him reading an outdated copy of *The Times* while she darned a pair of his socks nearby, perhaps with a belly swollen with child. The intensity of that vision made her tremble.

"And more importantly, it's private." Once more he caught her up into his embrace. Blatant need reflected in his eye, the same force that had driven her to this decision. "I've waited long for this." Emotion left his voice rough and entirely too delicious.

"While I've only just realized how much I wanted it… wanted you." Elizabeth laid a palm against his cheek. "This night has been… beyond any dream I could possibly have," she admitted in a whisper.

"It's not nearly over, and hopefully, when it's done, you'll dream of me often." This time when his lips met hers, the tenderness in the touch transported her far away from Ipswich and her worries. Brand slid a hand along her back, undoing the tiny buttons until her gown gaped about her shoulders.

Shivers racked her body; awareness rippled over her skin as he eased the garment from her arms and helped it slide down her torso. When he tugged it over her hips, it pooled at her feet with a soft sigh. She looked into his face and swallowed to encourage moisture into her suddenly dry throat. "I… I'm not certain what I should do."

"Nothing except enjoy yourself." He rubbed his knuckles over one of her hardening nipples through the fabric of her petticoat and shift. A grin curved his sensual lips. "You're exquisite."

Intense sensation streaked from her breasts to settle between her thighs. When she whimpered, need flared deep in his eye, and spurred him into action. In short order, Brand divested her of the remainder of her clothing, even the slippers and stockings. As she stood completely nude before him—except for the opal necklace—a sudden fit of modesty overcame her. She attempted to cover her private parts as best she could, but he shook his head.

"No, Lizzy. You were made to be seen, either in your clothes or out of them." He slipped his arms around her. "A life of servitude beneath men who treat you little better than a slave in the church is not your destiny." Then he dipped his head and nibbled a path under her jaw, along the side of her neck while he fondled her breasts and brought the tips into tight, hard buds.

"Then what is?"

"I'm not certain."

"Neither am I, and I don't have much time to discover it. That's the problem." She tugged on his cravat until it came loose in her hands. "Let me see you." Oh, she couldn't wait to feel his body against hers.

"Of course." He shed his clothing with the ease of a man who is used to doing so at a moment's notice.

"Oh, my." Elizabeth lost the ability to think as she stared unabashedly at his erect member that bobbed in front of him. His torso, neck, and arms were a golden tan that spoke of hours of work in the sun, while the rest of him was as pale as a fish's belly. It made him approachable and a bit endearing. Such freedom men had! "I should hide in embarrassment." After all, she was as naked as he, and they weren't married. Even then, intercourse wasn't for recreation, was it? Not according to the church.

"Will you?" He prowled the brief space between them regardless of the various garments that littered the floor. "Will you cower under the counterpane so that I'll have to come hunting for you?"

"No." The one-word answer was naught but a squeak.

"Good, because there's so much I want to teach you." It took next to no effort on his part to tumble them both onto the bunk.

The weight of him was pleasing, but she wanted to explore. How to go about it? Did one wait for an invitation? Then it didn't matter, for he settled himself between her bent knees. The coarse hairs on his chest tickled her skin, and when he took a nipple into his mouth, her world shifted. She buried her fingers into his thick hair and held his head to her breast. Pleasure twined through her body and ignited tiny fires in her blood. When he teased her other nipple with a hand, her back arched, but there was nowhere to escape the torment, for his body blocked her flight.

Brand's hands were seemingly everywhere as he caressed her skin and played her body, touching her in places she'd not previously known were sensitive. When a moan left her throat, he chuckled. "I adore the sounds you make, Lizzy."

She couldn't form words even if she'd concentrated. Her world existed in sensation and pleasure, heat, and chills. His fingers were rough due to his work at fishing and sailing, but that texture only provided an additional layer of friction that drove her wild. When he moved to his side, she murmured a protest. It died prematurely as he delved a hand between her thighs like he'd done the other day. Quickly, his agile fingers found the center of her being, and when he rubbed it, circled it, she thought she might break apart from the exquisite delight.

Over and over, he worked that button. Elizabeth emptied her mind of everything except what he did to her. Terrible pressure built and stacked in her lower belly, seeking a release she had no idea how to find. "Brand…" Restlessly, she thrashed her head from side to side on the shallow pillow. Her thighs clamped about his hand, but that only deepened the sensations. "I need… something."

"I know." He increased the tension and friction on that nubbin while taking a nipple into the warm cavern of his mouth. The second he suckled the bud and teased her in just the right way, the mounting pressure inside broke.

A scream of surprise and gratification wrenched from her throat, and this time she didn't have the wherewithal to stifle it. Wave after wave of bliss rolled over her, throbbing in her core, until she had the strength of cooked porridge.

"I knew you'd be transcendent when you found release." Brand kissed her lips and once more maneuvered himself in the small space so that his body covered hers.

"Can I touch you?" If she played with his hardened shaft, would he experience the same pleasure that he gave to her?

"Later." His voice was hoarse with need as he pushed her thighs wide and settled between them, the tip of his member kissing her opening. "Right now, I want you so damned badly." He held her gaze as she drew her hands up his arms. "I apologize if this hurts." Then he flexed his hips and in one, powerful thrust, he impaled her on his rigid length.

A sharp prick of pain assailed her and brought quick tears stinging her eyes as her maidenhead was breached. There was no turning back now. She'd leave the sloop a different woman than the one who boarded it.

"Lizzy." The sound came from around clenched teeth. When she opened her eyes, a muscle flared in his cheek, a testament to his control. "All well?"

She wriggled beneath him as she accustomed to his girth and how well he filled her. When he hissed a warning, she giggled. "Yes, I'm fine. The pain is already fading."

"Good." Slowly, carefully, he withdrew only to join with her again with equally slow, tender strokes.

New sensations washed over her, different but the same as when he had his fingers on her sex. These were all-consuming, went deeper than anything else she'd experienced before. Nearly lost, Elizabeth looped her arms about his shoulders and held him close. She locked her ankles at the small of his back and gave herself into his care.

In and out he stroked, and with each movement need shivered through her belly and down her spine. A moan burst from her, for this was miraculous indeed. The man was all muscle, primed and taut, beneath her fingers and she couldn't wait to explore. Feeling a tad naughty, Elizabeth dared to trail a hand down his back, following his spine, past a collection of scars, to his buttock. When she squeezed the firm cheek, a moan and a curse escaped him.

Such power a woman could command! Oh, if only she had more time.

As she grinned, he claimed her lips in a hard, demanding kiss that vaulted her back to the present. She kissed him back as best she could while he pumped in and out. Pressure returned to circle inside her like a relentless beast, hungry for another release. "Brand, more." Was it proper for her to say that?

"I was only going slow because it's your first time." Urgency threaded through his voice. He shifted his position slightly by gripping her hips and tilting them upward.

"I'm not a shrinking violet… at least not anymore." He'd emboldened her on many levels. "Give me all of you."

"Gladly." This time he thrust so deeply she feared she'd faint from the intensity of the feelings swamping her. Faster, shorter, harder he moved, joining with her until there was no him and no her.

They were one being now, one person. That had to mean something.

The new angle hit different places inside her channel. Her breath came in pants. She'd drown in the shivery sensations—in him. Need slammed into her, demanding her surrender, but she didn't know how. When she caught Brand's gaze, a modicum of calm found her within the sea of frantic desire. She took refuge in that dark gray pool, communed with him on a different level than before. Silver flecks danced in his iris and he ceased his movements for the space of a few heartbeats. They stared at each other, locked in a moment beyond time. *Something* was exchanged between them. Elizabeth felt as if a piece of her soul had been given to him, and it was as natural as breathing.

Then urgency returned and demanded relief, for her body was tight and shaking with need. Brand's thrusts grew erratic, went deeper until she whimpered, pleaded with him to finish her. Over and over, he drove into her, but the terrible pressure wouldn't abate. Desperate to fall over that beautiful edge again, she pinched one of her nipples the same time he put a hand between them and found her swollen button.

She was lost.

Elizbeth shattered into a million shards of light as she found release. She screamed, so great was her surprise at the wave upon wave of pleasure that swept her away. As it throbbed between her thighs, he stroked into her again, and with a shout of his own, he spent, followed her into that great chasm without light or sound.

Perhaps it was a rift where one found heaven. That's how wonderful the act felt.

He collapsed on top of her, and she wrapped her arms around him. Tears of wonder and joy slipped from her eyes to stream down her cheeks and pool in her ears. She reveled in the rasp of his labored breathing as it blended with hers.

If this was a sin, it was worth every bit of the fall. "I rather think I've enjoyed being ruined." Then she buried her face into his chest and let the residual bliss have at her.

CHAPTER FIFTEEN

B RAND STOOD AT the stern, staring out over the dark water of
the harbor, somewhere between his side and that of Lord
Nelson's. Midnight had just passed, and now the night skies were
a velvety black, punctuated with thousands of twinkling stars.
The relatively cool summer air wafted over his bare chest; he'd
only thrown on a pair of breeches he'd grabbed from a drawer
beneath his bunk. For one second, he paused and looked up into
the heavens. It had never been his want to pray or even initiate a
conversation with the Creator, but his chest was tight from the
effort of holding back years' worth of straining emotions, and
after the time he'd spent with Elizabeth this night, he felt
compelled to say... something.

*Uh... Dear God, I'm merely one small human in a vast world full of
the same, yet I want to say how extremely grateful I am for what's been
given to me so far.*

He blew out a breath of frustration. That wasn't at all what
he'd wanted to convey. Since the advent of Elizabeth, his life had
tilted like a drunken sailor on deck. Perpetually, it seemed, he
found himself at sixes and sevens while around her, but when he
wasn't with her, he wanted to be. And not merely in the physical
sense... though when they'd finally coupled, it had been nothing
short of brilliant.

Lizzy, what have you done to me?

Not a half hour had passed since he'd claimed her body. She'd fallen asleep immediately afterward, while he'd at first held her, but then guilt had prompted him to leave the bed. Unfortunately, there was nowhere to flee while on a ship, so he'd opted for navigating the *Charlotte* into open waters and then pacing the deck once the anchor had been dropped.

Neither activity had cleared his thoughts, for he couldn't escape memories of Elizabeth. The softness of her skin had his fingers itching to touch her again, the faint apple blossom scent of her perfume haunted him, the tight snugness of her body made him crave the act of burying his prick into her heat once more. The way she'd looked, the tears of joy that had fallen when she'd hit release all worked together, called to him as if she were a siren of old.

And yet, none of it was real, for he'd bedded her to win a wager. Hadn't he?

"Brand?"

The tentative sound of his name in her voice brought him out of his whirling, tumbling thoughts. Though his mind remained conflicted, he turned, and then caught his breath. Elizabeth stood on deck, clad in her shift with the opal necklace almost gleaming in the moonlight. *Oh, God.* Earlier he'd stripped her down except for that bauble and it had been one of the most erotic things he'd ever seen.

"Elizabeth. I thought you were sleeping." Awareness rushed over his skin prompting every fiber of his being to pay attention.

"I was, but then I awoke and when you weren't beside me, I became worried." Her shrug was as elegant as any duchess. "I made use of a chamber pot and the wash basin. Everything is quite efficient on this sloop that I adore the coziness of it."

His heart squeezed and his breath once more stalled. "It makes for a certain ease, though if I had a larger vessel, there'd be more room for comfort." *Of all things holy on land and sea, I'm in a right proper fix.* He was invested too deeply in this woman, and if he didn't stop his current slide, he'd end up in unfamiliar territory that he might not escape.

"Oh, but then you'd require more hands to help pilot such a craft. The privacy of communing with the sea would vanish." She came forward, a veritable water spirit in the thin shift that revealed the hard outline of her nipples. "Were you... ah... satisfied with what we did tonight?"

How could she think he wasn't? Something intimate, dare he say special had been exchanged between them, almost as if she'd taken a part of his soul and had given him a portion of hers in its place. The knowledge rocked him to his core, for nothing of that sort had happened to him before. Not even when he'd fancied himself in love years ago.

No, no, no! Am I in love now? That simply wasn't possible!

But she waited for an answer. "I've not enjoyed anything quite as much as being with you." The whispered words squeezed from a suddenly tight throat. Emotions he'd long denied over the years battered his insides in a bit to be set free. He held them back as best he could, but soon he'd break, and they'd have at him.

"I'm glad." Her smile could rival the stars, and once more, the sensation of standing on shifting sand assailed him. "I found it wonderful, but I remain curious about the deed." When she paused in front of him, her smile faded around the edges. "Thank you for taking the time to show me at least part of that mystery."

Damn it all to hell. Because he'd bedded her on his sloop in an impromptu moment, he'd not given thought to wearing a sheath or even having one at hand. What if she began increasing due to their coupling? A touch of dizziness infused him, and he stumbled in the attempt to keep his footing. Would she demand marriage? Worse yet, would he even know? If she intended to travel to India with her brother, he'd probably never see her again.

Dear God, this is a disaster.

But she peered at him with a slight frown and a tilted head, so he said, "I wouldn't have missed what we shared for the world." At least that was the truth, and he'd told precious little of that to her since they'd met.

"Good." Instantly, the worry cleared from her expression. Joy lit her eyes. "Will you take me home?"

"Is that what you wish?" The thought of quitting her company so soon left him in a cold sweat. Now that it was after midnight, he only had this one day left with her. One day remaining to win that damned wager…

"Not really." She glanced over his shoulder at the dark and quiet harbor. "Such a pleasant sight to see the glimmer of a few candles burning and the stars reflected in the water. How fortunate you are to be able to enjoy this whenever you please."

"Aye." Desperate to keep her with him in the hopes he'd forget the despicable thing he'd done to her—was still doing—he threw his gaze about the deck. "Care to watch the stars with me?" When she nodded, he drew her over to a pile of sails that needed mending. "It's not a luxurious bed, but you have to admit the view is worth all the riches in the world."

"Do you know any romantic seafaring tales?" she asked as soon as he'd settled her into his arms as she reclined on his side.

"Not really. Most of the stories and legends I've picked up are about sirens and mermaids luring unfortunate men to their deaths beneath the water. Or those of beings like the selkies who pick up and leave love and family behind to answer the call of the sea."

"How odd that sailors are so resistant to happily ever afters." A sigh escaped her, and she smiled into the night sky. "I never realized how beautiful Ipswich was, but perhaps that's because I've not seen it by starlight."

"I quite agree." Except he wasn't looking at the stars, but at her. How had he ever thought her as plain or mousy? "Shall I tell you a story about some of the constellations? This one has a happy ending. During my time in the Navy, some of my mates educated me on the constellations while we were taught how to navigate by the stars."

She turned her head and met his gaze. "I would enjoy that."

"This tale is about Andromeda. She was rumored as a beautiful princess—as such stories often say—but her parents, Queen Cassiopeia and King Cepheus of Ethiopia, were quite horrid."

"Why?"

"No one has ever said, so that might have been added to the tale for local color." Brand chuckled. "You know how the ancients were."

"Perhaps."

He glanced into the heavens again, located the northern section where the constellation in question rested and pointed. "Despite Andromeda's looks, her mother was also famed for her beauty. However, the queen adored talking about it. As the legend goes, one day the queen bragged about herself before quite a large company. She claimed she was more lovely and striking than all the Nereids—sea nymphs."

"That can't be good." Elizabeth's eyes were wide as she looked between the sky and his face.

"Of course it wasn't." Brand chuckled, for being with her was so easy, and he truly enjoyed sharing his knowledge. "Suffice it to say, Poseidon—the god of the sea—was deeply offended by this blasphemy. He was obligated to retaliate; else he'd lose face. So, Poseidon sent the sea waters to flood the king and queen's land. Not nearly satisfied, he also sent the great sea monster Cetus to gobble them all up."

"A fitting punishment for vain humans?" Elizabeth snickered. "As if the gods were blameless in all these stories."

"Precisely. Oh, but the story grows worse." Brand stroked his fingers up and down her ribcage. "Like any self-worried and superstitious parents would do, the king and queen decided to sacrifice Andromeda to Cetus in the hopes this would quench the monster's thirst for blood and halt the flood waters. Despite her protests, they chained her to a bunch of rocks and ran away like cowards."

"That's horrible. To think a set of parents would love a god more than their own child..." Her swallow was audible. "Yet, that is exactly the mindset of too many elders in the church, and William especially." A shiver went through her body and transferred to him. "I couldn't imagine abandoning my child, or even putting them into harm's way, even if God commanded it."

"Thankfully, we are a more intelligent set of humans these days." He hoped, for he'd certainly not used much of that when entering into that damned wager. "As luck would have it, Perseus—the grand hero, of course—had only just finished slaying Medusa."

"Ooh, the woman with snakes for her hair that turned people to stone, right?"

"Correct." For a few seconds Brand lost himself in nuzzling the soft, faintly perfumed skin of her neck where it met her shoulder. Then he continued his story. "The legend says he was on his way home with the intention of killing his enemies with the severed head of Medusa. Much like slaying two birds with one stone."

She giggled then groaned and playfully swatted at his shoulder. "That was a bad joke."

"Indeed." Oh, how easy and wonderful it was to talk with her! "On his travels home, Perseus spied the princess Andromeda chained to a pillar on sacred ground. Quickly, he released her, but Cetus was approaching."

"Did he fall in love with her at first sight?" The question was couched in a dreamy, sing-song voice that had the power to sweep Brand away on images of his own.

"No doubt he did, for how could he not? Perseus unveiled Medusa's head from the bag he carried it in. The sea monster turned to stone, fell over at the edge of the sea, thereby sparing the land of his foul presence."

"I wonder if it was truly that easy for him." When Elizabeth laid a hand on his chest, Brand nearly jumped out of his skin from the contact. "I adore it when the hero is made to overcome a large obstacle to win the hand of his lady."

"Yes, well, the details are scandalously absent from tales of this nature." He brushed his lips over hers for the mere fact that he could. "Eventually, once the king and queen realized the danger had passed—

"—and were properly compelled to ask their daughter's forgiveness, I hope," she interrupted with a fair amount of spirit in her voice.

"—Andromeda and Perseus married. No doubt they were quite happy and devoted to each other." He stared at the constellations. "As a reward, Andromeda was placed in the sky next to Perseus when she died, along with her parents and the sea monster Cetus. I suppose the gods didn't want anyone to forget the story. To this day, the constellation Andromeda shares a star with Pegasus."

"What a wonderful tale. Thank you for sharing it with me." She combed her fingers through the hair on his chest, and with every pass of her fingers, tiny fires erupted in his blood. "It's comforting to know their story has been immortalized in the stars."

For long moments, they lay there watching the heavens.

Eventually, Elizabeth sighed, and that tiny sound of contentment lodged into his heart. "What do you want for your life, Brand? If you don't choose to reside in London, where will you go?"

"I'm not certain. Perhaps I won't leave Ipswich." He held her more comfortably in his arms and reveled in her warmth, in how easily they fit together. God, he could become all too used to this. When once he'd rather die than spend post-intercourse time with a woman, now he found he rather adored the intimacy, the... bonding. "To be honest, if I had my druthers, I'd sail wherever I could, anywhere in the world. Yet, that requires coin and a bigger ship than the *Charlotte*."

Those words brought reality crashing through the blissful haze of peace that had wrapped around them. Now that he'd bedded her, the wager was nearly completed.

The warmth of her breath skated over his neck and upper

portion of his chest. "What of a wife or children? You'd previously stated you didn't wish to marry, but what if you change your mind?" A hint of hesitancy had entered her voice. "It's quite possible, you know."

An image of Elizabeth swam into his mind, her belly swollen with child while he held a toddler in his arms. The boy's hair was brown and wavy like hers, his eyes a stormy bluish gray. Brand's heart trembled. A thrill of anticipation went down his spine. For the first time in his life, he lusted after the security and contentment the image represented. A tiny grin curved his lips, but then another thought occurred that knocked the image astray.

Once Elizabeth discovered the wager and the details therein, she'd cut him from her life with alacrity. Any woman of substance would. How could she not? What he'd done, with malice aforethought, was callous and selfish and horrid. He'd manipulated her emotions, did it still, but he sorely wanted that schooner, needed it to launch a business that might make a proper gentleman of him.

No matter his intentions, hot guilt twisted in his belly. The pain of it caught his breath. "I don't know if a life of domestication is possible for me." Because he didn't deserve it, didn't deserve the love that should come along with such a scenario.

"I see." She pulled back from him enough to peer into his face. "Are you opposed to that state, or are you loathe to give up your life of sin?" A cool note had entered her voice. Uncertainty and disappointment flickered in her sapphire eyes.

The knife of his own creation turned and slashed through his gut ever deeper. He wanted to cry out from the pain his deception was bringing both of them, but fear—and wanting that damned ship—held him back. Of course she would have assumed the end result of his courtship and subsequent bedding would be a proposal. He swallowed down the sour bile that had crept into his throat. "It seems like a dream, really." Despite his confliction, he held her gaze, willed her to understand. "How can I offer for a woman when I have nothing of consequence to my name?"

"Oh, Brand, none of that is important, not when there's love as the foundation."

Damn my soul. Emotions clogged his throat, clawed at his chest to escape their tight prisons where he'd stored them for years. He glanced away lest she see the truth in his eye. "I'm not that good of a man, Lizzy," he admitted in a graveled voice. "No doubt a wife of mine would leave by some way or another, for I would disappoint them. That's a truth I can't ignore. Because of that, folks always leave me."

She would, once the horrible lies were discovered. Terror shivered down his spine. It cooled his insides and left him shaking from the enormity of it.

What if I don't want her to go?

"You can't let yourself think such things. Fear of the unknown plagues us all."

Oh, God. That's what she thought his hesitation and distress stemmed from. He could hardly bear her innocent trust in him.

Once more, Elizabeth snuggled into his arms, which only twisted that proverbial knife deeper. "You're a wonderful man, Captain. Honorable with great integrity. Any woman would be happy to have you for a husband. In order to reach your dreams, you need only a wife to support you."

Sweat broke out on his forehead. Every word she uttered added layers of shame and self-loathing to the storm brewing in his chest. "If only you knew the truth," he whispered and pressed his lips to her hair as unshed tears prickled the backs of his eyelids.

"I have faith in the Lord and in you." Her lips brushed his skin as she spoke. "Things will come out right and as they ought, you'll see."

Too bad the best scenario he could hope for was disaster. Not having the words to say in comfort or affirmation, Brand held her close and hoped his life wasn't heading for the rubbish pile like he feared.

The rhythmic slap of the water against the hull of the sloop, coupled with the steady thrum of her heartbeat lulled him into a sense of peace that offered a brief escape from what he'd done. Eventually, he stirred. She watched him with sleep-heavy eyes that sparkled.

I must tell her. Perhaps he could salvage their relationship, begin again with no lies between them. Make it right and proper and real.

As his pulse raced in his veins, Brand pushed into a sitting position. He scrambled for the compass around his neck, peered at it in the dim light. It always pointed north, and it just so happened the bold red arrow directed his attention to the very direction where Elizabeth reclined. A coincidence, of course, but perhaps it was a sign. She lay on her side, her hair a tangled brown mess, with one hand tucked beneath her cheek. His heart skipped a beat, for he wanted her for much more than a quick toss between the sheets. Perhaps he always had, but the wager had stood in his way and blinded him to the truth. "Lizzy, I must tell you something." He gently shook her shoulder lest she fall back into slumber.

"Mmm?" The sleep roughened purr of her voice went straight to his length. Arousal hardened the shaft. She blinked open her eyes. So much trust and dare he say love reflected there that he wanted to sob at the irony of it all. "Is there something amiss?"

"I…" He couldn't find the words he wanted to say, for fear held him captive. Above all, he didn't wish to lose her over those wagers that meant nothing to him now.

She propped herself up on one elbow. The opals glittered about her neck; they were part of his grandmother's wedding jewelry she'd left to him upon her death. Why he'd kept them tucked away on the sloop instead of safe in London, he couldn't say, but he always like the look of those jewels.

Perhaps he'd carried a stupid kernel of hope in his heart…

Elizabeth frowned. "Do you need something?"

I need you to forgive me. But at the last second, he lost his nerve. The words sitting at the tip of his tongue flew away like frightened birds. How could he confess such a huge sin—a crime really—against her? The knife deep inside his chest twisted once more. "I just wanted to tell you how beautiful you are." *I'm such a bloody coward.* For a delay would only make matters worse. Then he leaned down and kissed her, unprepared when several pieces of his heart went into her keeping. It was extraordinary, this feeling of belonging with another person.

As he pulled away, her smile could rival the light of the moon. She laid a palm against his cheek, kept him steady as she held his gaze. "I love you, Brand. You've completely changed my life, and I'm forever grateful that you chose me."

"Oh, God." He was a con, a blackheart, the worst sort of villain. His chest tightened so hard that he couldn't draw a proper breath. With those words, he'd won the schooner fair and square, but that victory rang hollow, for he didn't want the prize any longer. He pressed a hand to his heart where that traitorous organ ached. "Ah, Lizzy. I don't deserve you." Desperately needing approval and wanting her forgiveness, but swimming with disgust for himself, Brand covered her body with his. He kissed her long and deep, intent to lose himself in her shining light and perfection in the illogical hope that he'd find her goodness and wash himself clean.

That all of what he'd done might be forgotten.

That somehow he'd never need to tell her…

Yet, for all of that, she wasn't his, never had been, and now his time with her was limited.

At the last second, he stifled a sob against the soft skin of her neck. He didn't merit her, not in any capacity, yet here she was, loving him because all she saw was what she expected to see—a decent man. "I'm so, so sorry," he whispered in a choked, barely audible voice before claiming her mouth, bullying her into a surrender as he settled her more comfortably in his arms.

The imminent loss of this creature, this amazing woman he hadn't been searching for was staggering, much more so than losing the ownership of the schooner, for that second, in the joy of having her in his arms beneath the stars, he vowed not to complete the wager. He wouldn't tell his friends; he'd call a halt to all the proceedings, pay them the original five hundred pounds for their silence and discretion. And, if fortune smiled upon him, he'd find a way to keep Elizabeth in his life and her remaining ignorant of his crime.

At least it was a plan. Feeling more like himself than he had in days, Brand applied himself to kissing her senseless and slid his hands beneath the hem of her shift. Oh yes, it would work. How could it not? Desire clouded his brain, worked to further muddle his thoughts. Another, stronger emotion he refused to identify wrapped around his heart. He would claim her body again this night before taking her home, and then he'd work at securing her promise to share his life.

With a sigh, he gave himself up to the wonders of Elizabeth's charms. All would be well, and he'd have a happily ever after, just like that fellow Perseus.

CHAPTER SIXTEEN

August 31, 1817

O F COURSE, FOR her last day in Ipswich, rain had chosen to bedevil the area, one of those light mist-type rains that didn't immediately see one drenched, but it was annoying for its dampness all the same. The fog that had stolen over the harbor from this morning had thankfully dissipated, but still, the rain was a mockery. If she were honest with herself, she'd say the dreary weather matched her mood.

Regardless of the wonderful night she spent with Brand, first going to a ball, and then lying with him on his sloop and knowing him in the Biblical sense, the fact remained that tomorrow she would leave for India. Despite her admitting that she loved him, he'd not returned the sentiment and neither had he said anything else along those lines.

But the emotion in his eye! As she recalled that look and the intensity in the way he'd joined with her on the deck, gooseflesh raced over her bare arms. After that coupling, she was hard-pressed to deny he didn't feel *something* for her, yet why wouldn't he say it? Time was clearly running out.

She adjusted her shawl over her head and chest as she hurried up the main road that went around the harbor. William had taken their only umbrella, for he intended one last time to minister to the lost of Ipswich. He'd been abed by the time she returned home early in the morning, exhausted but happy. By the time she'd risen to give him his breakfast, his mind was already on his mission. Thankfully, he hadn't asked many questions about the ball or about Captain Storme. Perhaps he'd lost interest, or more to the point, he probably didn't care, for they'd leave on the morrow and she'd be removed from temptation.

I don't want to go.

The knots in Elizabeth's stomach pulled tight. Too many emotions went through her mind and heart, as fast as racehorses, so she couldn't quite encourage one of them to stay long enough to focus upon it. So, she called an image of Brand into her mind and ignored everything else. How could she make him understand that they were good together and that God had brought them together?

Perhaps she couldn't, and he was merely the rake he continued to liken himself to. Oh, how she hoped that weren't true, but why wouldn't he declare himself? If he were afraid, she'd help him work through that morass. She couldn't do anything unless he talked to her about it. Above everything, she loved him, adored the man that he was. Others might classify it as reckless or even appalling that she'd fallen in such a short period of time, and she supposed they were entitled to their opinion. However, in her heart of hearts, she knew the truth. He'd won her over by being nothing except kind and considerate, charming and honorable.

And if he doesn't ask for your hand?

Elizabeth chose to ignore that niggle of common-sense flaring at the back of her mind, mostly because she couldn't bear to think about a future that didn't include the captain... or the life of servitude that awaited. The worst thing to do was live out someone else's dream, and that's exactly what would happen if William had his way.

Oh, Mama, Papa, would that you were here and could give me counsel.

Of course, they would most likely side with William, for it

was inconceivable she could fall in love with a man who didn't attend church, who regularly took the Lord's name in vain, and had things in his past that even God himself would shudder at.

Eventually, she arrived at the Great White Horse hotel, for Brand had asked her to meet him there for a dinner in one of the private dining rooms and then he'd take her out for a twilight cruise around the harbor. Being that it was overcast, there wouldn't be much of a sunset, but the sentiment was the same. Any time spent in his company was better than listening to William lament the number of sinners unwilling to hear his message. If she were fortunate, he would use that time alone to declare his feelings for her and ask for her hand. Then her immediate future would be settled, and she wouldn't need to depart for India.

Please God, if that is Your will, make it so.

And if it wasn't… Well, she wouldn't think about that right now.

Once Elizabeth stepped into the corridor, she removed her damp shawl and hoped the moisture hadn't done much damage to the plum-colored dress. The hem was a bit soiled, but it couldn't be helped. The buzz of conversation and laughter drifted to her location the closer she moved toward the tavern's common room. A faint smile curved her lips, for despite the patrons' penchant for swearing and drinking, sometimes even smoking horrid pipes that filled the air with stinky clouds, she liked the sense of camaraderie the men seemed to have and the friendships that had been born in that room over time.

A barmaid drifted over to Elizabeth. Slightly older than the other one Elizabeth had spoken with the other day, this one wasn't as buxom. Lines of exhaustion filled her face. "You're here for dinner?"

"Yes."

"Mr. Hayhurst is already in your customary private dining room."

Why is William here? Elizabeth frowned. "He told me he had business to attend."

The barmaid snorted. "Oh, he's attending to something, all right, but it ain't *his* business." She rolled her eyes. "Who are you meeting, then?"

"Captain Storme. He promised to reserve a room."

"He did. Number three."

"Ah." Then, his laughter wafted through the air, and anticipation shivered down her spine. "Never mind. I'll find him myself." With a murmur of thanks, Elizabeth made her way through the tavern's dining hall. How incredibly sad this would be the last time she'd observe the ambience or see the smiling faces of hardworking fishermen and merchants. Her brother never acted as if he truly enjoyed the life he led. As a Christian, shouldn't happiness be at the forefront of one's existence that might draw the lost to them like a flame to a moth?

Once she reached the table in the corner where Brand and his friends held court—seemingly in high spirits as they lifted their tankards in some sort of toast—she stopped and softly cleared her throat. Immediately, the conversation and laughter between the group of friends ceased. "Good evening, Brand, er, I mean Captain Storme."

Since his back was to her, he scrambled to his feet and turned to face her. The three other men shot into standing positions as well. They exchanged glances with each other that ranged from speculative to knowing. "Uh, Elizabeth." Though pleasure lit the gray depth of his eye, guilt scudded through Brand's expression. Why did that one emotion keep popping up? "I thought we were to meet in one of the private dining rooms? It's already reserved."

"So I was told, but when I heard you, I decided to come over and fetch you myself." She looked between Brand and his friends. "Have I interrupted a celebration?" Worry snaked through her belly, coiling cold and precise. This was the last evening she had with him, but would he wish to spend it with his mates instead?

"Uh, not really…" Brand hedged. He flicked his attention to something over her left shoulder while the men behind him snickered.

A man with a scruffy beard snorted. "Not true. The captain has just acquired a schooner."

"Now that *is* good news." She peered at the captain. "You've long wished for such an opportunity. I'm glad it's finally come your way."

Brand huffed out a breath as two of the men exchanged wild snickers. "Miss Hayhurst, this is Mr. George Cantwell."

"I'm pleased to meet you." The fact that Brand had formally introduced her was a positive sign.

Another man, this one tall and thin with a shock of red hair, vigorously nodded. "Aye, and we've all signed a partnership agreement to form a shipping outfit."

After a low growl, Brand said, "And this is Mr. Philip Van-Cleve."

"Good evening. How wonderful that news is!" That meant Brand was serious about making something of himself and providing a steady income. The worry that had previously plagued her vanished. In its place came joy. Surely, he would offer for her now.

"Yes. It is." But he seemed anything but thrilled. In fact, he held his jaw tight and anguish clouded his eye.

The last man standing about the table nodded. He possessed a barrel chest and golden hair, but his kind eyes reflected worry. "Good evening, Miss Hayhurst. I'm the captain's best friend, Mr. John Butler. Used to be his first mate."

She sucked in a breath. "The man who saved him the day he lost his eye."

"Yes." A hint of red color infused his face. "I must say, the captain has told us much about you, and I believe he's fully smitten."

"God damn it, John," Brand hissed. "Enough of this gammon." With a groan that could only signify annoyance, Brand took her upper arm and pulled her a bit away from the table to a relatively open spot a few feet from the watchful eyes of his friends. "Why don't you go ahead into the private dining room? No doubt you'll feel more comfortable there."

"Are you not planning to join me?" Why did he act as if he were on edge? And why did he want her away from his friends?

"Oh, I will, of course. I was just talking with the men until you arrived." The grin he flashed was no less charming than it always was, but this time it didn't reflect in his eye. Neither did the delicate skin at the corner wrinkle. "They're a rather rowdy bunch, especially once they've downed a few pints. I wished to spare you embarrassment."

"That's sweet, but I'm not embarrassed. I find your friends interesting." She searched his face. "Are you quite well?"

"Yes, why?" He released her arm as worry entered his expression.

"You're tense. I can sense you're concerned about something." She frowned. "Are you worried about your new partnership?"

"Not as much as you'd think." For the space of a heartbeat, his mood shifted into pleasure. "Did you receive my package this morning?"

"Yes." Her cheeks heated with a flush, for until this moment she'd forgotten about the delivery, so consumed had she been in her own thoughts. A courier had dropped off a lovely floral bouquet as well as a large, flat box. When she'd opened the package and parted the thin tissue paper, the gorgeous golden ballgown they'd spied in a shop window that seemingly long-ago day met her gaze. Complete with matching slippers. "It's an exquisite gift and far too expensive."

"You're worth every farthing I paid." Fondness lingered in his voice. His sensual lips curved in a grin. "I can't wait to see you in it."

She rolled her eyes, but then a wave of sadness washed over her. "I have no occasion to do so, and besides, this is my last evening here."

"It might not need to be," he said in a whisper. He looked at his best friend, who arched an eyebrow and made a motion with a hand as if to say get on with it. Brand's Adam's apple bobbed with a hard swallow. "Elizabeth, there is something I must say to you, and I'd much prefer to do so in private."

Excitement danced down her spine while flutters filled her lower belly. This was it! He'd ask for her hand tonight, she was certain of it. She couldn't hold back her smile. "Oh, Brand." Her voice was decidedly breathless. "I knew God brought us together for a purpose."

"Uh…" He tugged at his already sloppy cravat. Shame and self-loathing fought for dominance in his expression. In fact, he looked a bit green about the mouth as if he wished to cast up his accounts, and soon. "I'm not sure I'd go that far…"

One of the men at his table let loose a loud guffaw. He collapsed into his chair. "That's not exactly true, Miss Hayhurst," the man, Mr. Cantwell, said. Mirth was clearly stamped across his face. "God had nothing to do with it."

With a glance at Brand, who had gone even greener, she returned her attention to the other man. "What do you mean?" When he declined to answer, another man, Mr. VanCleve, took up the story.

"That day at the fair? *We* arranged that meeting." When he grinned, a gold tooth flashed in place of one of his molars. "It was the best dare we've ever put forth."

Unease dripped down her back. Chill bumps immediately covered her arms. "A dare?" She didn't understand why he would say such a thing. "Captain Storme told me he was captivated by me from the moment he saw me…" Had that been a lie? With more than a little trepidation brewing in her chest, she sought out Brand's gaze. "What does he mean?"

"I…" Desolate crept into his expression. "They… we…" He put a hand to his chest and rubbed the spot where his heart was located. "Oh, God." The whisper was fraught with horror.

As the two men shared another laugh, Mr. Butler slowly moved toward her. "Miss Hayhurst, you and I have only just met.

However, the captain has been nothing but distracted since you came into his life. Please bear that in mind over the next few minutes."

"What shall occur in the next few moments?" She couldn't separate herself from the cloud of confusion seeping into her brain. What did this man know? What did they all know? Why were they hiding it from her?

His frown, as well as the worry and sadness pooled deep in the depths of his hazel eyes, tightened the knots already in her belly. "I've seen for myself how animated the captain is when he speaks about you, how respectful he is, how utterly infatuated he's become." He flicked his regard between her and Brand, but the words did nothing to alleviate the concern that had caused the muscles in her stomach to cramp. "Just as I see with my own eyes how much you've come to care for the captain. Despite everything, does it really matter how your association came about?"

"I'm afraid I don't know what you mean." Panic built and stacked within her chest. Something was afoot and it wouldn't bode well for her. She slammed her gaze back to Brand. "Please, tell me what's wrong." Perhaps he owed gambling debts and was embarrassed about it. Or perhaps he'd lied about having a mistress. As long as he hadn't lain with the woman during the time Brand had been with her, she could forgive his past. Men were men; but having faith and knowing salvation meant sins were covered, wiped out, forgotten. "No matter what the obstacle, if we talk about it, we can overcome it."

A red wash of color crept over Brand's collar and surged into his cheeks. "Elizabeth, please. For all things holy on land or sea, please go to the private dining room I've reserved for us." The plea, couched in a rough, whispered voice, intensified her misgivings. When she didn't move, he sighed and hung his head. "You must understand this was all thought up before you and I met."

"What was?"

He shook his head. "The wager."

"What are you talking about?"

Brand didn't answer.

She glanced at Mr. Butler. "What is he trying to say?" Quick tears pricked the backs of her eyelids, for whatever the omission was, it was large enough and horrible enough that Brand and his best friend were both racked with embarrassment and shame about it.

"John, for the love of God, do something." Stark desolation raged over Brand's face.

"Go ahead into the room you've reserved." He waved the captain away. "I'll attempt to mitigate the blow if I can."

Gratitude briefly shined in Brand's eye before fear trampled on it. "Thank you." He looked at Elizabeth, and instead of fondness or affection, there was nothing but self-loathing in his face. "Give me ten minutes to gather my thoughts. Then I'll tell you everything and I hope…" A heavy swallow followed. "I hope you'll forgive me." Without another word, he turned tail and ran through the public room to the door that opened into the private dining corridor.

What did he mean? He'd whispered those words to her last night before he'd sent her flying on the deck of his sloop. Why did he so desperately want her forgiveness? With shaking hands, she clutched her damp shawl as she peered at Mr. Butler. "What is happening?"

"Let me ask you a question in answer." The man rubbed a hand over his chin. When his two fellows at the table continued to laugh and whisper, he sent them a fierce look that instantly quelled their noise. "Please show some respect. Put yourself in her position and see what you'd possibly feel." As they avoided directly looking at both him and her, Mr. Butler sighed. He met her gaze. Sorrow pooled deep in his eyes. "Do you truly love Brand?"

"Yes." Elizabeth nodded even though the uncertainty tore at her insides. "At least, I thought I did after last night." Her chin trembled, but she ignored it. "Yet your behavior and that of your friends has given me pause." She held his gaze, willing him to relieve her sudden fears. "Unless you know of a reason why my feelings are misplaced."

"The fact that you can see into the soul of my best friend, look past his fears and insecurities, is a good first step. I worry often about him, for he chooses to avoid anything that makes him uncomfortable or requires him to peer inward for self-reflection."

"Yes, he has a tendency to ignore his feelings."

"Indeed." He paused, his lips pressed together in a tight line before speaking again. "I'm sorry that I had a part in this deception."

"Deception?" Cold foreboding sat heavy in the pit of her belly.

The man waved a hand. "I fear what was done in the spur of the moment as a lark will now tear apart something that would have ultimately seen the captain push himself into being a better man."

A sick feeling rose into her throat, the origin of which she still couldn't say. "Will you not give me a hint, Mr. Butler? I shall go mad shortly."

"I'm afraid that's not for me to say, Miss Hayhurst. You need to speak with—"

"Oh, for heaven's sake!" Needing an end to the delay, Elizabeth spun on her heel. She marched across the floor, ignoring the curious glances from a few patrons. At the door, she wrenched it open and then surged into the narrow, dimly lit corridor, traversing it quickly until she arrived at the third dining room. The second she stepped over the threshold and into the room, her world tilted.

Brand was locked in a passionate embrace with the buxom barmaid. His back was against an ornate longcase clock that didn't keep the correct time, his hands seemingly all over her chest and shoulders. When the barmaid shifted her stance, Elizabeth caught a glimpse of her bodice eschew with one breast on display.

"How could you, Brand Storme!" Her heart shattered into a million pieces the longer the kiss continued. The pain in her chest caught her by surprise as her heart squeezed. She couldn't breathe, couldn't think properly. Why had he done this knowing she was just outside the room?

In the heavy silence that followed, Brand shoved the barmaid away from his person. He dragged the back of his hand across his mouth. "Elizabeth, this is not what it looks like."

Her eyebrows rose. "Really? Because it seems you've rather developed a taste for used goods." Oh, goodness, that wasn't at all charitable of her to say, but these were extreme circumstances.

"You should talk," the barmaid said as she set her bodice to rights. "You fucked him same as me, so which one of us is the better woman?" A bruise was forming on her left cheekbone. Had Brand given her that? Never had he been prone to violence before. Embarrassment burned in her cheeks from the other woman's use of vulgarity.

"Bloody hell!" Brand uttered a strangled sort of sound. "That's not true! But I can guess at who's given her that shiner. The bastard's lurking about, I'll wager."

She frowned, couldn't follow the convoluted pattern of thought.

"Listen to him, acting like he doesn't want the secret out." A knowing light had entered the barmaid's eyes as she glanced between them. "I'll wager I service him better since I know all the tricks, especially what he likes."

"For the love of God, stop talking, wench." A warning growl had entered Brand's tone. His eye flashed gray fire. Never had she seen him so upset. "She's lying, Elizabeth. I swear, I never bedded her."

"Ha!" The barmaid sauntered toward her. "Better leave him be, miss. He'll soon grow bored with you." With a wink, she left the room.

Elizabeth cheeks were hot with humiliation and alternately fury. After everything she and Brand had shared together, *this* is

how he would honor their bond? She trembled from embarrassment while images of his body wrapped around the barmaid's
filled her mind. "I can't believe you would disrespect me like
this," she finally managed to whisper.

"I didn't." He shoved a hand through his hair, leaving it in
disarray. "I swear to you on my father's grave or a Bible if you
have it handy, I didn't lie with her and neither did I do anything
to which she referred."

"Did you kiss her?"

Guilt was stamped all over his face. "She attacked me when I
entered the room. The second her lips touched mine, I tried to
shove her away, untangle her from me, but she clung on like a
demented octopus." His were came so fast they tripped over each
other.

Yes, he was a known rake, but over the course of their time
together, she thought she'd come to know him. He'd certainly
acted as if he were enamored of her. Perhaps the barmaid lied; the
wasn't outside the realm of possibility. Elizabeth softened toward
him slightly, but he hadn't answered her question. "Have you
ever willingly kissed that woman *after* you and I were intimate...
at any time?"

Please say no. Please say that you were faithful to me.

Desolation reflected in his eye. "Yes." His whispered admission caused another few pieces of her heart to fall with a clatter. "I
did kiss her, but that was before I knew—"

"Enough." The shawl fell from her grasp as Elizabeth held up
a hand. Tears crowded into her throat while her chest felt tight
and ready to burst open. At least he was honest, yet that meant
there was a chance he'd bedded the woman too. How many
others? "I've heard enough."

"Please believe me. I've never had intercourse with her." His
stricken expression tugged at her compassion. "Or let her do
anything else carnal to me." Would a man who lied be able to call
forth such depth of emotion on command?

She had no idea. Perhaps it was a tool in a rake's arsenal.

With a hard swallow, Elizabeth shook her head. "I need to go. There is packing to finish." Somehow, she turned away from him as all her dreams withered and died.

"Lizzy, please! None of this is what you think."

"I thought you might have returned my feelings, that you would have declared yourself this evening. Instead, I'm trapped in a Drury Lane production with horrible actors." Elizabeth ignored the plea, ignored the flutters in her belly from his use of the dear little nickname, ignored the pain, for there would be plenty of time to nurse her wounds on the passage to India. She walked out of the private dining room and didn't look back.

What a naïve idiot I've been. Men never change.

CHAPTER SEVENTEEN

N*O, NO, NO, no, no!* How the hell had things gotten this far?

Brand didn't have time to wonder at the lies the barmaid had told, even though white-hot anger surged through his person. He didn't care why the devil she'd done it, for the damage had already been done… and he hadn't even had the chance to confess about the wager yet. "Lizzy, wait!" Regret and fear sat heavy on his chest, forcing him into shallow breathing.

It can't end like this.

Fortunately, John Butler had waylaid her in the tavern room. He'd handed her a pristine white handkerchief, which she used to dab at her eyes. They spoke in low tones that Brand couldn't hear, but she was quite upset, if the flush on her cheeks and the animation of her hands was any indication. George and Philip observed the drama with expressions of interest. *Damn their eyes.* Once things had settled and he won Elizabeth, he'd offer John the sloop. Hell, the man could have the schooner if he'd but help Lizzy stay. And then he'd give his other friends the dressing down they richly deserved.

But winning Elizabeth was his priority.

By the time Brand joined them, the tears were more evident. "Elizabeth." Gently, he turned her about to face him. "Let me explain."

"Can you without making things worse?" she asked in a soft

voice, her eyes luminous, while John stood by, his expression pained.

Across the room, the buxom barmaid watched them with glittering eyes and a smug smile. Would that she'd pay for what she'd done. Then he dismissed the woman from his mind, but that shiner on her cheek was a veritable calling card. No doubt William was here, lurking, waiting for his moment to condemn them all or usher Elizabeth away.

That bastard probably paid her to drive a wedge between me and Elizabeth.

"I can but try, if you'll listen to me." He took her free hand and held onto the fingers as if she'd suddenly vanish. "I would never do anything to hurt you." Except... he had. Guilt and shame twisted through his gut in twin hot threads. If he could win her back now, did he necessarily need to confess to the wager?

"I'll admit, in all the time I've known you, you've never acted with malice toward me," she said in a soft voice.

That was all to the good. It was merely a matter of coaxing and soothing her as if she were a skittish colt. "After these weeks together, don't you feel I have your best interests at heart?" It was true, in the beginning he didn't, but now, he only wanted to make her happy and give her everything she'd never had in her life.

"I suppose, but..." She pressed her lips together. Oh, how he wished he could kiss her, show her how much he cared for her instead of trying to puzzle it out with words. "...but if that is true, why were you tarrying with the barmaid to begin with?"

"I wasn't. She wanted that kiss, not me. I *didn't* kiss her back, and I certainly wasn't embracing her." Was this the hill that she would die upon? He held out a hand, hoped to God she'd take it. "Come, let's discuss this in private."

Elizabeth had almost put her fingers into his palm when his damned friend Philip opened his mouth.

"You should believe 'im, Miss Hayhurst. He's been so tangled up in seducing you that he's had no time to go chasing after another woman."

No doubt Philip thought he was helping, but the surprise that jumped into her eyes told him that matters were about to grow even worse. "Do shut up, Philip."

"But, you have to know we're curious, Captain," he said, clearly not heeding the warning look Brand sent him as Elizabeth bounced her gaze between them. "Has she fallen in love with you? I don't see the lock of hair we requested."

The heat of anger pushed up the back of Brand's neck. "Enough."

"A lock of hair?" Elizabeth frowned as she rested her gaze on Brand. "What does he mean?"

"It was to signify you'd fallen for me," he finally admitted. In for a penny, in for a pound. Perhaps it was best to have it all out into the light.

Philip nodded. He drained his tankard. "He's got a right proper gift of that. How many women have you seduced in Ipswich, Captain? 'Cept none of them won him a schooner."

"What?" All the blood drained from Elizabeth's face while George knocked Philip on the side of his head and called him an idiot. Her eyes rounded. "You won a schooner in return for seducing me, making me fall in love with you?"

Oh, God. A sick feeling rose in Brand's throat. "I'd rather not do this with an audience." Not giving her the choice, he grabbed her hand and quickly escorted her through the public tavern room to the private dining room he'd reserved with a completely different conversation in mind for the evening. As soon as they crossed the threshold, she wrenched from his grip.

"Answer the question, Captain Storme." Never had he heard such a waspish tone from her before. "I demand the truth. All of it, no matter how hideous. I think I deserve at least that."

"You do, I agree." He closed the door and then moved back into her full eyesight. "Yes, I won a schooner, and yes, part of the wager was to seduce you."

With a gasp, she pressed the borrowed handkerchief to her lips. "So, everything that happened between us wasn't real?"

"No." Brand's chest felt flayed open. He died a thousand deaths at the look of betrayal on her face. "Yes. I mean, at first it wasn't real, but not now." Damn, but he was mucking this up. Why couldn't he find the words to tell her how he felt? Nothing in life had prepared him for an event such as this.

Where someone else's feelings mattered.

"How can that be true?" Despair pooled in the cool depths of her eyes. "From your own admission, you deceived me." The tiny waver in her voice, that barely discernable hitch pulled the knots in his belly tight. "You used me. You made me fall for you, all to win a bloody wager?" She twisted the handkerchief in her fingers. Each accusation fell like a blow upon his shoulders. "I shared my body with you." Tears shimmered in her eyes as horror lined her face. "I sinned with you because... because I thought you cared, that you would offer for me, wish to be with me for a lifetime."

Bloody, bloody hell.

Emotions battered his insides—guilt, self-loathing, shame, regret—with the intent to harm, to beat a hole through his body, but he couldn't let her see that her statement had gotten to him. "I'm so terribly sorry." As with everything else he'd experienced in life, he shoved all of it deep inside, ignored it, for it would break him completely apart if he allowed even one feeling to escape. As he watched her, he curled one hand into a fist and then relaxed it. The ownership of the schooner slipped through his fingers but suddenly it wasn't the most valuable loss he faced. "You must know how I care for you after these weeks we've spent together."

That wasn't what he'd meant to say, but the words he needed simply wouldn't come.

She dabbed at the moisture on her cheeks. "How can I when everything you've done has been a lie?"

"Not everything." Unable to remain parted from her, he

closed the distance, needed to touch her to help convince her of his honesty. "Things changed for me that night at the ball, perhaps before that." His jaw worked. How could he express all that his heart begged him to when he'd not been taught? "I no longer thought of the wager and what I'd win, for there was you and—"

"Stop!" She moved so quickly he wasn't prepared. When her palm connected with his cheek, the slap resounded in the sudden quiet of the room. "Just stop." Her eyes flashed blue fire. "You're naught but a parasite, Brand, feeding off others' feelings because you can't—won't—examine your own."

His cheek stung from her slap and he welcomed that heat, for it meant he was still alive, and he had a chance to change her mind. "Now see here—"

She continued as if he hadn't spoken. "You're content to exist in that void where you feel nothing, where you care about nothing all due to the fact you are terrified of being hurt—of left."

That was fair, but he had developed feelings above and beyond those he'd stuffed deep down inside him. "What you say is true to a point. However, once I met you, spent time with you, everything began to change."

"Has it though?" The anger in her eyes faded. Profound sadness took its place. The longer she looked at him, the more her chin quivered. "How many times have I asked you personal questions and you answered them with the bare minimum of information? You've struggled in revealing anything too deep for fear people—or I—might see you as weak."

"Yes, but—"

She shook her head. "You are afraid of going home and making things right with your brothers."

"If you knew them, you would wish to stay away too." A trace of annoyance threaded through the words. Who was she to tell him how to live his life?

When another few tears fell to her cheeks, he pressed a hand to his heart, for each one of those crystalline drops cut him deeply for the mere fact that he caused them. "You refuse to acknowledge all that you've seen in the war or how that makes you feel. You won't let yourself mourn for the friends you've lost or even for the death of your father because deep down you're afraid."

"I'm not," he whispered, but there was no conviction in behind the rebuttal.

A tiny sigh escaped her. She raised a hand, perhaps to cup his cheek, but then she apparently thought against it and put another few steps between them. "Perhaps you can't feel emotions for you are incapable to taking anything seriously. I don't know." She pressed her lips together, and he died a thousand deaths as he stood there knowing that never again would he kiss that mouth or know the joy of being with her. "It's readily obvious I know you not at all, and some of that is my fault. I was swept away with joy thinking you'd paid attention to me out of genuine attraction." Her voice broke on that last word, and it shredded through his insides.

Say something, you nodcock!

Yet the words she needed, the words he wanted to utter stuck stubbornly to the tip of his tongue. He was paralyzed with fear, just as she'd said. If he said nothing, he couldn't hear the words of rejection that he'd tried to avoid since he'd lost his eye, since he'd turned his back on his family. But if he didn't do *something*, he'd lose her anyway. "Elizabeth I... I..." What was the point? She intended to leave, just as everyone he'd ever cared for in life did. He'd be a fool to show any sort of emotion or tie to her, for that would give her power over him.

"Oh, Brand. I thought just this once you might have truly changed." The tears grew into sobs that washed away any hope that he had of reclaiming what they'd shared not twenty-four hours prior. Slowly, she shook her head. Her eyes were pools of infinite sadness while his heart began to shatter into a thousand shards. "Have a good life. I'm sure you'll land on your feet and will have me replaced in a thrice."

Those words sent icy fear into his chest and down his spine. "There can be no one else for me *except* you, Elizabeth," he managed to choke out in a whisper. *Please don't go. Please show me patience. I'm trying to grow, but I need your help.*

She laughed, but it wasn't a mirthful sound. "That is exactly what a rake would say, a man who played with my emotions all to win a ship. A man who took what I gave him and didn't care that it was a gift, never thought of me as something special." Though she attempted to stifle another sob, it escaped her chest as a ragged wail full of despair.

"No! I didn't… I mean, it wasn't… After a time, I learned how to lo…" But when it came down to brass tacks, he was a coward, still afraid of being hurt, and he drew the last of his battered dignity about him as if it would protect a heart that had already been pierced. "I need time."

"There is none." The hurt, betrayal, and infinite grief in her eyes would haunt him for the rest of his days. "You've squandered it, and when you had the opportunity to show me you aren't the horrid man I fear you are, you've remained mute because…" She broke into another round of tears, but then shook her head. "…because you'd rather be alone in your shallow life, never connecting with anyone. You'd rather remain in the prison of your own making while I return to mine." She turned to leave so quickly her skirts flared.

Panic welled in Brand's chest. The opportunity to win her was slipping away, but his mind was so clogged with the things he'd ignored over the years, he couldn't think straight. "Please don't go." *No! That's not what I what to tell her!*

"Why?" She glanced at him from over her shoulder. The light of hope shimmered in those luminous depths. "Is there a reason for me to stay?"

Say it, you fool! As his heartbeat pounded out a quick rhythm, he stared at her, the most valuable thing he'd ever found in the whole of his life, and yet the bloody words wouldn't leave his throat. *I need to weigh the risk against the reward.* Taking a deep breath, Brand let it ease slowly out. He nodded, screwed his courage to the sticking point, and said, "I don't want you to go, for I—"

The door flew open with enough force that it crashed against the wall. William stood on the threshold looking like a thundercloud with victory in his dark eyes. "I was told you'd be here, Elizabeth," he said without preamble. He grabbed her upper arm, but his focus remained on him. "Come away from this vile place, and *him*." As he pulled her toward the corridor beyond, she once more looked at Brand, longing and disappointment warring for dominance in her watery eyes. "I warned you about men of his ilk. Once we're underway on the ship, I'll appeal to the Lord to save your soul after its corruption from the detestable Captain Storme."

Then they were gone, and he was indeed, alone.

For long moments, he stood there, staring at the place she'd occupied, mulling over her words in his head. His chest ached from the labor of holding back the emotions he'd denied himself over the years, to say nothing of the pain from the breaking in his heart. Nay, he no longer had such an organ, for she'd ripped it from his body and had taken it with her. Perhaps that was the reason for the sensation of hollowness inside him.

Then the heat of embarrassment and shame swept in. Damn, but he'd treated her horribly. He'd been a blackheart, a cad, probably even worse, and the pain of her loss almost brought him to his knees. "Fine. Run to India. See if I care!" His shouting at the empty room had no effect on the state of affairs. "Perhaps I'm better off without you." Oh, but that was one hell of a lie. Anger rushed into the emptiness of his soul, white-hot and consuming, like a long-lost friend. Hell, but he wanted a drink. Afterward, he'd prowl the harbor and perhaps coerce a willing woman into his bed.

Of all things holy on land and sea! He shook his head and tossed the thought away as soon as it occurred. That wasn't the man he was any longer. If he couldn't have Elizabeth, then he didn't want anyone. *Devil take it.* That wasn't the truth of the matter. As the dam holding back the emotions strained its boundaries, Brand took a few gasping breaths. He pressed a hand to his chest where his heart used to be. He didn't have Elizabeth, for he'd lost her due to his pride and his inability let himself feel everything in life. Good or bad, it was part of him, the process of living.

"I need her so damned much," he whispered to himself, but she was gone. Not for carnal relations, not to win a wager, not for the joy her companionship brought, but for herself, for no other reason than he was a better man when he was around her and that he was… himself in her company.

And he'd realized all that much too late.

"Oh, God." With nothing else to do, Brand quit the room. He made his way through the ponderous, twisting corridors until he shut himself into his rooms. "What am I to do now?" Never in his most outlandish dreams did he think his penchant for scandal and bedding women would tear the best thing to ever happen to him away. "I've done this to myself. Perhaps losing her is my penance."

With a straining chest and the sense of hovering on the edge of a knife, Brand wrenched off his jacket. When he tossed it to the floor, hair pins and two tortoiseshell combs tumbled from the inside pocket to clatter on the hardwood. How many times had he plucked those fripperies from her locks for no other reason than to see those tresses flow free?

Never would he have cause to do so again. "Ah Elizabeth, I'm so incredibly sorry I wasn't the man you deserved, the man I needed to be—for both of us."

The emotions he'd held back, refused to acknowledge for years, came pouring forth as if the sea itself wished to claim him, and he was helpless to stem the tide.

All the hurts, the slights, the anger, the sadness, the grief, the love, the exhilaration took hold and carried him away, showing him scenes and flashes from his life. The fact that he was never taken seriously as a youth or that he was made to feel he wasn't as important as his brothers. Brand cried out, but the emotional scenes were relentless.

While in the Navy, he'd never been given a promotion in rank until he'd become an order-follower despite his natural talent and affinity for sailing and leadership. That anger and jealousy bubbled up in the attempt to drown him.

The grief and sensation of hopelessness he'd had when his father had died. He hadn't been there, hadn't made his peace with the man, and now it was too late. Regret plowed into him, for his brothers had their own lives now and he probably didn't fit into them.

The fury at being bested by the French in the battle that had lost him his eye and his respect when the ridiculous court martial had followed.

The confusion and embarrassment he'd met when his heart was broken by a woman more concerned with his looks than his soul.

And still the emotional torrent raged. The aspects of war he could never learn to stomach and the disgust and self-loathing he had every time he'd been forced to kill a man took hold and shook him like a dog with a bone.

Brand fell to his knees as he gasped for breath. Only then did he become aware that he cried, sobbed really, as the waves of feeling continued to batter him. Hopelessness from having to come to terms with his new life and navigating with only one eye. The loss of that still made his breath hitch.

Emptiness and loneliness from playing the rake crashed into him next. Never had he wished to continue that path, but it had been easier than finding himself invested, his heart vulnerable.

It didn't matter that his body shook from the onslaught, they still came, fast and furious. The unrelenting call of the sea that urged him to do whatever it took to keep it in his life.

As he scrabbled his fingers over the floor to grasp those combs, their teeth biting into his palms and keeping part of his mind clear, the confusion and exhilaration of falling in love again slammed into his chest. Yes, it was true. He'd fallen for Elizabeth so far and so fast there'd been no way he could have stopped it, but in doing so, it had been the most amazing thing he'd ever known outside of being on the sea.

Finally, the crushing grief of losing that love had him kneeling on the floor, bent at the waist, and crying out his frustration, pressing his forehead to the floor while his chest heaved, and his stomach knotted. He'd lost her in his refusal to grow, in the midst of that ill-advised wager. *Oh, God,* how would he survive without her, without her light and her enthusiasm that made him remember why he'd wanted to sail in the first place or why he'd settled in Ipswich? Knowing Elizabeth had changed him when he hadn't been aware of it. Because of her, he wasn't the man he used to be. Shock and pleasure filled his chest before self-loathing chased it away.

"I'm not that man anymore!" he cried out to the empty rooms. All because of Elizabeth. He wanted her still. Nay, he *needed* her, for he loved her to distraction, and if given the chance, he would tell her that in as many ways he could until she believed him. Hell, he'd spend the rest of his life showing her... if only she'd come back.

If only she'd not left.

If only he'd not pushed her into it.

The torrent swirled around him, battering him, making him remember, giving him no choice except to feel each emotion and recognize it for what it was. This storm that had brewed for years had finally unleashed its fury upon him, and he was lost, so very lost, but there was nothing to do but ride it out.

From the depths of his emotionally storm-tossed memories, one recollection came to the forefront stronger than the rest. Years and years ago, when he'd been just a small lad, his father had taken him and his brothers fishing. There was a lake on the Derbyshire property that always yielded a good catch. That day, however, the fish weren't biting, but his father hadn't seemed perturbed by that. As they stood looking out over the blue water with the sunlight sparkling upon the surface, Brand had learned how to skip stones under his father's tutelage.

His father had unhooked a pretty little trout and let it escape back into the water while Drew put yet another fish onto his string of recent catches. "Listen, Francis, it's not the quantity of the fish you catch. It's the quality of the ones that you do. Some men keep catching fish out of boredom instead of appreciating them for themselves."

Brand had been mystified by the notion. "What happens to the ones that aren't worthy of us taking them home?"

"We throw them back into the water for another day."

"What then?" Brand had wanted to know. "When that day comes, you might not catch any fish and you'll be hungry."

His father had shrugged. "Try harder for the next one and remember that not every fish is meant for you." Their gazes had connected, and, in that moment, it felt as if they'd understood each other. "Sooner or later, you'll find yourself satisfied with the fish you *do* catch, and you won't want any others."

The memory faded. Brand shook from the message in that long-ago time. Had the conversation been merely about fish or had it been a metaphor for life? He sat upright on his knees, gasping from the insight. That was how it had been once he'd found Elizabeth; he hadn't wanted another woman since then.

The storms faded, as did the emotional torrent, and at the end, like the aftermath of a cyclone at sea, his mind was clear. Finally, he saw his path again, shining before him as bright as it ever was, but he was exhausted. He fumbled a hand inside his shirt and brought forth the compass. As always, the tiny red arrow pointed to the north… and in that direction, the harbor lay.

Elizabeth.

Her ship left tomorrow morning, but he'd forgotten to inquire as to a time. Spent and shaking, he staggered to his feet and then collapsed, fully dressed, onto his bed. He'd need every ounce of his strength on the morrow, but for now, a sense of peace stole over him and he smiled.

Yes, this was exactly what he needed to do.

CHAPTER EIGHTEEN

September 1, 1817

W HEN A KNOCK sounded on his door just after sunrise the next morning, his breath stalled in his chest. With a yawn, he tumbled out of bed and to his feet, holding out hope that perhaps Elizabeth had returned to give him a second chance, but when he wrenched open the door, John Butler stood there, concern lining his visage. "John." Cold disappointment sank into his chest like an anchor.

"Are you well, my friend?" The bigger man shooed him out of the way so he could enter the room. "When you didn't return to the taproom last night, I grew worried."

Brand swallowed the ball of unshed tears in his throat. He didn't care that the evidence of his personal storm from the night before probably still showed on his face, but he did scrub at some of the dried moisture on his cheeks. "For the first time in years, I think that I am."

"Good. I figured you needed time alone, so I didn't come looking for you." John nodded. "By the by, I gave the boys a tongue lashing and sent them on their way last evening. They didn't know any better and wanted to help in their own ways."

"I know." Brand waved a hand. His stomach growled. Damn, but he required nourishment if he were to survive the ordeals the day would bring. "Once I put my affairs in order, I'll talk to them."

"So then, what now?" His friend's deep voice echoed in the empty chamber. "You have the look of a resolute man even if you do resemble a dog's breakfast presently."

Despite the gravity of the situation, a laugh escaped Brand. Oh, it felt so good, so freeing to do such a thing. "Perhaps I *am* resolute." He glanced at the floor beside his bed. The tortoiseshell combs glittered there in the morning sunlight. "I'm going after Elizabeth."

John's brow creased with worry. "Her ship has no doubt left. Harbor's been abuzz with activity this morning already."

Damn it all to hell. But he'd fought against greater odds before. "Perhaps it has, but it hasn't had that much of a head start. You know how slow and delayed passenger ships are, especially ones loaded with cargo for the East India Company." With urgency plucking at every nerve, Brand quickly changed out of his rumpled clothes into the dark evening suit he'd worn two nights before when he'd discovered that he loved Elizabeth. "Will you come with me?"

"Of course." John sent a speculative glance at his attire. "I'll always be your first mate."

Brand tucked the combs into an interior pocket of the jacket and hoped to God he didn't look too much of a desperate suitor. "Glad to have your support. You've been closer than a brother to me these years—the Storme I chose, the brother I actually wanted."

A faint wash of red infused John's cheeks. "I don't know about that…"

"Well, I do, and brothers stick together." Damn it all to hell. With that statement, the realization that he needed to make up with his own slammed into him. *She* had done that. He pulled on a pair of boots. "Speaking of brothers, I'm certain Elizabeth's had something to do with splitting us up downstairs, and I mean to get to the bottom of that as well. That buggar beat the barmaid, of that I'm certain."

"I look forward to you giving him his just desserts, Captain."

"Not as much as I am, I'll wager." Then he sucked in a breath. "Forget that. As God is my witness, I will *never* wager again."

John snorted. "Can't say as I blame you, since this one caused such chaos."

"And brought me exactly to the place I needed to be," he added with a wink.

"Aye." John laid a staying hand on Brand's arm. "Best pack a bag, at least, unless you wish to return to Ipswich after your daring rescue."

"Right." He tapped his temple. "You're always thinking ahead." Then another thought occurred. "If all goes well and I snatch Elizabeth off that ship, she'll need rigged out as well." He looked at John, who shrugged. "I'll need to make a quick stop at a shop before we go."

BY THE TIME Brand reached the harbor and made a few inquiries, he discovered that the *HMS Bright Hope* had already sailed, its destination Bombay, India, about ninety minutes before.

A sense of cold desolation chilled him to the bone even though the summer sun lay at the ten o'clock position in the cerulean blue sky. He rubbed a hand over the side of his face and the stubble there, for he'd forgotten to shave in his haste to leave. Then shoved it through his hair, equally unkempt. "I've lost her."

"Perhaps not." John glanced over the harbor where a bustle of activity filled the waterway and the River Orwell beyond. It was Monday and time for the fishermen and merchants to resume their workaday lives. "For as long as I've known you, you've never given up without a fight for the things you believe in."

"I can't fight for her if she's not here, mate." Brand put his hands on his hips while inside his heart broke anew. It was odd, this letting emotions have at him in the moments they occurred, but he hoped it would prove beneficial later when they wouldn't have a foothold to crush him.

"Sounds like giving up to me." John shook his head. "Isn't love worth doing anything to claim it?" He slid his gaze to Brand's. "If it were me and I'd just been given the news that the love of my life had sailed away from me, you wouldn't even have to think twice that I'd go after her. Nothing in heaven or hell could keep me from that mission."

"Of course, you're right." A slow grin curved Brand's lips. "What would I do without you?"

John shrugged. "Die of loneliness as a confirmed rake, I suspect." He dropped a hand on Brand's shoulder. "She's been good for you these past weeks. Don't discount that and don't let her go without fighting for her. Go be the man she believes you are, the man *I* know you can be."

Gratitude surged through his chest. "Thank you." Then urgency spurred him into action. "Is the schooner ready for sailing?" Damn, he really needed to give the ship a new name.

"I think so. George just saw supplies laid on yesterday in preparation for deploying it for the shipping outfit's maiden run."

"Good." Brand nodded. "I need to borrow it."

"It's yours anyway."

"No." He shook his head. "It belongs to the four of us, to the business, but first I'll have use of it."

"Why?" Astonishment lit John's face. "I thought you were going after Miss Hayhurst."

"I am. I'll need a decent ship to carry the woman I love to London to marry her, won't I? She'll need to meet my family before that occurs." Shock took hold as soon as the words left his mouth. Yes, it was time to make amends with his family. "Then I shall take her on a wedding trip worthy of her dreams." His confidence soared. He *would* win his lady back, of that he had no doubts. This time, it was a matter of being himself.

"Aye, sounds like a worthy endeavor." John heaved a sigh.

"I'll go with you, not as your first mate." He held up a hand. "Unless you want me to. However, while you're tarrying in London, I might as well have a visit with my father. You know, if I'm there anyway to stand up with you at your wedding."

Brand's mouth worked but no sound came forth. Finally, he nodded. His eyes misted with moisture. "Thank you." Without the help of his best friend, he wouldn't be here today. "I owe you so much."

"Ha!" John shook his head. "Seeing you wed and happy is payment enough."

"Then, let us not tarry any longer." This time he didn't turn away when emotion overcame him. He let his friend see it with no shame. Feeling things were what made him human, and a broken one at that, but it didn't mean he was weak. "I have a life to begin."

"Aye, Captain. It's good to have a purpose again."

It took nigh unto an hour to catch up with the *HMS Bright Hope*. Since the schooner was much lighter and smaller, it cut through the water like a knife to butter and made better time. Overhead, the sun was nearing its spot directly overhead that would proclaim the noon hour.

Brand wiped the sweat on his brow with a jacket sleeve. It'd be devilishly warm by teatime. "Bring her abreast of the *Bright Hope* as close as you can. I'm going to swim for it."

At the wheel, John nodded. "Do you wish me to drop anchor and wait?"

"Or you could circle about. We should know soon enough if she'll take me back." He drifted to the port side railing. "Wish me luck, John."

"You'll have that and more, Captain."

With a quick nod, Brand dove over the side. Seconds later, the familiar coolness of the North Sea closed over him. He pushed himself to the surface and then swam for all he was worth until he reached the hull of the *Bright Hope*. Thank goodness the ship was much like the one he used to captain in the Navy, for there was an iron ladder bolted to the side. It took next to no time to grab hold of one of the rungs and then pull himself upward until he reached the railing.

Dripping wet, he hoisted himself over the side and plopped ignobly onto the decking. Three sailors darted forward with shouts of alarm. One had a pistol drawn, another a saber, while the third had his fists raised and ready to defend the ship. As soon as Brand found his footing, he raised his hands, palms up. "Easy, boys. I'm not here as a threat."

"On your knees!" The man without a weapon ordered. From his uniform, he was a midshipman, not an officer, but the one wielding the pistol was.

"If you'll but listen." Slowly, Brand kneeled but kept one hand up. "I need to speak with one of your passengers."

The officer, a lieutenant, leveled the nose of his pistol on Brand's head. "Now is not the time for social calls. And this is hardly the place. You're a threat to this crew and its passengers. Why are you here?"

"The time is as perfect as any, and as I told you before, I'm here to speak to one of your passengers." A trace of annoyance wove through his words. "Please, let me explain." If his words were rather breathless, it was to be expected. This was what felt like the pinnacle of his life, and it all depended on the grace of this young pup of an officer. He stared at the man, refusing to give quarter. His presence here was too important.

"Fine." The officer lowered his pistol but gestured to the man with the saber. "Locate Captain Bingham, post haste."

"Right away, sir." As the man ran off on his mission, Brand slowly rose to his feet.

There was nothing for his appearance—the image he'd wished to make for her destroyed by the sea—but perhaps that was in his favor. Elizabeth often adored it when he looked a mess. He glanced at a burly man who hadn't lowered his fists. The man glared. Brand blinked at him with a faint grin. How well he remembered those heady first days of sailing when he'd do anything to defend King and country.

A commotion broke out once the man he assumed was the captain came onto deck. Various men about saluted, but the man sent them back to their positions with a nod and a soft set of orders. He was a tall man with a regal bearing and clean-shaven face. Blond hair gleamed beneath his hat. As he approached his position, he clasped his hands behind his back, but his hazel gaze never left Brand's face.

"Good morning. I'm Captain Gregory Bingham. Now then, what's this?" His tone was cultured and spoke to breeding. "Lieutenant Summerford said you wished to speak with a passenger on my ship."

"I do." Brand glanced at the young lieutenant as he belatedly rejoined the party.

"This is highly improper."

He snorted. "Captain, everything I've done in my life up until now has been that, but now I believe I'm ready to walk the straight and narrow."

"Why is that?" Curiosity lined his expression. "The least you can do is answer my question before I toss you overboard."

"Fine. But this delay is most regretful." Brand shook out his arms and sent water droplets flying in all directions. He shoved his fingers through his hair, putting the wet mass from his eye. "I love a woman listed on your manifest and I've only just realized it." He huffed out a breath of frustration when the three men surrounding him stared blankly back. "She needs to know even if she chooses to reject me."

"This is about a romance gone bad?" Confusion clouded his eyes.

"Perhaps, but I deserve to say those words to her, regardless of the outcome." Panic took hold of Brand's insides and twisted until he wished to cast up his accounts.

For the space of several heartbeats, the captain assessed Brand's face. Finally, he asked, "Who is this woman that has driven you to this desperate pass?"

"Miss Elizabeth Hayhurst. She's the sister of missionary William Hayhurst."

"I see." The captain narrowed his eyes. "Why should I do this?"

Fine, if the man wanted his credentials in order to take him at his word, so be it. "I'm Captain Francis Storme. I've spent years in the Navy and have missed it since. I lost my career as well as my eye in the battle of the Isle de France." He paused, carefully considering his next words. "When a Navy man knows what he wants or has a suspicion, it's more than a hunch. Don't you agree?"

"I do." The captain crossed his arms at his chest. A hint of admiration lingered on his face. "I've heard stories of you, Captain Storme."

"Oh, I'll wager you have."

"You're rumored to be one of the best England's ever put on the sea."

The praise warmed Brand's cheeks. He ignored it, for there were more pressing matters at hand. "Aye, so about my current mission?"

"Ah." Captain Bingham's lips twitched. "The last I heard, you were making your way through England playing at being a rake. You've fallen into the parson's mousetrap at last, have you?"

A tremor went down his spine. "If Elizabeth will have me." There was no shame, no fear, no aversion to becoming wed. Only hope remained, and it burned bright in his chest. "However, I've been an arse and made rather a muck of things with her yesterday."

"So have we all been at one time because of a woman." Captain Bingham grinned, but the gesture didn't reach his eyes, and they were haunted by memories only he knew. "I myself have recently become engaged to a woman I've met, but you're right. When a Navy man knows, he just *knows*."

Some of the anxiety clawing at Brand's insides quieted. "Then, you'll let me see her?"

"Aye." Captain Bingham nodded. He glanced at the lieutenant. "Fetch Miss Hayhurst to this deck. Tell her she'd be smart to dress in her best, for unless I miss my guess, this will be a day she won't want to forget. And she'll at least wish to match her man's effort of looking proper."

"Aye, sir." Once more the man loped off.

The captain landed his gaze on Brand once more. The heat of embarrassment went through his cheeks. "Where will you go should you win the heart of your lady?"

"Wherever the wind takes me." He shrugged. "Wherever she wants to go." His voice broke. "I have a schooner…" Obliged to swallow heavily to clear his throat, he then continued. "…but it means nothing without her."

"Aye, I understand all too well. The sea and a woman go hand in hand." Amusement twinkled in the captain's eyes. Then he transferred his attention to the men around him. "Drop anchor, boys. We'll allow a half hour delay so one of our own can win the heart of his lady."

"Oh, thank God." Brand nodded his thanks as relief shivered through him.

"It's the least I can do for a Naval hero whom we all rallied around in the early days of our careers." Captain Bingham smiled. "I wish you good fortune."

The wait wasn't long, for soon Elizabeth was escorted onto the deck by the young lieutenant, and every thought flew out of Brand's head. He couldn't remember how to breathe let alone his own name as the sunlight shimmered off the golden gown he'd sent her just days ago. She was a vision of loveliness, a siren direct from the sea, but the closer she came, the more clearly he discerned the anger and confusion in her expression. She'd been crying, that much was true, for her gorgeous eyes were red-rimmed and her cheeks were stained with muddled pink.

Surprise flickered over her face for an instant before grief stole it away. She glanced at him. "Why are you here?"

"To see you." Obviously, he'd need to work twice as hard to

make things right between them.

One of her brown eyebrows shot upward. "To humiliate me again? Didn't you have enough of that yesterday?"

"No." The words he wished to say were stuck in his throat. Why was it so bloody difficult? She was nothing like the other woman he'd fallen for; she'd shown that time and time again. Doing anything of this magnitude was a risk and made a man vulnerable, put him out there for hurt and ridicule, but Elizabeth was well worth that risk. "I…" *Say it, man! You can see your path, so take it!* "I needed to see you one last time."

Devil take it, that wasn't it!

CHAPTER NINETEEN

*O*H, WHY CAN'T *he just leave me alone to grieve in peace?* Elizabeth had no time for this. Brand had broken her trust. He'd made jest of her feelings for him. He'd stolen her heart and then trampled it beneath his heel. And now he wished to talk? She owed him nothing, yet her traitorous heart fluttered at the sight of him. He'd dressed in his fine evening clothes, had apparently *swam* after the ship?

How was that possible? Perhaps it didn't matter, for she couldn't tear her gaze away from him. He was adorable wet and wondering, with his silver-streaked midnight hair slicked back from his forehead and the days' worth of stubble clinging to his cheeks and jaw.

"Lizzy, there is something I must say to you," he said, emotion graveling his voice. "And it can't be said in a letter, even if you've not given me your new address."

Captain Bingham as well as a few of his officers and crew stood around them in a circle, all looking on in various degrees of expectation and interest. What had Brand said to them that warranted such attention? And why the deuce had the captain demanded she come clad in her best dress?

It had been sinfully vain of her to don the exquisite golden taffeta gown with the golden sparkling overskirt and the delicate tulle at the neckline, but it gave her confidence to stand and face

Brand for one last time. "Yes?" She crossed her arms beneath her breasts, and when Brand's gaze briefly dipped to the scandalously low bodice of the gown, tingles of need danced down her spine.

Several seconds passed. He said nothing further, but a muscle worked in his clenched jaw.

Elizabeth stifled a sigh. "Cat got your tongue, Captain Storme?" Despite a few snickers from the onlookers, she peered more closely at him. A gasp followed, for on second look, he was magnificent. "You look like a storm, all wet and bedraggled, lightning in your eye." Or a man laboring beneath passionate beliefs with his muscles taut and clenched—a man on a mission. She swallowed to force moisture into her suddenly dry throat. "Why are you here?"

Dare I hope? It was folly to fall for him the first time. Surely, it would make her the biggest goose in the world to do so a second.

"Let me start at the beginning." Brand cleared his throat. He tugged on the wet lapels of his evening jacket. "Last night I was forced to acknowledge the storm of my own making. All the emotions I'd held back came due after you walked out of my life, and I had no recourse but to let them have at me."

She trembled. Her hands shook so badly that she clasped them in front of her to hide her reaction. "How did that make you feel?"

"Horrible. Wretched even." Nothing except honesty reflected in his eye. "Every single thing that had hurt me, wounded me in some way from my past came back to haunt me on the heels of your rejection, so I gave each one of them their due."

"Did you set them free?" The fact he'd had the capacity for even that was the change she'd been hoping to see in him from the first.

"I did, and in the process, I found freedom myself. I broke from my prison." His grin was small and tight. "This morning, I woke up and knew exactly what—and who—I wanted for my life, but by the time I arrived at the harbor, your ship had already sailed."

Oh, he was skilled in words, but she refused to let her hopes soar in the event he dashed them out from under her again. "William was insistent we leave. He lectured me for hours after we returned home, told me numerous times I was destined for hell unless I put you from my mind."

Brand growled. "If that's the case, then he'll be one of the first you see there, for he is as evil as the day is long."

"I'm not certain…" She pressed her lips together. "I cried myself to sleep," she admitted in a soft voice as she strove to ignore their audience. "You hurt me deeply."

"I know, and I'm heartily sorry for my behavior." He came forward a step but paused, doubt in his expression. "So, I swam over to this ship—"

"You swam." It wasn't a question. She glanced out into the sea and frowned. A ship, a tad larger than his sloop slowly cruised about the area but stuck close to hers.

"Yes… Well, John and I took out the schooner—"

Disappointment stabbed through her chest. She was forced to stifle a sob. "The one you won in the wager that broke my heart."

"That is also true, but hear me out."

She gave him a sharp nod. "You swam from your vessel to this one. Why? That smacks of desperation and illogical thought."

"Aye, it does indeed." He exchanged a speaking glance with Captain Bingham, who nodded with encouragement. Brand's grin stole her ability to breathe for all its wicked intent. "A man in love is seldom rational."

"Oh. You're in love." It wasn't a question. Why did he come all this way to tell her that? Did he wish to harm her anew? Was *that* the urgent thing he needed to say?

"Yes." The gleam in his eye intensified. "Can you guess with whom?"

Why must he be so cruel? She blinked the tears back from her eyes. "That woman I saw you with in the tavern, that barmaid who had more breasts than brains." When surprised laughter circled through their onlookers, heat slapped at her cheeks. "Why would you do this to me? Just let me be so I can mourn your loss." Her strength flagging, Elizabeth drooped and rested a hand on a nearby barrel for support. It simply wouldn't do to collapse in front of him.

"No." He shook his head, a frown curving down his tempting mouth. "That's not true."

"No, you're not in love with her, or no, it's a different woman altogether?" He *was* a rake, after all. No doubt he probably had a bevy of women all hanging for his notice.

A sound of exasperation issued from him. "Good God, Elizabeth, will you let me explain without interrupting or leaping to assumptions?"

"Y…yes." Her hand on the barrel shook. Surely, he couldn't mean… her.

"Good. I want no lies between us this time." Brand took a deep breath and let it ease out. "Since the day I met you at that fair, I knew my life would forever change."

"The day you set out to deceive me."

This time it was Captain Bingham who answered. "Miss, I don't know either of you from Adam, but I do know Captain Storme's reputation. He's as good as they come, so please, hear him out."

"I'll try, but he broke my heart, Captain. A woman doesn't soon forget that." And now that she'd experienced what it felt like to show a little backbone and spirit, she wasn't keen on returning to a life that stifled them. Never again would she let men have control over her future or how she should act.

"I understand. However, men in love often act rashly. That only means they'll be extremely faithful and loyal." He looked at Brand. "Please, continue. Your half hour is rapidly coming to an end, and we must maintain our schedule."

"Right." Brand rubbed a hand over the side of his face. Then he landed his gaze on her. The gray depth was a summer storm. "I've apologized for my behavior time out of hand, so I won't waste this precious second chance with you by doing that." He paused, his head slightly tilted. "The second I kissed you, I was intrigued. But when you showed an affinity for sailing, when you accepted me without questions or disgust because of my missing eye, when you didn't push me on things I wasn't ready to square with, I knew you were a woman unparalleled."

"Oh," she breathed as tears prickled the backs of her eyelids.

"You've brought light to illuminate my darkness; you gave me back hope when I thought I had none. You showed me there is more than one way to portray myself as a decent man, and you make me want to be a better one every day that goes by. For you... for me." He came a step closer, but there was too much space between them for her to touch him. "I adore seeing you on my sloop with the wind in your unbound hair. I rejoice watching you come into your own confidence and seeing your eyes light with joy at the littlest things like tying a knot correctly."

"Well, some of them are frustrating buggars," she whispered, to the murmured agreement of a few sailors who'd joined the circle around them.

"Indeed, and they're just like trying to navigate emotions. You unlocked all of that for me the longer we came to know each other." His smile was sad, and her heart ached for him. "However, none of that compares to how I feel when we're lying together watching the stars at night, sharing our hopes and dreams. So much so that I began dreaming a new one after the night we went to Lord Nelson's ball."

The night when they'd come together twice and each time she'd felt as if they'd exchanged pieces of their souls with each other. "And?" She could hardly force out the word, so great was the tightness in her throat.

"I knew then I wanted you in my life forever. At that moment, I didn't wish to win the damned wager; I only I wanted you. But my past was a count against me, as were the lies I'd told in the beginning."

"Everyone has a past, Brand," she whispered. "Everyone has chapters we don't let anyone else read for fear of what people will think of us, but love helps us overlook that, just as God wipes all of it clean."

"I don't know if God would forgive my trespasses against you. I hope you can forgive me... eventually." He shook his head, implored her with his gaze, but she remained silent. "You distracted me in the best of all ways each time I spent time with you, and I had already developed feelings for you, but I fell in love with you at the ball and afterward..." As his words drifted off, heat infused her cheeks. "There is nothing for me if you're not in my life; *I* am nothing if you leave."

Her breathing came in short pants. She dug her fingernails into the wood of the barrel's top lest she faint away in the heat and beneath the dozens of stares. Her heart squeezed first with anticipation and then joy. "Give me a reason to stay, Captain Storme. That's all I ever asked of you, but everything else got in the way." That was exactly how life worked, a balance of good and bad, and the conscious effort to keep hold of the good.

"Indeed." A shuddering sigh escaped him. Slowly, he sank to his knees before her and he took one of her hands. "All of this is to ask you a most important: Elizabeth Hayhurst, will you do me the great honor of becoming my wife?" The hand holding hers shook. "I have nothing but a sloop to my name—"

"You have the schooner," she couldn't help interrupting.

"No, I gave it up. I'll share it with John Butler and the others, for our shipping business. There is something else I wanted much more." Such love shone in his eye that she bit her bottom lip to keep from crying. "Despite everything, I vow to keep you in comfort and happiness if you'll have me."

Oh, good heavens, he's finally declared himself! But she tamped on the pure joy that rose in her chest for fear all of this would dissolve. "Will we remain in Ipswich?"

"Do you wish to?"

"Not particularly, but I do want to be close to the sea." Yet... "But Ipswich holds a dear place in my heart."

Brand and some of the sailors surrounding them chuckled. "I

think we can all appreciate that sentiment." The smile he flashed her warmed her insides. "We'll go wherever you wish. It matters not to me as long as I have you."

Flutters filled her heart and echoed low in her belly. "You're a risk. I can't deny that."

"Aye, but only you can say if I'm worth it."

Hadn't she always kept that in mind during their courtship, make believe though it was? "Can you promise me you'll remain faithful to me for the rest of your life?" This was unconditional. If he continued his rakish ways, she wouldn't have him.

A faint flush swept over his sodden collar and into his neck. "Sweeting, *you* taught me how to love, *you* brought it out in me, showed me what it is to feel belonging to one person. How could I ever want that with any other woman?"

Her heart trembled. That was one of the most romantic things he'd ever said. For long moments, she regarded him, thought everything through, examined every aspect of their relationship and its hastened, premature ending, weighed the risk against the reward. Despite all of it, she loved him still. Each beat of her heart called his name, and she would never feel whole unless he was in her life. The remainder of her hurt and anger faded, and gladly she ushered in the waiting joy. It filled her, left her breathless, swept the pain from her soul and left her new. "You look like a dog's breakfast." But he was the dearest man she'd ever seen.

"John told me that this morning." He quickly finger combed his hair.

"You have no livelihood." She'd be a ninny to agree to his suit.

"I know, but I have a plan in starting a shipping outfit with my men. We're not all layabouts, you see, and John will keep us honest."

"Somehow, I believe you." Elizabeth couldn't help her grin. "I haven't met your family."

"I know that too, but one of the reasons I brought the

schooner was to take you to London after this should you accept me, but please, Lizzy, you *must* answer my question, or I shall go mad." Emotion graveled his voice, and his gaze was quite strained.

Captain Bingham chuckled. "He rather does need to be put out of his misery, Miss Hayhurst. I'd say he's groveled and explained enough."

"Yes." She smiled down at Brand as awareness of him tingled over her person. "I *will* marry you, for I'm scandalously in love with you."

"Oh, thank God." Brand uttered a loud whoop of victory. He shot to his feet, happiness illuminating his expression. "Truly?"

"Yes. What else is there to say?"

"Indeed." Finally, he closed the distance between them, held her face between his large, rough palms and kissed her soundly to applause and cat calls from the gathered crew. When he pulled slightly away, he put his lips to the shell of her ear and whispered, "Thank you for saving me, Lizzy. I'd never have seen the light if not for you."

The heat of embarrassment filled her cheeks, but she didn't mind. Never had she been so happy. "Perhaps you weren't the only one in need of saving, for you did the same for me, showed me there was more to life than the limited exposure I had." It was she who lifted onto her toes and claimed his lips a second time. Oh, he felt so good, much like coming home, but to a place she'd never been before. He took the hint and treated her to long, drugging kisses that had the power to melt every bone in her body, but she adored being lost in him, loved the way she felt safe in his arms. At the end, she added, "So scandalous."

"I can't help it." His eye darkened to charcoal with desire and love he could never hide again. "How often does a man go tip over tail for a woman?"

Captain Bingham cleared his throat. "Once in a lifetime if you're lucky."

"Just what I was thinking, Captain." Brand tugged her close

once more and claimed her lips again. When he finally let her up for air, her head spun, and her knees had the strength of cooked porridge. But his grin held a victorious air that awoke butterflies in her belly. "Are you ready for adventure, Lizzy?"

"Oh, yes." She could hardly wait to begin their lives together.

"You're certain you're quite healthy?"

"I am." Her lungs had felt strong for some time. It hadn't pained her to breathe except when she'd spied him kissing that dratted barmaid. She trembled in his hold. "Why?"

"You'll see in a second." He winked but then looked at the captain. "Thank you for letting me ask my question."

"It was my pleasure, Captain Storme. We aren't treated to much joyful news as this." His grin was as wide as Brand's. "She'll continue to lead you on a merry chase, you know."

"Oh, I hope she does, but then, only the best women do."

It was on the tip of her tongue to say something witty, but a commotion on deck interrupted the scene. The circle of sailors parted as William came forth with a pistol, waving it madly and scattering sailors in his wake.

"My sister isn't going anywhere with you, Captain Storme." Abject hate glittered in his dark eyes. His gaze bored into hers. "How can you trust a man who repeatedly has intercourse with prostitutes at that tavern, Elizabeth? No matter that they flaunt their bodies, he hasn't the integrity needed for a husband of yours."

What is happening? She stumbled when Brand abruptly released her. Then his words took root in her brain. "Wait, how do you know that? I never told you of the conversation between the captain and myself and the barmaid."

William shrugged. In his dark suit, even if he did wear his clergy collar, he no longer resembled the emissary of God. No, now, with animosity seething through him, he looked more like he belonged to the devil's minions. "Rumors surround men like Captain Storme. If some of them weren't true, there wouldn't be the need for gossip, would there?"

"I trust Brand." She laid a hand on his arm. His muscles went taut beneath her fingertips. "No matter what he's done in the past, it's forgiven. As God does for us, we should do for those we love." She smiled at him, her husband-to-be, and her heart squeezed. "I know the kind of man he is, and I couldn't be happier."

"Ha!" Her brother shook his head and waved his pistol again. "People don't change, Elizabeth. It's merely desperation talking, for you're an old maid without prospects. You don't wish to go to India with me, so you'll take any man who offered for you."

"Enough!" Brand bristled. He shook off her touch. "That's a bit of the pot calling the kettle black, eh Hayhurst?" A warning rumbled through his voice that quivered the hair on her nape.

Before she could speak, William flicked a glance at him, looking at Brand as if he were excrement on the bottom of his shoe. "I don't know what you mean."

"No?" Brand glanced at Elizabeth, who frowned with confusion. "Let me tell you something about your good, Christian brother. He's been—if you'll pardon my coarse language. It's needed here to make the point." When she nodded, he continued. "He's been fucking that barmaid at least once a week, but in addition to paying her—and cheating her on those wages—he beats her when she doesn't fall in line with his preaching. I've seen the bruises, and so have you. No doubt he's done more than that to humiliate her, for she needs the coin more than she needs the reputation. He probably conspired with her to tell you that lie about me, for I'll swear until Judgment Day that I never took her to my bed."

"What?" Elizabeth gasped, for she had indeed spied the bruise forming on the barmaid's cheek that night. She peered at her brother. "Is that true?" There had been so much to take in during the past two days that she couldn't absorb anything else.

At least William had the grace to blush. "Sometimes a man must minister to the fallen at their own level."

"Did you pay her to tell that lie?" Oh, she should have trusted

Brand from the first, but she'd let emotion carry her away.

William shrugged. "Does it matter? The lie did what I needed it to."

"Lies and sin from a man of the cloth." Brand shook his head. "Does that include having her service your prick?" He snorted while a few of the remaining sailors clustered about murmured. Captain Bingham watched the whole drama as if it were the worst Drury Lane play he'd ever seen. "How do you explain beating her?"

"Enough! I don't need to hear this. My behavior is not up for discussion." William aimed the pistol at Brand. "You have vexed me for the last time, Captain Storme."

Captain Bingham shook his head. "Lay down the firearm, Mr. Hayhurst. There are consequences on this ship for such actions."

"I won't, for sometimes God's will doesn't extend far enough, so I must intervene."

Elizabeth gawked at him. Her brother had gone insane.

Beside her, Brand shook his head. "So then you'll add murder to your list of sins? As long as you ask for forgiveness, you don't care how many crimes you'll commit in the name of the Lord, is that it?" Annoyance and pity threaded through his voice. "You disgust me."

"If it saves my sister from a lifetime with you, absolutely." William's eyes glittered with a fervor all his own. Behind him, Captain Bingham silently maneuvered two of his officers into position to presumably wrestle William to the deck. "I'm ridding the world of an evil man, doing the work our Lord won't." When he cocked the pistol, the sound of it echoed loudly across the deck.

Bang!

Fear shivered down Elizabeth's spine. "No!" Her heartbeat skittered into a rapid pace as she darted in front of Brand, stretching out her arms and shielding him from William's wrath. The pungent scent of gunpowder drifted to her nose, for her brother had indeed fired the shot, but Brand yanked her hard to him at the last second. Even still, the whizz of the ball flying past her ear was too close for comfort. She stared at William with horror clogging her veins. "You would have shot me, your own flesh and blood."

"He's demented," Brand whispered, his hold still tight on her.

She shook from reaction as Captain Bingham gestured. The two officers each grabbed one of William's arms while a third sailor took the pistol from his fingers. Brand's arms around her were the only things that kept her upright. "I see now exactly what sort of man you are."

"I'm one of the righteous!" William screamed while he struggled with his captors. "It's my sworn duty to rid the world of sinners who don't listen, who won't follow God's law!"

How could she have ever doubted Brand's integrity, his honor, his love when her religious zealot of a brother was so much worse than she could have ever imagined? "William, I'm done letting you order me about and using the church's dictates to bully me." Tears filled her eyes from fear and horror. "Somewhere along the way you've misinterpreted what the Bible says. You've been trying to impose *your* will upon everyone around you, not His."

"This is an abomination!" William's screech echoed over the deck. "You are all going to hell for daring to thwart me."

Captain Bingham shook his head. "Take the *good* Mr. Hayhurst into custody, Lieutenant." His emphasis of the word *good* cast doubt and put forth his opinion on William's character. "Put him in the brig for attempted murder."

"Aye, sir." In short order, the officers led her still shouting brother away.

Brand let her go long enough to extend a hand to Captain Bingham. "Thank you."

"It was my pleasure. At least this livened up the voyage." He shook Brand's hand. "I wish you good fortune."

"Fair winds and fallowing seas, my friend."

Elizabeth cleared her throat. Her limbs felt made of water.

"What will become of my brother?"

"He'll remain in the brig for the duration of the journey to India. After that, I'll hand him over to the English authorities in Bombay. They can decide what becomes of him. If they want to ship him back to Ipswich to answer for his crimes here, that's their prerogative."

"And if they don't?" She feared she knew the answer.

His eyes were kind as he looked at her. "He'll be held in an Indian prison for attempting to murder Captain Storme. I have no issue in giving a written statement to that fact."

Perhaps that was what her brother needed to see how twisted his thoughts had become, how far he'd moved away from the love of God. She nodded. "Thank you. I apologize for the trouble and interruption we've caused."

"Live a good life, Miss Hayhurst. That's all I ask in return."

"I promise I will." Though she was sad at William's fate, excitement fell over her when she glanced at Brand. She was exactly where she needed to be. "What happens now?"

"This." He winked at Captain Bingham. Seconds later, he tossed her overboard.

CHAPTER TWENTY

"**B**RAND, YOU BASTARD!" Elizabeth's shout echoed against the hull of the *Bright Hope*. A splash followed as she hit the water.

He glanced at Captain Bingham and shrugged. "Best to keep her guessing."

The other man grinned. "Be the husband she needs, Captain Storme, for in her you've found your redemption, I think."

"Aye." With a salute and anticipation buzzing at the base of his spine, Brand dove over the side of the ship. As soon as the cool water closed about his body, he quickly surfaced and searched for her. "Lizzy?"

"Brand?" A bit of fright rang in that one word.

"I've got you." He swam over to her location as she splashed, and once he held her about the waist, he pulled her close. She grabbed onto his shoulders while he paddled the water.

"As much as I appreciate the cool water, why did you do that?"

"How else was I supposed to get you to the schooner?" He pressed a quick kiss to her forehead. "Right now, we're going to sail to London. I'll introduce you to my family and procure a common license to marry." As he talked, he propelled them through the water toward the schooner. When John poked his head over the side, Brand grinned. "John!"

"All right, Captain?" John's grin was as wide as his own.

"Aye, but I'll need assistance with my bride-to-be." God, but it felt good to say that and know that Elizabeth would soon be his wife.

"Gladly, and might I offer my congratulations?" John extended an arm while Brand grasped her about the waist and hefted her upward until she'd grabbed his friend's hand.

"You can." As soon as John had reeled her onto the deck, Brand scrambled over the edge himself. His gaze went directly to Elizabeth, who stood sopping wet with the golden creation of a gown clinging indecently to her person as John stared at her. "Manners," Brand whispered. He gave his best friend a light smack on the shoulder.

Elizabeth shivered. "What now?" Confusion filled her lovely eyes.

"Now I'm going to show you exactly how I feel about you so that you'll have no doubts." Awareness of her as a woman—*his* woman—rippled over his person and tightened his member, and he swept her into his arms.

"Right here?" Excitement and alarm twined through those words as her eyes rounded.

"Yes. Why not?" He angled his head for a kiss, but she planted a palm against his chest, holding him at bay, much to John's amusement.

"Mr. Butler will see."

"Let him." Brand didn't care, for he'd won her.

"I'm not decent in this dripping gown."

Oh, how he wanted her! "You'll be a fat lot more indecent in a few seconds, and *that* is something I don't wish to share with John, no matter that he is my best friend."

"Merciful heavens," Elizabeth breathed. She looked away from John. A sigh escaped. "I don't know that I'll ever forgive you for the toss in the sea that ruined this beautiful garment." She shook out the drenched skirts and the sunlight danced upon the numerous beads and spangles.

He exchanged a glance with John. It was undecided which one of them wore the bigger grin. "I've taken care of that. There are clothes in my cabin."

A faint blush stained her cheeks. "Brand, have *some* decorum."

"Can I help it that I want everyone to know how happy you've made me?" Again, he looked at his best friend. "Do you mind piloting the *Lizzy* for a while? I would like to have a private conversation with Miss Hayhurst."

"I'll wager you do." John waved him off. "It'll take at least ten hours to reach London. You have plenty of time… to talk." He winked.

It was Brand's turn to feel the heat on his neck and cheeks. "One day soon, I hope you'll understand exactly what I'm going through."

"From your lips to God's ears, Captain." John's wide grin showed too many teeth as he waggled his eyebrows.

Elizabeth sucked in a breath as Brand took her hand and ushered her over the deck. "You named the schooner after me?"

"Aye. Once in London, I'll hire a painter to make the changes upon the hull. Now you know you'll never be forgotten." It was the least he could do. "Come. I don't want you falling ill, not when our lives together are just beginning."

She snorted. "It's summer, so I won't catch a head cold."

Brand led her down a short set of wooden stairs to the deck below. "Still, we shouldn't take chances." There were two doors opposite each other in a short, narrow corridor. He pushed open the door on the starboard side. "This is my cabin. The other belongs to whomever else is sailing with me."

"This is marvelous." She glanced about the tight quarters, and he saw the cabin through her eyes. Cherrywood cabinets and cupboards gleamed and lined every wall but the one the wide bed was shoved against. On the top of one cabinet, a carriage clock rested. Directly opposite the bed was a small secretary that could also be used as a lady's vanity, for there was an ornate mirror with legs that rested on the smooth top. In one corner a cheval mirror with carved waves in the wood frame rested. "It's like a luxurious home upon the sea."

"That it is." As soon as he'd ushered her inside, he closed the door behind them. "In the event that you should feel a chill, I'd be glad to warm you."

"You haven't lost your charm." She sighed when he came up behind her and maneuvered them in front of the cheval glass.

"Aye, and I vow to you right now that I'll never lose you again either." He manipulated the tiny buttons from their holes, and when the golden gown sagged, he encouraged it down her arms and torso, and then finally off her body. A groan rose in his throat, for the outline of her hardened nipples was evident behind her damp and clinging shift.

"Somehow, I don't think you will." She leaned back against him and raised a hand to cup his cheek. "You're mine, now and always."

"Yes." He tugged the remaining pins from her disheveled hair. They clattered upon the deck with soft *pings*. "I brought the tortoiseshell combs. I remembered you said they belonged to your mother." In a bout of panic, he patted his wet jacket, feeling for the outline of the fripperies. Yes, they hadn't been lost to the sea.

"You're a wonderful man, Brand Storme." Her eyes brimmed with tears. "Thank you."

"It's the least I could do." He stepped away long enough to divest himself of his boots and clothing. Soon the hardwood was littered with his garments and hers, for he couldn't wait any longer to see her nude. "I don't know how to be a husband, one you'll be proud to call your own, but I'll do my level best to be the man you need." He stood behind her once more, cupping her breasts, watching her in the cheval glass.

When she smiled, his world tipped sideways, and he fell into the sapphire depths of her eyes. "We'll learn together, for I've never been a wife. I don't want to fail either." She shivered as he rolled her nipples. "But it's inevitable, for we're fallible."

"Indeed, yet at the end of the day, I'll still have you, and that alone is something to find pride in, regardless if it is one of the deadly sins." He didn't want to talk anymore; there was no need. Everything he wanted to say could be accomplished by touch, by caress… by love.

The warmth of her beneath his hands was as comforting as his favorite pair of gloves, and the silkiness of her skin pushed him to the borders of madness. Brand nuzzled the crook of her shoulder as he teased her breasts, plucked at her nipples. When she trembled, he walked her over to the wide bed and gently tumbled them onto it, where he spent copious minutes learning every inch of her body with his fingers, tongue, and lips.

Each moan and gasp she made went straight to his stones, but he didn't stop showing her how much he adored her. The faint scents of apple blossoms and the sea filled his nose. A slight tang of the salt from the water lingering on her skin added a comforting flavor to his play. Elizabeth writhed beneath him. Each time she reached for him, he batted her hands away, for he wasn't nearly done worshipping her form.

Slowly, he kissed and suckled her breasts, teasing her nipples with his tongue until she arched her back and begged him to leave off. Randy bastard that he was, Brand slipped a hand between her thighs and encouraged the tiny bundle of nerves out from hiding. He manipulated that bud, that center of her pleasure, within an inch of its life, applying various degrees of friction. When she cried out, tumbling over the edge of a gentle, cresting release, he grinned against her soft skin. Not nearly done, he nibbled a path between her breasts and down her torso, lifting her hips as he went. When he buried his head between her thighs, licking the place he'd just touched with his fingers, a curious sound of a moan mixed with a scream issued from her.

"Brand, stop!" The urgency of her whisper only pushed him to continue. "Surely this is too wicked and sinful."

"Don't you think God wished to endow the humans He loves

with the ability to show that love to each other?" He chuckled when she pressed her fingertips to her lips in an effort not to utter any more sound. "I *am* endeavoring to love you, Lizzy, now that I know exactly what that means." Then he resumed the exquisite torture designed to send her flying a second time.

Which she did in short order. Despite her attempt to quell her response, the muffled scream sent pleasure directly into his engorged length. A flush appeared on her chest and cheeks, a sure sign he'd worked her properly over. As she went pliant on the bed, Brand situated himself between her splayed thighs. He took her hands, threaded their fingers together, and brought them up above her head, pinning them to the pillows.

"You've shown me what it's like to go into a relationship with my eyes free of the blinders I'd had, which is quite the feat, for I only have one." With a gentle thrust, he entered her honeyed heat and didn't stop moving until he was fully seated in her snug passage. "This act is so much better, more meaningful, when there are genuine feelings behind it." Awe from that fact lingered in his voice as he stared into her eyes. "I love you, Elizabeth."

Dear God, it's wonderful being able to say that to someone!

"I love you too, but for the love of everything, if you don't finish me, Brand Storme, I shall refuse to marry you out of principle!"

He laughed at that, for she was adorable in her desire. So many little things he adored about her, it might take a lifetime to discover them all. "I'll strive to never disappoint you in the future." Then he moved within her, treating her to long, smooth strokes designed to titillate and tease, to draw out her pleasure as well as his.

Oh, but his Lizzy would have none of that. She tightened her hold on his fingers, nipped at his chin while squirming beneath him. "Don't hold back today. I want to feel the full effect of you and rejoice in knowing you are mine, and that no other woman will ever have access to your body as long as we both shall live."

If he hadn't already been tip over tail for her, that would have done it. With a soft cry, he claimed her lips in a hard kiss at the same time he thrust deep. Over and over, he tangled his tongue with her as his hips pumped, his strokes fast and hard. He released her hands so he could grip her hips, tilt them up to allow for greater penetration. With every push, the mattress rocked, and her breasts bounced. She wrapped her hands about his forearms, encouraged him with murmured words while she tried to move her hips to match his rhythm.

When that still wasn't enough closeness, Brand left off. He slid from the bed, brought her with him until her hips and bum were balanced on the end, then he took her legs in hand, held them steady while he thrust his full length into her passage.

A scream issued from Elizabeth, unmuffled. She twisted her hands in the bedclothes, thrashed her head back and forth while her eyes shuttered closed. With the damp tendrils of her hair spread about his pillows and her body flushed with desire, never would he forget the picture she made.

Urgency rode his member as he stroked into her for all he was worth. All too soon, the familiar tingling in his stones signaled he'd find imminent release. Her body was too lush, too exquisite, too new that he couldn't rein in his excitement or passion. "Lizzy, I'm coming." But he didn't want to explode without bringing her with him.

"Give me all of you," she whispered as one of her hands drifted to her nipple and plucked the hardened bud.

Brand did that and more. One of his frenzied thrusts, her body went stiff and then relaxed. She cried out his name, over and over, like a litany. Her feminine walls fluttered around his shaft, pulling him deeper. Tears rolled down her cheeks and she went pliant in his hold. "Of all things holy on land or sea," he murmured seconds before he lost himself to bliss. He didn't just fall over the edge into pleasure. Oh, no, this time he hurtled through that wilderness and into a new place where white light enveloped him, and his body literally let go. Never had he spent so powerfully or as long. He ground his pelvis into hers as his prick pulsed, shot out his seed.

As before with her, he hadn't worn a sheath, but now, the thought of possibly having a child with this woman enhanced the sensations currently threatening to tear him apart.

With a quiet shout, Brand collapsed against her, his face between her breasts. Elizabeth wrapped her arms around him and held him close. The sounds of their ragged breathing filled the air, competing with the drum of his heartbeat loud in his ears.

Eventually, he stirred, only enough to resettle her on the bed and join her, holding her close in his arms. Now, he wasn't afraid of the fall, for she would always be there to catch him if things went awry. A satisfied grin took possession of his lips. Loving Elizabeth was like steering a ship—a delicate touch and a firm hand—and he couldn't wait to see where life would take them, for, after everything, he was a wildly fortunate man.

EPILOGUE

November 1, 1817
Somewhere off the southeast coast of America

F OR THE FIRST time in his life, Brand Storme was content and happy. He stood on the starboard deck of the *Lizzy* while the afternoon sun beat down upon his head. They'd been married for just shy of six weeks, and in that time, he'd found everything he'd ever wanted in life. Movement from the corner of his eye caught his attention, and he glanced at his wife as she came onto the deck from below, for she'd wished for a nap after a particularly vigorous round of copulation.

"Hello, sleepy head," he greeted softly, unable to hide his grin or his appreciation. After spending time in the sun, they were both tanned golden. She wore her hair down more often than not, and it was now streaked through with threads of blonde. During their trip they'd sailed and swam, coupled with obscene regularity, but they'd also talked and laughed and had come to know each other better.

"Hello, Husband," she greeted and peeked over the edge of the schooner, as always checking for interesting fish in the water.

Tomorrow they would head home—for a visit to London—before going back to Ipswich where his shipping business awaited. But he'd promised her a tour of Town and an extended visit with his family where he had vowed to find common ground with his brothers.

When he shifted his gaze and looked at the woman he'd completely changed his life for, his heart squeezed. Still, after all these weeks, he couldn't believe he'd won her. "Lizzy, are you happy in this life?"

"Marvelously so." She straightened and faced him, creeping ever closer to his position. "I never knew I could be this happy." A blush stained her cheeks. "You'll scoff but I thank God for bringing you to me that day at the fair."

"Perhaps I'm coming around to your way of thinking." How else could he explain why he'd chosen to kiss her despite the wager? He could have refused.

"Are *you* happy, Brand?" The dulcet tones of her voice continued to have a soothing effect on him. "You don't carry worry in your eye or a heavy burden on your shoulders any longer."

"I am." He adjusted the sails, kept a hand on the wheel while they talked. "Every day is a new start. I hope I'll do you proud, be the man you need through every season of our lives."

"I have faith you will—you are." A serene smile curved her highly kissable lips. "You'll also make a wonderful father."

For long moments, he stared at her as his breath stalled and his heartbeat hammered out a frantic tattoo. "I beg your pardon?" He could barely force out the words from his suddenly tight throat.

She nodded, her eyes luminous. "I'm increasing."

His hand shook on the wheel. "Are you certain?"

"Yes. At least two months." Her smile widened.

"So, you weren't sick from the sea when we wed and embarked on this trip?" He raked his gaze up and down her still slim figure but saw no discernable signs of pregnancy.

"No." She chuckled, and his world tilted once more. "All is well though. I'll request a visit from a midwife once we arrive in London."

"We'll have Finn's surgeon, or no one at all. He's the best." He shook his head. "You should rest. Can I get you anything?" How did one act when one's wife announced news like that?

"Stop. I'm not an invalid. Women have carried children for centuries while living their customary lives, so I shall be fine." Her eyes sparkled like blue jewels. "Are you pleased?"

"Yes. So much." His chest relaxed as joy bubbled through it. Quite an odd sensation, that. Then the reality of the matter crashed into him. "Dear God, a child. I'm to be a father." He gripped the wheel with both hands to remain upright. What if he was a proper mess of it like his own father had been? "I never dreamed…"

"Now you can." Elizabeth drifted to his location. She kissed his cheek. "Your mother will be pleased."

"No doubt." He snorted. In the brief time they'd been in London, his mother had constantly talked of Drew's impending addition. His child and Drew's would be cousins. They had to make a concentrated effort not to muck this up like their father had. "I shouldn't waste time. When you and I return to Ipswich, I need to throw my full attention into the business."

"You'll do well enough, for the four of you are a good fit."

"I need to, for I have a family to care for now." Shock and then elation swamped him. He could hardly believe how much his fortunes had changed. As he looked at her, he couldn't help his grin. "For now, we'll hold our course and enjoy the remainder of our wedding trip." Brand took her into his arms and eased the bodice of her mint-green dress down, baring her breasts. "Let's make the best of it."

"Cheeky." But she tugged his head to hers and kissed him soundly.

"Indeed." Brand sighed, and then gave himself over to the wonder that was his wife. Life was amazing then horrid and then magnificent once more. The trick was finding a comfortable balance. He couldn't wait to see where his path would lead now that he had a partner to traverse it with.

Thank you, God, for giving me this second chance.

Never had he been more grateful for being led out of the storm and into the light.

The End

About the Author

Sandra Sookoo is a *USA Today* bestselling author who firmly believes every person deserves acceptance and a happy ending. Most days you can find her creating scandal and mischief in the Regency-era, serendipity and happenstance in Victorian America or snarky, sweet humor in the contemporary world. Most recently she's moved into infusing her books with mystery and intrigue. Reading is a lot like eating fine chocolates—you can't just have one. Good thing books don't have calories!

When she's not wearing out computer keyboards, Sandra spends time with her real-life Prince Charming in central Indiana where she's been known to goof off and make moments count because the key to life is laughter. A Disney fan since the age of ten, when her soul gets bogged down and her imagination flags, a trip to Walt Disney World is in order. Nothing fuels her dreams more than the land of eternal happy endings, hope and love stories.

Stay in Touch

Sign up for Sandra's bi-monthly newsletter and you'll be given exclusive excerpts, cover reveals before the general public as well as opportunities to enter contests you won't find anywhere else.

Just send an email to sandrasookoo@yahoo.com with SUBSCRIBE in the subject line.

Or follow/friend her on social media:
Facebook: facebook.com/sandra.sookoo
Facebook Author Page: facebook.com/sandrasookooauthor
Pinterest: pinterest.com/sandrasookoo
Instagram: instagram.com/sandrasookoo
BookBub Page: bookbub.com/authors/sandra-sookoo